D0006763

The Accomplice

Also by Kathryn Heyman

The Breaking
Keep Your Hands on the Wheel

The Accomplice

Kathryn Heyman

First published in 2003
by Review

An imprint of Headline Book Publishing

Quotation from *The Drowned and the Saved* by Primo Levi reproduced by kind permission of Time Warner Books

10 9 8 7 6 5 4 3 2 1

The Accomplice is a work of fiction based on, and inspired by, the shipwreck of the *Batavia*.

Cataloguing in Publication Data is available from the British Library

ISBN 0 7553 0215 X

Typeset in Perpetua by
Letterpart Limited, Reigate, Surrey

Printed and bound in Great Britain by
Mackays of Chatham plc, Chatham, Kent

HEADLINE BOOK PUBLISHING
A division of Hodder Headline
338 Euston Road
LONDON NW1 3BH

www.reviewbooks.co.uk
www.hodderheadline.com

For my nieces, Pippa and Alana
For my nephew, Jake
And for Sharon, my sister

November 2004
Hopefully you'll enjoy a bit of old Dutch history.
Happy Birthday

The harsher the oppression, the more widespread among the oppressed is the willingness to collaborate with the powerful.

‘The harsher the oppression, the more widespread among the oppressed is the willingness to collaborate with the power’

Primo Levi
The Drowned and the Saved

Chapter One

My daughter has [illegible]
curving beneath her [illegible]
husband scarcely buried. [illegible] beneath her
eyes and she eats nothing but [illegible]. The ground
was too cold when they laid him down [illegible]
that I could only think of his [illegible]
his—him. She cups her hands [illegible]
not kiss his child.

[illegible] coffee cools on the [illegible]
scouring the air. Hours pass; [illegible] is cold [illegible]
thick soup.

My daughter says, 'There was [illegible]
bruises beneath her eyes turn [illegible]
fingers tapping at the white [illegible]

[illegible] sip the cold coffee. Hold it in my mouth for a moment then
spit it into my cup.

She came often to the dispensary [illegible]
[illegible] and for nervousness [illegible]

Chapter One

My daughter has returned from Amsterdam, her belly curving beneath her winter cloak, her young apothecary husband scarcely buried. Grey moons have formed beneath her eyes and she eats nothing but pickled fish. She says, 'The ground was too cold when they laid him down. Ice was everywhere, so that I could only think of his lips turning blue, and I could not kiss him.' She cups her hands beneath her swell. 'And he could not kiss his child.'

Coffee cools on the board between us, its sharp scent scouring the air. Hours pass; days. The coffee is cold, turned to thick soup.

My daughter says, 'There was a woman in Amsterdam.' The bruises beneath her eyes turn black as she watches me, her long fingers tapping at the white pot.

I sip the cold coffee. Hold it in my mouth for a moment then spit it into my cup.

'She came often to the dispensary, seeking remedies for sleeplessness, and for nervousness. She stopped coming sometime before Hans –' she pauses, presses her hands together, 'she stopped some time ago. She was on the ship, Mama. Had a husband in Java who died just before she arrived.'

Lucretia. Sour coffee aftertaste fills my mouth and suddenly I long to taste my daughter's pickled fish.

'She did not know who I was. It was only that Hans's apprentice knew a boy who was her godson. Of course I never spoke. Hans said –' her mouth stretches, becomes a thick track across her face. One high note, again and again, pushes through those lips and then, worse, the sound stops and her shoulders shudder noiselessly.

When she speaks again, it is a borrowed voice, a child's cry. 'How will I do this, Mama? How can I raise his child alone?'

'You are not alone, and neither shall your child be.'

Days pass; hours. And then her crying stops. And then she says to me, 'The woman. In Amsterdam. Later, she came for smallpox remedies. Then her maid came. Then no one, and we knew she had died.' She sits on the cool floor, as though she is a boy. 'You are the last one, Mama. You should speak.'

'Too much has been said already. Everyone has spoken. I have spoken.'

'But not to your grandchild. And not to me.'

The wood of the chair is hard, aching beneath my back. I close my eyes, as I always have done, until the silence becomes too loud to bear.

Chapter Two

Birth. It is always best to begin with birth.

Here is my mother. The doctor beside her, his long thin hands rubbing at his cuffs. I am beside him, watching the bony fingers. My father pacing downstairs, smoke curling from his pipe, his mouth in a tight-drawn line. Screams. Wails. Lashing about. This is what I expected, is that a wrong thing?

My father took me aside, when my mother was still round with the child, said, 'Judith, be strong, for your mother will be unable. She will be crying, even wailing. You must not fear, not for her, not for yourself. Do you understand me, little Jude?'

Yes, I told him, yes, I did understand. But he was wrong. My mother is able to be strong and she is not weeping. All is still but for deep breathing. Her forehead creased with concentration, her hands stretched out, the veins blue and raised.

The doctor picks at his teeth, then raises my mother's gown. 'Yes,' he says, 'you will soon be ready. Perhaps, Judith, some ale?'

Downstairs, I pour the rich red brew. My father takes my wrist, spilling a drop of the ale onto his shirtfront. It spreads, like blood. His voice is anxious, desperate. 'Judith,' he says, 'tell me how she is, tell me. Don't spare me.'

He is a good man, you see. He worries for my mother, his wife, that she will be lost to him. It is important that you understand this: that he loves her deeply, that he loves us all so deeply. It is important that you understand from the start his willingness to love.

Laughing, I say that really my mother is so well, she is adored by the angels and the saints. For a moment my father's face goes shadowed. For we have neither angels nor saints in our house; they do not belong in the house of God, and to speak of them is godless papist sport. My sisters are asleep, knowing nothing of my mother's pains which have called to her in the night. Knowing nothing of this vigil. It is true that it is not usual even for the eldest daughter to be present for this moment. But I am seventeen, and this is my mother's gift to me, this moment. Allowing me my presence. For I have waited for the arrival of this new child for long months. I have even felt his feet as he swelled within her. I feel sure that it is to be a boy, although my mother insists that the child is carried high which is a sure sign for a girl, being as each of we three girls were carried so high as to be almost below her ribs. Deep in the nights, I have whispered to him, as though he were in the very heavens waiting for my words. Fanciful, my father calls me. He jokes that I am to be kept away from the papists, for all their fluff is sure to fill my head. Which only makes me wish to meet one.

'My mother is truly well,' I tell my father. 'Now please, let me take the ale to the good doctor, or he will faint away and be no help to your wife at all.'

He releases my hand and I run upstairs, hearing the wood clucking beneath my feet and the water beneath the wood whispering. The door to the chamber is dark and heavy, takes much of my weight to push and I spill another drop of ale. Silence inside, except for the deep, deep breathing of my mother. She is on her side, eyes tight shut and her body shuddering.

Dr Volkerson waves his hand, calls, 'Come.'

He is going to tell me she is dying, that her shudders are unnatural indicators, that her very silence is a sign of death – I am sure of these things and full of repentance for my calling on angels.

'Hush,' he says, 'he is coming. The child is coming. Wipe her brow, she is wet with strain.'

I sprinkle ale on her head, for it is what I hold in the cup and I cannot bear even to cross the room for the water pitcher, not now, not with him coming.

My mother's eyes open wide, so that I think she has an entire sky forced between the lids. Her lips pull back and she does not look like my mother, but rather like an old and ugly horse. Her chin is thrust forward and I am thinking about these things, about her chin and the grotesque horse and such because I know that something terrible is coming. Her face tells it to me, her body shaking tells it to me, the doctor bowing over with his face frowning tells it to me. The whole impossibility of the thing tells it to me. My mother's thin body with her white gown twisted about her knees. Hair sticks to her face, and I pull it back carefully.

'Don't touch,' she yells. 'Want. No one. Damn. God. Uh.' Creasing up her body, leaning down into herself.

'Hush,' Dr Volkerson says, 'all is well, hush.' Looking at me, eyebrows up near his cap.

'Get damned away,' she snaps out. 'Damned away.'

Her words are short, short as her breaths, and I back myself towards the door. Before I am there, though, at the door, there it is: her whole secret self widened out, dark on the edges, but wide and round and through the middle, holding tight, a slippery shining surface. Flat as a table and wet as an eye. Then somehow not flat, but round, tilted, though still wet. As round as a head.

'Aaah, Lord, Lord, Lord,' says my mother. 'Ahhhh, my Lord, oh, oh.'

The sound is of water, of the slap of water, and he slips out so fast that I think he will fall, but he does not fall, he is held by the long hands of Dr Volkerson, Saint Dr Volkerson. Small and red and his lips like bubbles, he is my brother, he is born and I do not care what my good father says, there are angels and they are singing a deafening, wonderful tune.

Chapter Three

The flagstones in our long kitchen are ice to the touch: my hands are dappled with cold spots as I scrub. Wylbrecht is beside me, scouring more fiercely, more quickly. Beneath her grey apron, her arms are round and strong; I watch the curve in them as she heaves back and forth across the stones. She sits back, folds her red hands in her lap and watches me. Her eyes are still, and my scrubbing slows beneath her gaze.

'What is it, Wylbrecht?' My hands, like hers, fold into my lap.

Her fair eyelashes bat against her cheek and she looks over to the door, left open to the hall.

Lowering my voice, I say, 'Father is in his office. There is no one else to hear.'

Wylbrecht, I believe, has a mortal terror of my father. She becomes quite silent when he is near, and stumbles over her most basic duties. She, too, speaks softly; so soft that I have to lean in close to hear her.

'Your brother Jan wishes to learn to swim. He has asked me to teach him. Here, in the harbour.'

I take up my brush again, begin to scrub across the stones. 'My father would not wish to know.'

'I told him I could not, Judith. Your father would not – I do not believe he would be pleased with me.'

'No.'

'He told me he would teach himself, whether or not I would help. I should have come to you, or to your mother. I should have said yes. You always say yes to him. Your father says it will be his undoing.'

I glance up at her, trying to look stern. 'Someone must say yes to him, at least sometimes. If not me, then who? Mama is distracted and Father says yes to nothing.'

Each of my fingers is thick with polish, slipping through the white cloth. Sweet smelling, and as solid as lard, it warms my hands. I rub them on my apron, already criss-crossed with black, grey and silver marks. Wylbrecht's apron stays crisp, clean, all day long. She is naturally neat, temperamentally ordered. For me, cleanliness is a battle which is never won, even my hair creeps from under my cap when I scrub at these stones. Beneath my fingernails there are always pebbles, black lines, even slivers of paint where I have scraped at the white walls of the church. Mama says I must stop pawing at everything; I am always hungry for touch, for taste.

Wylbrecht has returned her attention to the flagstones, her whole body shifting back and forth, a line of sweat running from her cap to her chin. Outside, in the hall, a sudden rush of voices: my sister, Myntgie, and my brother, Jan. Calling, 'Good boy, clever boy!' and 'Judith, Mama – come see Roelant. Come quick.'

In the hall, my baby brother takes a step to me, then another and another, clapping hands all the while. His fat legs are wide apart, so that he could be straddling a canal, and his hands are stretched in front, grasping at the air. His laugh, though, is victorious. When he tumbles into my lap, I rub my polish-covered hand against his soft cheek. He is as warm and sweet as the beeswax staining my fingers.

Perhaps if Roelant had not learned to walk, my father would have stayed there, safe in the Blue House in Dordrecht, and our family would grow old and happy together and I would never marry but stay and take care of Roelant and my mother, watching the water of the harbour turn grey with storms and green with promise. Sometimes, in my dreams, this is the way it happened. Firelight in the evening, the sound of words passed by the docks, Roelant a plump and possibly spoilt child, demanding an extra kiss for bedtime. Father praying by the window: oh Lord, protect your flock.

Four weeks after Roelant's first steps, he wobbles past Wylbrecht beating at the red rug, past Anna placing flowers in a blue bowl, past me dreaming my dreams. Off he totters, out towards the docks. Mr Jan de Royt, from the Honourable Company, pulls Roelant by the scruff, picks him up moments before he would wobble himself right into the harbour. Jan de Royt lifts our brass knocker, notices the black tarnish on the underside of the brass hand and pauses to rub at the tarnish with his own grey handkerchief. Holding Roelant on his hip as he might hold an unsavoury parcel, Mr de Royt at last lets the knocker fall. Wylbrecht drops the heavy wooden brush and begins to push herself along the hall, all clumsy with haste.

'I have it, Wylbrecht.' I hold my hand up to stop her stumbling any further, hurry down the hall, and swing the heavy door open.

'I believe I have a piece of your property,' Mr de Royt says, smiling as though he has made a clever joke.

Roelant lifts his hands and calls to me, 'Oodick.' He points back to the water, completely delighted, and says, 'Wa-wa.'

The water of the harbour is grey today and for a moment I imagine the round body of my brother floating past the bridge.

Unsure of the words I need, I hesitate. 'Please,' I say. Then, 'Thank you, we did not realise he was gone. I cannot imagine . . . thank you.'

Mr de Royt looks well pleased and clicks his heels, ready to turn and leave. He wears a long cape, very dark, and there is the glint of a buckle near his waist. 'You are most welcome,' he smiles.

My father's voice carries across the hall, gruff and loud in the office. 'Well, they must, that is all, or else they shall all become as godless as the Jesuits.'

Jan de Royt pauses beneath the lintel and says, 'Do you know, I think I will have a word with your father. Yes, yes indeed, now that I am here it occurs to me that I should speak with him.'

Wylbrecht, hovering behind me, runs to the office door and knocks for my father. He is pink near his scalp when he arrives, a sign of agitation in his spirit. He invites Jan de Royt in and offers him ale, calls Wylbrecht to bring a plate of cheeses. They sit in my father's office, each man leaning close to hear what the other has to say, their heads nodding. Yes, my father seems to say, everything that you bring to us is good, and I can only agree to all you say. Yes, yes, yes.

Inside the office, this is what happens: Jan de Royt, senior merchant to the Honourable Company, says, 'How is it for you, being an elder here in the city, now that your mill has gone?'

My father sucks at his teeth, a poor habit suited, so my mother says, to servants only, and one which my father finds hard to break.

'Hum,' he says. 'Hum.' Wondering what it is that is being asked, wondering about the correct answer, wondering what the rewards are likely to be. Finally, 'Why do you ask?'

'Simply that certain positions, certain –' and here I think that Mr de Royt pauses, delicately – '*influential, senior* positions are soon to become available.'

'Oh,' my father says. 'Oh.'

'And I would not want to discuss them with you if you weren't, as it were, willing to consider. More responsibility. More influence, certainly, and more respect. But more responsibility with it. And of course there is the question of calling. One must be called to the Lord's work. As an elder you see this. Have you felt any sense of calling, dear Mr Bastiaansz?'

My father is quick to jump. 'Why yes, I have pondered just these last months whether the heavy hand I have felt upon my heart has been the hand of the Lord. In fact, I have asked the Lord for a sign, for a messenger. Perhaps you are he?'

Perhaps if my father had asked me, I could have illuminated for him the cause of the heavy hand upon his heart. For I have observed that one's sense of the Lord's heavy hand becomes considerably lighter if one does not partake of generous dishes of pickled herrings and cheeses and sweetbreads before retiring in the evening. But, no matter, the questioning did take place and good Mr de Royt decided – in partnership with my father – that the heavy hand was indeed the call of the Lord. And would he feel called, my father, to undertake a Company appointment? Why yes, my father would feel called, would feel humbled by the honour. And would he feel called to undertake an examination on matters of doctrine and conduct? Again, he would be honoured.

And what about this, called to carry out the duties of a predikant in a far green island, in the fort of Batavia, where flowers grow all year long and the scent of spices fills the nostrils and the sun is always warm on the arms and face; where the faithful Dutch are surrounded by godless natives and disease; where predikants are few and the need is so very great? Would he, with no work to turn to in Dordrecht, feel called to this duty? Yes indeed, my father would feel called.

Lastly, this: to travel as a predikant on a ship – the queen of ships, the head of the fleet – defending the spirits of all who sail on her?

It is this last which makes my father cease from the infernal sucking of his teeth and begin tapping his fingers on his knees, a sure sign of anxiety. Water is not a welcome friend to my dear father. The grey waters of the harbour are tolerated by him, in the way that the papists are tolerated by the council. He is endlessly grateful that our fair land was liberated from the sea and has spoken of the brutish nature of the waves, of sailors, of the sea itself. No, he is not a man who desires ships.

Seeing the anxiously tapping fingers, Jan de Royt asks, 'How would you expect to travel to the fair green island without a ship, my dear friend? The Company needs you, needs good pastors to care for the flock and to ensure that the goods – for they are many, and of great value – are kept safe. There are rewards commensurate.'

We are seven hungry mouths to feed, seven bodies to dress, and my father's mill is signed away. Admittedly my brother Gisbert is now himself a Company clerk, but it is also true that our house is small and our needs are not.

So it is that my father emerges from the office with the black-coated Jan de Royt and has my mother call us all together. When we gather in the Welcome Room, he announces to us, as to an assembled flock, 'My children, we are going across the sea to the fair green island. To Batavia! We are going to a better life.'

My mother looks straight at my father and says, 'How do you know the life will be better, how do you know that?'

My father says nothing, only sucks his teeth and taps his fingers on his thighs. He takes a breath and says, 'We are going to do the work of the Company; to do the Company's will.'

Later I consider this, what he said. For one would think that he would say: we are going to do the Lord's will. It is only much later, after my own daughter is wed, that I consider this: that for my father, as for so many of my countryfolk, there is no difference between the Company and the Lord. Even now, after everything that has happened, there are those who say this. The love of mammon, my father would say, is the root of all evil. And with the next breath: we desire only to serve the Honourable Company.

With the waters of Dordrecht harbour beginning to turn black, my mother wraps her cloak about her shoulders, shrugging away the sudden chill. Roelant totters back and forth across the hall, shrieking with laughter each time he hits the wall. We each of us stand silent, watching him wobble and fall. Measured against our wordlessness, his laughter seems louder and louder until it resembles thunder, or perhaps the sound of tears.

Chapter Four

So much of this story is familiar. It has been spoken of over and over again, as though repetition can wear terror into a comfortable shape. The world is full of musings, full of longing to understand how such horror happened. Longing to believe that it was just that once – a rare moment, a freak of history – that it will never happen again. For some years, I was quite the exhibit. Invited to give talks, to open functions; invitations which I declined, for the most part. I was a mere curiosity, for all I had survived. There was, I suppose, a kind of titillation. But they did not want to draw too close for fear of being infected with my grief. One woman said – I remember her pale, round face, peering too closely: 'It must have been such a relief, that you were spared.'

Oh, I held my tongue, though I did want to hiss and scream and spit at her: 'There is no relief, not ever, from the memory of what they did.' Wanted to call her Stupid and Devil besides, but did not. This was long ago, too, in the days when I had forgotten how to count sweet moments; it was in the time when I could not see the presence of the Lord, no matter where I looked. After that, I stopped attending such gatherings. Stopped attending gatherings of any kind and hid away, gnawing at the memory of it all, as if it were my own leg. For some time, I spoke only to my husband. Like my father, he was a predikant. Like my father, he did not know what to do with me. It was as though I were a troublesome pet, needing to be placed somewhere and given bowls of mush.

My daughter forces me to speak. She sits with her eyes upon me, until my mouth opens, and words begin to fall. She stands arm in arm with me and I am somehow given courage to speak.

There are halls of strangers, still, waiting to hear this story. To remind themselves, perhaps, that they are not like those beasts, the murderers of men. And perhaps you like to hear this story to tell yourself this: that if you had been there, you would have survived, like me. And to tell yourself this also: that if you had been there, you would have kept your kindness, kept your faith, kept your hope alive. That you would not be silent, that you would be strong, resistant. That you would have a different story to tell. Yes. Perhaps it is true.

But you were not there and this is not your story.

I thank the Lord that not everyone is a victim. But I ask forgiveness, too. Because I was there and I know that not every victim is innocent.

Chapter Five

Rain pours for three days before our sailing and I fancy the ocean has been made deeper for our departing, and therefore perhaps kinder. My father grows quite pale as we are rowed out to the ship. The sailors deliver us from the dock to the ship in batches, as though we are brown loaves fresh from the oven. There are perhaps two hundred folk boarding, not including sailors and soldiers and officers, and I cannot see how we will manage to live together on a ship for so many months.

A thin, brown-skinned man separates us from those who are not boarding. 'Say your farewells while you have the chance,' he shouts out, but no one is listening much.

Who would have thought such a multitude would gather? The sea herself can barely be glimpsed for all the crowd of boats floating on its surface. The noise would swamp the loudest storm, I swear that to be true. Many folk are waving coloured cloaks, though a good number are crying. No one is on the dock weeping for us, the Bastiaansz family. Gisbert will be a company clerk in Java, and a ship's clerk on board the *Batavia*, and so we are all together, travelling together to the far island. New Israel: green and full of promise. Even Wylbrecht has come with us. Hoping to find herself a husband, Myntgie has whispered to me, giggling. For Wylbrecht is boney and flat of face and my sister supposes this would make the search for a husband an impossible one. It is my opinion, though, that when love strikes, one would not notice the flatness of the face. My sister does not believe in love in this way, only in duty or convenience. For one so young, she has a very hardened heart.

'Come then, say your farewells.' The man gathers about forty people at a time into long flat boats and single-masted sloops.

Amongst the rush and crush, some folk leave badly, forgetting to embrace their loved ones. One woman turns right around and stands up in the sloop, calling out, 'Sara! Sara! You've been such a good sister, I love you so,' as though she will never see her family again. Another man, quite fat and red, suddenly hesitates, calling that he cannot get in the sloop. His hands flail about, become flapping birds. The man's wife is already seated on one of the long benches and I watch her beckoning him, pleading with him to come. I cannot hear their words, only see the fat man being pushed into the boat, where he holds the edges and sobs, staring down into the sea.

How the Lord tries to save us, warning us of danger, even when we are not listening. Even now, I weep for this man and his wife, who were almost able to hear the Lord speaking.

'Quick step, on you come!' The brown-skinned man is a human bridge, guiding us on to the rocking piece of wood beneath our feet.

Suddenly the ship, the queen of ships, looks far away. One brown speck on cold blue. My brother Jan, who has been so full of boasting and brave talk, holds to the edge of the boat each time it rocks. Every time another person arrives, the little craft tipples and topples until I am sure that we will tumble in before we have even seen our ship. My heart fills my ribs, fills my whole body. So much water! With each slap of the oars, a spray of sea hits us in the face. Wind chills me, though I have my stole, and my heart has long gone across the stretch of water to the ship. For Jan and Pieter, I smile and make myself brave, telling them that this is the safest of journeys, the happiest of boats. Soon, speaking it makes me believe it, though my father is looking grey, clutching his hands in prayer while my brave-hearted mother smiles at the sky, so that it would be impossible to tell that she has spent these last weeks weeping in the kitchen, pleading with my father. After midnight just three nights ago, I heard her hiss, 'It will destroy me, I swear.'

There are seven ships, docked together like sisters, each one more brightly coloured than her neighbour. And there she is at last: *Batavia*, the leader of the fleet. Seeing her, solid and richly painted, surrounded by sloops and yawls and smaller ships, a sigh fills my mouth, like a ripe fruit. Oh, the colours! Red and blue all along the edges, and stripes of gold and bronze. Grey-blue wavelets tossing about. Roelant reaches his hands out, trying to touch the waves. Wriggling in my arms, he slips towards the water, so that my hands clasp his round legs. Fearing he will squirm right out of my arms and topple into the sea, I gather him close to me, ignoring his cries and holding his arms by his sides.

'Look,' I say, 'see the pretty ship. Our big ship.'

Sails fly high, fluttering like bird's wings. Looking at them billowing, my spirit lifts as high as the mast, lifts right to the Lord. When I touch my father's hand and whisper to him, 'My spirit is soaring, Father, I am so enormously excited,' he shakes his head at me.

'Fanciful,' he says. 'You are too fanciful, girl. Like Lot's wife. Fanciful thoughts did her no good. Just watch out for the children. Think about that, not soaring spirits.'

'Well,' my mother says, white-faced, looking up at the sails, 'this shall be our home for some months. Glory be.'

When we are finally on board I hold Myntgie's hand and stare down at the flat water. Pieter and Jan immediately tag behind a tall soldier, asking if they may carry this, if they may touch that, if they could eat with the soldiers instead of at the commander's table. He does not speak, though he looks kindly on them, and my mother tries to pull them away, whispering, 'You are not to speak to soldiers, boys. I do believe they should not even be on deck.'

Though I would never notice from looking at the ship, it is said that below the deck are huge carved stones, ready to be assembled as a new city gate. Imagine this: entering the new city through new gates, on our very arrival. Processing beneath the stone arches, bowing to the natives, who will present us with the spices they have grown for the Company. Naturally enough, I know this to be a foolish fancy, for the gate has to be erected and this will take some time; yet the fancy comforts me and so I shall persist. It saddens me that we leave Dordrecht with so little ado. There were perhaps one hundred folk who journeyed to Texel to farewell those they love and not one of them for me.

When I tell Myntgie of my sadness, she says, 'But Judith, we are all here. You are bringing those you love with you. Isn't that true?'

Yes, it is true; it is the truth. Yet still I ache as the calls of 'Anchor up' echo around the deck, and the dock becomes smaller and smaller in my sight. The leaving seems sudden; I feel that I am unprepared. Sudden, too, the scurrying action on the deck. Sailors dash about, I can scarcely fathom their actions. Pushing us aside as though we are mere goods, calling to each other in accents that are thick and unfamiliar. Wind fills the sails above me, they are thrust out and it seems that the land shifts away from us as we stand still.

There is no solid earth beneath my feet, nothing stable at all. Each foot slips away from the other and my knees bend when I try to move. Sailors run past me as if there is ground beneath them instead of this ridiculous rocking floor. Perhaps if I were to make it inside to our cabin beneath the deck, I would not feel so bewildered by the strange motion of my legs. They seem to not obey my commands, as it is in dreams. Even my mind is disobedient, drifting away in all directions. My eyes as well; for I look to the land and can see none. Texel is gone and there is nothing to steady myself with. Only a fine line ahead of me: the horizon. Straight and distant, it is an edge which frightens me but does not give me strength.

I have a talisman though, a picture to bring me courage. For a moment I think of my mother and my baby brother; I think of her calmness, of his arrival, and I place one foot carefully down after the other. It is true that my hands are stretched on either side of me as though I am a windmill. Also true that my whole body sways left and right so that if anyone were watching I would look a fool, but I am moving nonetheless, each terrible step bringing me closer to the darkness of below deck, where I will no longer see the shifting mast, the infernal water.

Perhaps I have taken five clumsy steps, perhaps seven, when I see the tall soldier who so excited my brothers as we stumbled onto the deck. He is walking briskly towards me, swinging his long arms. Although I attempt to remain still until he passes – for like most folk, I do not like to look foolish, even in front of a soldier – I cannot help but sway and as I do so, my arms spring out from my sides. No doubt I do look slightly comical, and the soldier gives a snuffle of a laugh.

'Would you like some help to your cabin, madam?' He offers me his arm, still laughing. Red marks cover his cheeks, his skin is mottled, his teeth square.

Yes, yes, I would like some help to my cabin, for I am not happy wobbling along as though I am a child's toy. Yet he has laughed at me and I am still innocent enough to be proud.

'Thank you, no,' I say. 'I do not believe it is proper for a soldier to be seen with a passenger, and I would not wish to cause difficulty. And after all, I am merely enjoying the sea air. I appreciate the wind on my arms.' To prove myself, I spread my arms out again, sighing with feigned pleasure.

'Certainly. The wind is pleasing before the storms start. Watch for the light as the sun sinks, the colours are marvellous.'

Often at night now, I see him in my dreams, with his sawdust voice, his tangle of red hair. I hear the thick accent and see myself, the young Judith, holding herself in so tightly that she is unable to recognise what is before her. Whoever does recognise angels? When I wake from these dreams, I am calling out, crying out to myself to listen, to look. But I do not listen, it is not possible; I hear only my own skittering thoughts, and I speak with an unbecoming sneer. 'I did not think soldiers would appreciate delicate colours.'

'Some of us have eyes to see what is before us.' He smiles at me and I notice the crookedness of his teeth, though there does appear to be a dimple in one cheek. 'It can be helpful to stand and get the measure of a ship before beginning to walk. If any of your family, your younger sisters perhaps, were to find it difficult walking about on deck, you could suggest that they stand and sway with the ship, let their legs be soft. This can help get the sea legs, if they are hoping to find them.' He pauses again. 'Your brothers speak very highly of you, if you are the sister called Judith.'

'Indeed I am, and my brothers are inclined to speak well of everyone. They have been brought up well and do not mock others, not even soldiers.' My jaw feels tight as I say this, for now I know I am being absurd. 'An admirable quality others would do well to emulate.'

'Soldier! What are you doing on deck?' The words come from behind me; a deep voice, warm and full. A reedy man steps alongside me. Though his arms are stretched out a little like mine, he makes me think of a musical pipe, and for a moment, I imagine the wind fluting through him, high notes echoing in a grand hall. When he speaks again, the tones are deep. 'I'm sorry, girl, the man should not be bothering you. He is out of his place.'

The soldier looks down at the deck and a plum-coloured flush travels up his neck.

'Please, no. I spoke to him, asked his assistance. It was my error.'

The thin man holds his hand up. Each finger is as pale as soap. 'You must know better the next time, for the soldier could be well punished for your folly. If you wish assistance, come to me. I am Jeronimus Cornelisz, undermerchant to the Honourable Company.' He bows down low, twirling his pale hand in the most peculiar manner. 'I offer assistance. Soldier, you should return immediately to the –' he straightens up, appears to hesitate – 'to the soldiers' quarters.'

'The gun deck, Undermerchant.' The soldier nods his head at me, his thick arms hanging by his side.

Jeronimus Cornelisz does not look at the soldier as he leaves, but keeps his dark eyes on me. I cannot tell if I am to be allowed to leave, and it is many moments before he speaks. 'You should not be without your husband. Soldiers are an ignorant lot, and you should be protected.'

'I do not travel with my husband, but with my family. My father is the predikant.'

'Oh, yes. The predikant. Where should we be without the ministers of the Lord? You should return to your family. The predikant will wonder about you.' Staring at me as though I am a curiosity, he is as smooth as cotton. After long moments, he nods his head, though his stare continues. I turn and stumble off, arms grasping the air, until I feel that his eyes are no longer on me. Yet the sensation of his gaze remains until I have retreated below deck, and the thought of it makes me stumble even more.

Chapter Six

Despite the grandeur of the queen of ships, our living quarters are small and dark, making our home in Dordrecht seem as expansive as the Company offices. This is good; I am glad for an opportunity to be grateful for what I previously complained of. We are to sleep on top of each other, on wooden ledges hammered into the wall, surrounded by the smell of skin and salt and old breath. Our three boxes, full of clothes and books and the few jewels which my mother has, are piled high in the gallery, a narrow corridor smelling of spices. We have one trunk with us in the cabin. Father is pulling out the two copies of the Lord's Book which sit alongside the folded dresses and coats. Pieter lies stretched out on the cabin deck, his stick-like arms tucked behind his head. Now and then, Jan kicks at him, laughing.

Father looks around at his family squeezed into the dark wooden womb and asks if we are happy to be on board such a ship. Are we not glad to be on our way to the fair island, glad to leave Dordrecht with all her gossip and bitterness? Mother says nothing, only strokes Roelant's hair and looks at the curved wall as she nurses him, his hungry guzzling louder than the slap-slap on the outer surface of the ship.

There was a whale stranded in Dordrecht when I was a girl. A huge creature, reefed on the rocky shore of the harbour. For some weeks, Dordrecht was quite famous for the whale, though the stench was terrible. I remember little of it, only the smell. Jonah, caught in the terrible smell of the whale's belly. We are like Jonah, swallowed up into the dark belly of the whale; saved from the sea by this great rocking ship. We are settling into the belly of the *Batavia*, curving ourselves round its ribs.

Looking over at my father, at his jutting chin and dark beard, I become full of thoughts for the new island, Java. 'Father, is the green island like Nineveh? Full of sinners?'

'Sinners abandoned by the Lord, for they are not a chosen nation. And our own flock, waiting for us.' The ship gives a lurch and Father clutches for the edge of his bed.

Holding myself rigid, I watch the wooden deck tilting beneath me. 'I confess I felt a moment of sadness, leaving our land. Watching the earth slide away.'

'There should be no sadness for doing the Lord's work.' Father is distant, already thinking of something else, something greater than my tiny concerns.

Jan laughs and says, 'Oh, Judith, land does not leave us, we leave the land.'

'Really?' I ask. 'And how did you come to be such an expert in the ways of the sea? You who had to be cajoled and coaxed into the sloop just this morning?'

Jan smiles at me, a look of triumph, and says, 'Wiebbe Hayes has told Pieter and me, for though he is a soldier this is his third sailing and he has promised to show us which stars the sailors use to guide the ship.'

'And who is Wiebbe Hayes that we should hear him?'

'The soldier we found this afternoon. He has no family. He is going to live forever in Batavia, to shield the fort from rebellious natives.'

'The rude soldier? He with the ugly face? And we are not to mix with soldiers. Undermerchant Cornelisz has told me so.' I am still smarting from my encounter on the deck.

Mama turns her face to me. 'Could even a soldier be ruder than my daughter who was yesterday so courteous to all, so inclined to think well of all? This is not my Judith, to speak so ill of another.'

'Perhaps you do not know your Judith as well as you think.' It is unbecoming of me to speak to my mother so harshly. I scarcely understand my own irritation, yet my patience is somehow worn away already by the salt, the endless slap of waves, the tilting back and forth so that I never know quite where I am.

Unpacking the heavy box, surrounded by strangers, her own daughter hissing at her, my mother holds in her tears. She bites her lip and puts her head down so that I cannot see her face. One tear does drop, though, onto her hand.

'I am sorry, Mama. I had no purpose in speaking to you harshly.' I fold my hands into the cloth of my apron.

My mother raises her face, looks not at me but at my father.

'It is not you, Judith. I do not weep because of you. I weep for all of us.' She waves her hand at the dark walls, the narrow wooden ledges, our beds, cut into the walls. 'Because of this I weep.'

My father says nothing, only opens the Holy Book. Not the family Bible, but the predikant's Holy Book: perhaps this will carry more inspiration. Searching for the correct rebuke, he lifts out a fine leaf, an illustration of Lot's wife, looking over her shoulder. Lips parted in sorrow, as her feet turn to salt. My father runs his finger over the picture. 'Do not look back, for the Lord's will is being done.' He snaps the predikant's book shut and lifts out the family Bible. The predikant's book, I think, makes him nervous, with its heavy pages and leaves of illustrations ready to flutter out at any time. More, I think, he is nervous of the weight of the book, of what it may require.

My mother repeats his words quietly. 'Do not look back.' Her face is whiter than I have ever know it and I hear the memory of her whispered words: it shall destroy me. Here, in the deep half-dark of the cold cabin, it seems like prophecy.

Perhaps it is the truth that we leave the land, as my too-clever brother has been told by his new too-clever friend. Yet this is how it seemed to me, watching through the wet mist – that we stayed in one place while the green and brown edge of earth slipped further away, everything familiar and known slipping with it. Perhaps it is like this, after all: the whole earth is tilting and our fine, glorious land slides off to new oceans as the green island glides across the sea to find us. Where these fancies come from, I do not know. Too concerned with my own thinking, and with my own fancies, that is what my father tells me. Mama agrees with him, adding that it will bring me to no good. It is not that I wish to come to no good, and not that I wish to be disobedient, but I cannot seem to help it. One moment I am folding cloth, for example, not concerned with my own thoughts, concerned only with the folding of the cloth, and then with no warning I have gone. Thoughts arrive: thoughts of whether or not a baby thinks of the sky while he waits to be born, thoughts of whether or not the papists against whom my father warns are truly so wicked – all sorts of wonderings and wanderings. This is not the worst of it: the worst of it is my pleasure in my own thoughts, as though I am a creature of importance. Time and again I ask the Lord for forgiveness, yet even I am inclined to wonder if I mean it, for I do continue in the sin.

Myntgie and I eat dinner in the Great Cabin, the commander's quarters, full of dark leather and wood. So many of us gathered around the table, and who would have thought that such a room was possible on a ship? It is as though we are in one of the miniature paintings which are such a wonder, where the whole world unfolds in a scene the size of a handkerchief. Here, though, it is not the world which unfolds, but the elegant dining room. Anna and the boys eat in the passengers' dining room; for Anna is yet only twelve, and there are more than enough men around our table. Throughout our meal I can hear songs and calls for jokes and stories rising from the poop deck. The music is loud and forms a pleasing accompaniment to our meal, but secretly I wish to be outside with the noise and the calling. Mama has attempted to make me look like a lady, placing my cap far back on my head and loaning me her white collar. There are men on board, men requiring wives, who might be mine for the catching. She has not said this in words, has only insisted that I should make myself agreeable and keep myself looking fine even if water for washing is not so plentiful.

My father says the grace, and he takes so long about it, and makes so many requests of our Lord, for safety, for good food, for healthy trade, that all at the table begin to stir and I cannot help but wonder whether our good Lord might be wishing Father to get on with his meal and perhaps be a little thankful for what we have; that being the purpose of the grace after all. Myntgie begins giggling when Father starts on his long lists: oh Lord our gracious granter of all goodness who does make the sea to be calm and make the heathen to trade in proper goods. She giggles so much that I have to hide my head in my hands in order to prevent a fit of laughter from my own lips. When I raise my head, Jeronimus Cornelisz, the reedy undermerchant, is smiling across the table at me. Next to him is a man wearing a soldier's shirt; yet the coat over it is of fine grey cloth. His eyes are dark on me and he is paused, holding his cup in the air. Heat runs down my cheeks. He stares for many heartbeats before raising his cup at last.

Dinner is equal to any we would eat at home, though Father complains that the soup is too rich, the meat too salty, the beer too pale. Sometimes I believe that my father has the habit of unhappiness; for he complains so often of poor chest, poor back and a poor stomach which cannot tolerate good plain food that I fear he has forgotten how to praise. Our half-family forms the plainest corner of the commander's table. Such fine cloth! You would barely believe that we were on a ship, not in a grand town house. The commander is squeezed between the red-faced ship's skipper, and a woman who sits close, talking quietly as though she knows the commander well.

My mother moves close to me, looking at the woman, and says quietly, 'Hardly fitting for a Christian woman to be travelling alone, I would have thought, nor to be so well ornamented.' Though the woman's dress is decently black, like my mother's, her collar is of fine lace and her cap edged with the same.

I long to shake my head at my mother, to dispute her reasoning. Unlike her, I do not believe that the Lord requires us to be plain, to be hidden, to be haters of our own selves.

The woman looks up and smiles across at us, lowers her head.

The commander leans towards me, taking the woman's hand, and introduces her. 'Lucretia van der Mijlen. You shall be friends for each other, I am sure.'

Jollity hangs about our meal, for we have been let loose from the land. Good Commander Pelseart tells a tale of a wedding he attended where the predikant fell down dead, just like that, and his clerk, Salman Deschamps, a brown scar snaking across his forehead, adds that he once saw a predikant drop down in the middle of reading from the Lord's word. The undermerchant Jeronimus, running his pale fingers along his wine goblet, asks which book the predikant was reading from at the time.

The clerk scratches at his scar and says, 'Jeremiah, I believe. No, perhaps it was Isaiah.'

'Did he finish the reading?'

Salman Deschamps looks anxiously at the commander. 'I do not recall. Perhaps the shock . . .'

Jeronimus takes a long sip of wine, keeping his eyes on Salman. 'Yet one would think you would recall exactly the book. After viewing such a thing.' Wiping his lips, he calls to the table, 'Still, whichever book it was, we must recall that no one is above the work of God.'

All nod, and Father raises his glass.

'Indeed,' Jeronimus adds, 'everything in all creation is of God, after all. Book or no book.'

Again Father raises his glass in an act of blessing; but when I look at my mother, a frown is edging across her brow.

When a young cabin boy carries a glass of ale to him, Jeronimus whispers in the boy's ear and nods in our direction.

'Madam Bastiaansz?' The boy stands near my mother, bending close to her ear so she can hear him. He points to Jeronimus. 'The undermerchant wishes to show Lucretia van der Mijlen the ship and stars after dinner, with the predikant's wife and daughters. If you would oblige?'

'Why, yes, we would be glad, only too glad, of his kindness. He is too kind.'

Myntgie kicks me under the table. 'She'll have you a husband before we arrive at the Cape.' She grins benignly at the undermerchant.

'Actually, thank him for his offer, but explain that we will be busy after dinner.' I look straight at Mama, not at the boy.

'Judith! We are not busy, not at all. And we will be more than grateful for a tour of all the decks, which otherwise we shall not see.' The boy stands, apparently waiting for another defence from me, so Mama adds. 'That is all.' Her face has lost its earlier whiteness and is now rosy; as if the journey shall be lifeblood to her after all.

When dinner is ended, Jeronimus smoothes himself over to my mother. There is no other word for it, for we barely see him move.

'Shall we, madam?' He offers his arm and my mother runs out of words before she has begun.

The dark-eyed man stands to join us, and though it is improper to note such things, I see that his waist is fine like a girl's, though his arms are as solid as Gisbert's.

'Conraat van Hueson, ship's corporal.' Jeronimus nods in the man's direction.

My mother hesitates, looks towards my father for assurance. 'I do not think – I did not expect company.' Her face is shining with dampness.

'I see your concern, Madam Bastiaansz,' Jeronimus steps in close, lowering his voice, 'yet Conraat is not a soldier of the soldier class; how could he be at dinner here with us if that were so? He is the son of the Gelderland van Huesons, a noble family and fine friends of the commander. Does this settle you?'

My mother, for all her strength, is a woman easily cowed by

nobility. Already her face is tinged with red, her hands twisting at the tablecloth, in fear of what she may say wrong. Even with the elders of Dordrecht she is nervous, impressed by their fine manners and pretences.

Mama wipes her brow, smiles up at Jeronimus. 'Thank you, Merchant. I had no wish for my daughters to stand alongside soldiers.'

'You may trust me, Maria.' The way he speaks her name makes it sound like a whisper, though he has not lowered his voice. His other arm is offered for Lucretia, and my father nods enthusiastically at us as we sway out to the deck, legs buckling, bodies tilting with the ship.

'The poop deck, ladies. Home of entertainment, including star showings and lute strummings.' Jeronimus holds his hands out, shows the deck as though it is his stage.

Already there is a small gathering near the mast; a merry tune plays on a lute and a whistle, two women are dancing about each other. The deck is long and we can see the light from the Great Cabin, shadows dotting back and forth. Around us, though, are only sea and air. For a moment I am both frightened and lonely. The ship tilts and sways, never a moment of stillness. I stand, move with it, and let my sea legs develop.

'And here, my good ladies, are the stars.' Conraat van Hueson, the Gelderland noble, points upwards. 'Ursa Major. Pegasus. You will see the stars change as we move towards the Cape, so that everything begins to appear downside up. Here is the Hunter, do you see his belt? His arrow? Careful, for he might –' he moves behind me and touches my waist so that I jump – 'get you!'

Truly, despite my earlier protestations, it is marvellous to see the dotted handprints of Our Lord spread across the night sky. Each pattern of stars is named according to its likeness; and it could seem that there were indeed likenesses if one strove to see them. As with clouds of a day, drifting patterns which form any picture you may choose, so the constellations appear to me. Jeronimus and van Hueson guide us to them as though they are friends and the music of the lute grows warmer and rounder. My fear disappears: I may form any picture I choose. I am not lonely, I am only happy. My feet are stable now on the shifting deck. Myntgie is smiling and clapping and asking to dance with the ladies near the lute. A low brazier is alight and more people are dancing. Of course they would dance. All is possible now, now that the land has disappeared and we are in between times, in between lands and lives. Here we can be anything, want anything, do anything. Van Hueson is tall and fair-haired, with the light behind him as he smiles down at me in the starlight. With the stars behind him like this, he seems like an object to be painted. Indeed, I have never seen such a beautiful man. He is as beautiful as a woman.

Music, promise, happiness. We do not hear the wind squalling or see the waves rising. Here is hope. Just for a moment – as the brazier burns, and the storm builds out of sight – bright, bright hope makes a light in the dark sea.

Chapter Seven

My daughter knows little of this story, for I have told her the smallest fragments of what I remember. When she was a child, she would ask for the story of the storm and I would tell how there was once a girl on a ship, a magnificent ship, with red decked around her gunwale and a carved lion jumping from her prow. I would tell her how the ship left the port and set off to the shining sea, and the girl was full of promise. Here I began to blow like the wind, and held my daughter close; she was always a child who liked fanciful games. Just a little like her mother in that respect, but with far more sense to go with it. Yes, my daughter would say, and then what, then what? Oh, the wind began to blow and the waves got higher and higher – here I spoke louder, and she would tremble with excitement – and the waves began to wash over the ship until all the passengers were wet and cold, clinging to each other and weeping. Sailors who had sailed many voyages were swept away on the waves, and the soldiers stayed below deck, frightened of the storm. My daughter's round face would look up at me, tilting with worry as her hands rubbed against my skirt. Yes, I would say, and then everything changed, went well: the sun suddenly appeared, smiling down on the whole ship, and the girl and all her family sailed on to their new land where they lived for many years, each one happier than the last. Sometimes she would ask me for other stories of the ship, and I would reply that I knew only that one, of the storm which ended so happily.

It is sometimes necessary to give lies to children. Or at least to have untruths in stories.

For many years I tried to forget the journey to the fort of Batavia and all that happened after. This I do remember though, that my sister Myntgie was as sharp as pickling spices, as sharp and as lovely. There are days when I forget her, forget to miss her, and when I do remember I feel guilty for my own happiness.

My first husband was to be my saviour; he was to help me forget. On our wedding night, we lay alongside each other, skin not touching, while I wept silently. On the second night, he reached for me, and I lay quietly, waiting, but I could not speak. He turned away, then, and said, 'Why must you be silent, girl?' His back was thick with hair, grey-black; thicker hair than on his beard. On his shoulders the skin was pitted and brown. For half a year, until the bloody flux took him, he waited for me to speak, to give myself to him. In church, I held myself tightly in, waiting for the Lord's sentence to be called on me. This I added to my list of sins: that I had sent a man to his grave, cold with wanting me.

Many years ago, after my second husband, the predikant, went to his Lord, I found that I was penniless. My husband had nothing, barely six guilders, and the Honourable Seventeen gave me five hundred guilders 'in the light of all I had suffered'. As if this could make the suffering less, make the passing easier. Yet it did remind me of kindness, of its existence. The predikant was not unkind, you understand. He knew all that I had endured, all that had gone before, of course he did. Everyone knew, it was still in the days of hushed scandal. Intrigue, titillation: they did not appeal to him. He did not endlessly poke and prod at me, wishing to see my wounds sliced open for his inspection. Neither of us spoke, and silence, at last, became a dear friend. This was his kindness.

I have tried to be happy, to notice kindness and to remember all that I remember, without forgetting that there is goodness. Myntgie would – but no, I cannot do that, explain what Myntgie would think about my opinions on goodness, for my Myntgie is too frozen in memory; she is paused and infected by my rememberings. Harder and harder to decide how much of her I invent and how much is true recollection. Roelant is untouched though, I know that. I will never forget a moment, an edge of Roelant. In spite of happiness and in spite of the thirty years which have passed, he is as fresh to me as in his first breath. You could not imagine, you have no idea how fresh he is to me: his hands like flowers; his high voice, squeaking with questions; the dry yellow dust, catching in his hair.

My daughter is tall and broad of face. She has her father's strength, his goodness. My third husband, her father, was full of kindness, and I am thankful for him. When the water broke for my daughter, he wiped my face, whispered, 'You are the Lord's love, you are the Lord's child.' The little I have learnt about love, I learnt from him.

When my daughter was born, I took to my bed for several weeks, weeping into my pillow. He pulled me from the bed and poured cool water on my face. Insisted that I would not go the way of the dead. And so I did not. Here I am, yet again, with the living. Here I am, yet again, pulled to dry land. Reclaimed, as my people are reclaimed from the sea.

Every day I think of my blameworthiness for surviving; I know that their blood is on my hands, even as I know that it is an accident of sorts that I am here and they are not. Even as I am free, determined to live well and happily, I am swallowed by remorse, terrified of being submerged by these memories.

My daughter's child is carried low and I know he will be a boy. I pray he will not be beautiful.

Chapter Eight

Our first night is spent pitching from cabin wall to cabin wall, and it is Father who sobs through his prayer, convinced the Lord has destined us for death at sea. Mama holds Roelant to her, whispering the commandments. Retching and shivering, Myntgie and I hold tight to each other, and we do not dare to speak until morning comes and the sea is quiet again. All night, we have heard yelling and blaspheming from the deck, and we can barely look at each other for shame. We are separated from the fleet already, and the *Gavenhage* is so badly damaged that she must stay back.

In spite of this, day turns into day, meal into meal; for there is little else to mark our journey out. Storms at least provide diversion, but with fair weather and food which is still ripe we have only gossip to while away our hours. I take to waiting near the main deck, trying to catch glimpses of the soldier, Conraat van Hueson. Fair hair, curled thickly beneath his hat; those harbour-dark eyes; a straight and long mouth. Even Myntgie, who rarely notices such things, is inclined to whisper, 'Who can imagine anything more handsome?' When Conraat removes his hat and shows his face, men shiver, surprised. Women giggle behind their hands, reduced to the state of girlhood. Not all women, though. Not Lucretia.

Lucretia frowns, swatting the air with her hands, when Conraat comes near. When I speak of him, she turns her head away; it is so marked that Father has commented, asked if she has some jealousy over Conraat's attentions towards me, for though he is a soldier, he is a nobleman. Father's morning sermons have taken to concentrating on Joseph and his brothers, the evils which came from dissatisfaction and envy. Looking at Lucretia all the while. I have told him this is foolish, for why would Lucretia envy me? Everyone is in love with Lucretia, at least a little. With no reason, other than her fine skin and high forehead. Fine manners also. Manners which from a plainer face would be merely acceptable are from a fine face considered a marvel. It is not expected that the beautiful person should be courteous, or warm, or kind; it is not necessary.

Lucretia is kind and calm and never rude, if never warm. I am willing to stare at her for long hours, astonished by her smile, wishing that it were mine. Heiress, wife, benefactor, subject of shipboard gossip. Here are the things I have learnt from holding my silence and mending neatly while the whispers skittle past me: her husband is young and handsome and waits for her in Batavia; her husband is old, ugly and very rich; she has two children, both lost to the bloody flux; she has never had children, and has been alone these last six years; her father traded in diamonds and has left her all his wealth; she is the daughter of a miller who lives in Utrecht and all her wealth has come from her merchant husband. Some of this may be true. Certainly there are those on board who are smitten, and those are bitten by envy.

As for myself, my hands are smooth and white, my lips red, my hips plump. The ragman in Dordrecht told me that I was a true beauty, and my brother Gisbert laughed out loud. I am told that I appear younger than my eighteen years, that I seem almost as fresh as Anna, who is completely in love with Lucretia. In the first week on board, when my sister was green and bilious, Lucretia offered her a scarf to wipe her face with. It was woven from cloth as soft as air, a deep, dark grey. When Anna was well again, she sought Lucretia out to return the scarf.

'No,' Lucretia said, 'you must keep it, for I have much and you have little.'

She is kind in that way, so Anna tells me, always offering goods, always mindful that she is fortunate where others are not. Myntgie says that Lucretia simply wishes to remind people that she is fortunate; that all her offerings are a mere reminder of who she is. This is ungenerous, I think, for Lucretia even offered her servant a neckchain of gold.

Time shifts so in the midst of the endless sway of the ocean, I lose sight of where we may be, or when. On what may be my tenth or the twentieth night on the ship, Anna drags me to the poop deck. Leading me by the hand, as though I am a child, or a servant, she calls to Lucretia, 'Here she is.'

Lucretia smiles and says, 'Your sweet sister has been telling me stories of your family. You are ready for marriage, she says.'

'Anna! I am no such thing – I want no part of marriage if I can help it. Truly, I have no idea where such an idea came from. Who am I to be betrothed to?'

Anna looks at her feet and says nothing.

Lucretia laughs, her hands coming up to touch her mouth. 'No, I am sorry. She did not say that you are betrothed, only that you are of marrying age and that your parents are hoping for a husband for you.' She leans close to me and whispers, 'Your sweet sister has asked me to help find you a husband. She seems to think that I could help you with your presentation. And indeed, I do have some dresses, if you would like them. I find that I have brought too much with me, much more than I need, and we have squeezed two boxes into my cabin, can you imagine? Perhaps we could look at them together?'

'Wonderful,' I say, 'that would be wonderful. But I do not wish for a husband.'

'How old are you?' Lucretia touches my hand. 'I cannot tell from your face, for you look almost as young as your sister.'

'I am not yet nineteen.'

'I was eighteen when I married my husband. And I loved Boudewijn van der Mijlen dearly.'

'And now? Do you love him still?' Though it is perhaps ill-mannered of me to ask, the question is loud in my mind, and I cannot bear to leave it silent.

Lucretia does not answer the question, only says, 'I am travelling to him now, in Batavia.' As if this should be satisfactory.

Eyes wide as hazelnuts, she looks towards the Great Cabin, and I pull my breath in, draw my own conclusions.

And I am not the only one on the *Batavia* who follows Lucretia's gaze. As we sail closer to the Cape and the air becomes warmer, the sea calmer, there is much talk on the poop deck of Lucretia and the commander. No one is specific, no details are known: only that she has been seen with him, talking closely, listening intently, nodding her head as though he is her father. As for him, he seats her next to him at each meal, brushes her hand when he rises, licks his thread-like lips when he watches her drink.

Oh, look at us, clustered around a piece of gossip as we might crowd around a fine jewel. Tutting and pointing and all the while avoiding the gaze of our own selves, for fear we may not like what we see. Is not all gossip this, avoiding the pages of our own book, keeping attention away from our own nastiness? How quickly we have become sure of ourselves on the poop. Little societies and companies have already formed, each with a careful code, each with its own activity. The sky is watchful over us, larger than we have ever known. Salt stains our lips and we have learned to walk with a roll, to bend at the knees with each step. Servants rarely venture to the deck; even on board there is always much to be done. Wylbrecht hardly shows herself these days. She does come up to help Mama with Roelant and scrub our cabin deck and such, but all in all her duties are far fewer than in Dordrecht. She tells me that she sleeps on a hard mat, tossing in time to the snoring of others. And that she sleeps as soundly as could be hoped, given that she is worn to the bone.

No snoring could be worse than Father's snoring, I tell her. For the noise my father makes from his nostrils at night is louder than the seabirds above the ship calling for scraps of food.

Sometimes, Wylbrecht brings me a scrap of gossip, as though I am just one of those seabirds, and the gossip is a good wet slice of bacon fat. How greedily I gobble the morsel up, smacking my hungry lips. The cook is not happy, she tells me, nor the skipper. Always hungry, I edge closer, and she tells me more. She saw Jacobsz, the red-faced skipper, drinking below deck, slapping his hands together and calling out, 'Who would fight for Pelseart over me?' I shake my head, my teeth pressing down on my lips, and she whispers, 'The undermerchant Cornelisz, the dark snake of a man, has huddled with that same skipper, asking things such as, "Does the commander strike you as weak or weary?" and "Do you consider him incapable of authority?" ' Wylbrecht folds her arms, swears all to be true, and her words hang between us, as rich and fragmented as dew.

The morning after Lucretia's offer to me, my family have gathered on deck, listening to Father read the family lesson of the day. The good woman is above rubies, he tells us, reading from the Holy Book. She is clothed in strength and dignity and can laugh at the day to come. Father coughs and creaks as he reads, and his lips point downwards, but today even this cannot prevent me breathing in the words like a rich scent. Above rubies. My eyes begin to close and my head tilts back, so that my cap almost slips from my head. Birds – mostly gulls, I believe, although one has its wings spread like a bird of prey –

are circling overhead. With my eyes narrowed to slits like this, the sun is a jewel, my lashes form coloured patterns. Now and then, a bird dips down, diving for a piece of fat. On the lower deck, a huddle of sailors, soldiers and officers wave sticks in the air, hooks hidden beneath the bait. Tasty birds to grace our table, but I cannot help my sympathy for the poor creatures who never asked to be killed.

'Oh, they have caught one! Skipper Jacobsz has one.' Myntgie pulls herself up and is pointing down at the lower deck. 'He has it in his – oh the horrible man, he is holding it by the legs and swinging it about. Look, Judith, look at him.' She pokes my arm, so that I have little choice other than to sit up and join her watch. The skipper has an enormous gull caught in his hands. The neck of the bird is tied, yet it is not strangled, and Jacobsz swings it above his head, so that the gull screeches. No one watching stops him. No one speaks a word.

The skipper has a cluster of sailors gathered about him, all roaring with laughter at some ditty or other he is chanting. Roaring and swaying like drunk men, they clap their hands as the skipper swings the bird over his head. Myntgie grips my hand and leans forward, as though we are watching some travelling players performing in the market square. Truly, it is not unlike the way I imagine such a performance to be. Certainly Father would never allow us to see such things as travelling players, claming that they belong in the devil's camp, with papists and thieves, so I can only imagine what such a display would be.

This skipper is, I think, excited by his audience, for he steps back from his band of supporters and gives the bird's neck an almighty snap. 'Almost dead, a tasty meal for two.' His words carry over the deck gossip, over the waves. Lifting his arms as in prayer, he steps back and calls out, 'Come and get your gift, Lucretia van der Mijlen. Come while it's hot.'

While the laughter swells about him, the skipper throws the gull up to the top deck. Feathers scatter and there is a hard thud as the bird lands at Lucretia's feet. She stands at the end of the poop, hand over her mouth, staring down at the bird. Edging closer, I can see that it is still twitching. The skipper stands with his hands outspread, his face pointing up to our deck. He is like a child, looking up, wishing to be carried. Staring straight at Lucretia, as rude as a blind man. Yet in the Great Cabin he is as polite as a fish to me, with his cold scaly hands and an ape's face. Truly, the man is a natural marvel, he has so many parts of animal in him; it's a wonder he is able to sit up to eat.

'Thank you, but I have no need of this or any other gift.' Lucretia stands no closer to the ledge. 'And could you not have the courtesy to kill the thing properly? The poor creature has been toyed with so that blood has stained its feathers.'

She has her hands clasped in front of her, and we are all silent, waiting for – what? A sign?

Lucretia turns to face us, and calls to my father, 'Perhaps you would have the cook prepare the bird for the sailors?' She does not look over her shoulder as she descends to the stern cabins.

It seems that no one will speak against the skipper. Uncertain of the meaning of his actions, we cannot call out in defence of

Lucretia. Slowly, laughter and song begin to dance across the decks again.

Myntgie puts her head near mine and whispers, 'Perhaps not so perfect after all.'

She is a cold stranger to me in that moment; for I see envy forming neat icicles around her eyes. Yet I am not innocent, for I have not spoken a word. Though I could run after Lucretia, offering her my friendship, I do not. I swallow a strange kind of fear in my throat, but more than fear there is this: desire. For on the lower deck, the skipper takes a long gulp from a stone bottle. Alongside him, almost dark against the bright reflection of the sun, are two figures. One is the thin shape of Undermerchant Cornelisz. He shakes the hand of the other man, who looks up at me and lifts his hand to his heart. Conraat van Hueson. Lucretia is forgotten: I have no concerns other than the heat on my temples and the metal buttons on my overdress pressing into my chest with all the weight of the ship, a weight which makes me bite my lip and keep an unholy silence.

Chapter Nine

Roelant had a perfect head. Round and smooth. Amongst all the babies on board, Roelant had the sweetest, smoothest head, the finest hair. It was not just me who thought so; all agreed. Though perhaps they were abetted by me. Forced to say sweet things of my baby brother simply to please me. People will speak well when it serves them, I know this now. And yet, and yet; not always. Even in the midst of everything on the island, there were great kindnesses; there are always great kindnesses. If only I had been stronger, more generous. If only I had been less concerned with my own desires.

My third husband, Fransz, was the kindest man in the world. Yet it is easier to be kind when one's own life is not threatened – I know this to my shame. When I met him, he had barely time to fall in love, being busy with seven young prisoners. Each day, after his own work was done, he would visit them, read to them, carry victuals to them. His compassion made me love him, though I had to close my eyes to kiss him. With my first betrothed, I could not bear to miss even a glimpse. Strange, perhaps, that I should have married a papist. Or so it would have seemed. Certainly there were those who thought so; but by then I had returned to the Netherlands, settled here in Friesland, far from Dordrecht and even further from Batavia. We hold Mass in our upper rooms, a quiet affair for all the papists in our town. We are tolerated by the elders, and I learnt long ago to keep my eyes low, my speech soft. My Lord is soft, like this; it is as unlike my Father's religion as I could hope. Forever, above all else, I will be grateful to Fransz for bringing me to this balmy God with room for forgiveness, with room for those who have lost their way. Like my second husband, the predikant, my daughter's father was always a little afraid of asking me too much, or of asking too much of me. We had only one child, and I was terrified that it would be a boy; I could not bear the thought of comparisons. My daughter was born after thirty-three hours of pain, and that was not enough to wipe the memory of my baby brother.

Every night, even now, I remember Roelant's head, perfect and round. I force myself to this, to remember this roundness, this perfect thing. To count the bumps on his temple, to see his green eyes. Sometimes I confuse him with my daughter, the way she looked as a child. Brown hair, as straight as a bone. I meditate on these things, like the psalmist meditating on the wonders of the Lord. This is the way I can stop myself recalling Roelant's thin arms, raised to his face, covering his head. His perfect skull, broken.

Chapter Ten

Long days go by with the sun getting hotter and hotter. On the poop, we push our dress sleeves up to our shoulders, and Myntgie takes her stockings off. Each noontime, she rolls them down and wriggles her bare toes at the burning sun. My hands become hard and nutbrown, like the hands of a boy. We barely see my brothers; they spend their days playing dice with the Jansz boys, the sons of the provost, or else trailing about behind the sailors on watch, begging to be allowed to coil this bit of rigging, or wipe that bit of deck. In the cabin below deck, though, the sun has bored in through the plank walls of the ship, and made a stench as bad as any found in Amsterdam.

Wylbrecht tells us that between the decks it is worse, where three servants have been ill with a disease of the skin and there is no light to clean or wash by. Thank the Lord for our dank hole, though we are squeezed into it like locusts, and for the gallery, carrying our luggage; otherwise, how would we sleep, surrounded by boxes? There are many who never see the sun burning on the deck, but stay buried in the dark gaps between decks. I do not know, cannot imagine, what they do there for recreation. We have been generally safe from disease and storms, thank the heavens; for though we now seem to be sailing alone, only five men have died since leaving Texel, two from drunken brawling and three from disease. Jeronimus Cornelisz told my father that there have been journeys where half of the entire fleet is lost by storm and thirty men or more from disease. Yet I do not know how he can be sure of this fact, for at dinner one night I heard him confess to Lucretia that he has never been on board a ship of any kind before setting foot on the *Batavia*.

Kaaren Hendrickson is heavy with child and as the sun comes closer to us, and we come closer to the Cape, she becomes more and more blistered. Feet, hands, legs; all swollen and white with shining blisters, full of pale water. She has no friend to travel with, none to speak of, and no proper maid either. Her husband Jan Hendrickson spends his days gambling on the lower deck. Sometimes he rouses himself to ask if she is well. Once he picked some mustard cress from the salad box on the main deck and insisted that she eat it straight from his hand, just as if she was a cow, that the child within her might be well.

When it seems that the sun will collide with us, on the day when we are most sleepy with its overwhelming heat, Kaaren feels water trickle beneath her skirts. She pulls at my mother's arm and whispers that the child is coming. On the deck below, four men are playing a complicated game with long sticks and flat discs for markers; Jan Hendrickson is not among them.

Mama calls for Wylbrecht to search for him and also to search for the surgeon-barber while she gathers Kaaren up and bustles towards the Great Cabin. The commander appears some moments later, his hand held on his head as though in pain. He stumbles over to my father and asks, 'What shall I do, Predikant?'

My father looks about, nervously, his throat turning red. 'I do not know, Commander. It is your ship.'

Commander Pelseart looks behind him, then rubs his hands together. 'Yes. Thank you, Predikant.'

'Judith, do you think that you should go and help Mama?' Anna is standing at her full height, trying to bounce so that she can see a little of what might happen.

'If she wanted me she would have asked. No, I shall stay here and wait for her to call me.'

We three – Anna, Myntgie and I – close ourselves off in a circle, each of us looking towards the Great Cabin. Roelant tucks himself in and out of our skirts, playing peek-a-boo, and we are too distracted to pull our dresses away.

Myntgie reaches her arms out for him. 'Here, darling boy, come to Myntgie.'

We sit silently. My mind is full of rememberings: the quiet of the morning of Roelant's birth, and how distant it has grown; the fear which Father had for my mother's health; the smell of vinegar on wood. We hear nothing from the direction of the cabin, though we strain ourselves with trying. There has been one birth already on the ship, a boy born beneath the decks to a serving girl. We wait, as we did for Roelant. Nothing: no sound for such a long time that we almost forget we are waiting,

waiting for a birth to provide a diversion from day after day of salt and sea-rocking and the smell of sickness and worry. Though we are blessed by a lack of storms, the wind is still fierce when it wishes, and there is no escape from the constant motion. Sometimes I long for stillness. There are nights when I dream of the quiet days in Dordrecht, with only the sound of my cleaning cloth on the flagstones interrupting my thoughts. Long, still days.

Perhaps it is because I am so immersed in my own fancies that I do not hear the screams when they come. The game below is accompanied by shouts and curses, for it is true what I have heard said of sailors and soldiers, that their speech is peppered with brightly coloured words. Over the noise of the game, the provost is calling out the watch chant. So it is only when Myntgie sits up and shushes Anna from her babbling that I hear it. One sharp, shrill scream which sounds almost like a whistle, it is so high and so long. Wylbrecht is on the lower deck rushing from one group of men to another, though none of them seems to pay her any attention. She looks up at us and shakes her head. 'He is a scoundrel, that Jan.'

On the main deck, the sailors are hoisting a mainsail and chanting a loud and happy song. Some on the poop are clapping along. Beneath our feet, one hundred people are huddling. All of them waiting, though few knowing of the woman wailing in the Great Cabin. Each moment on the ship is one of waiting, one of anticipation. Talking daily of what the new land will be like, what it will be to walk on flat earth again; we have become masters of waiting.

Father offers to read aloud from the Lord's Book. His mouth is barely forming the words when the provost strikes his baton against the mainmast, and calls out the burial chant.

My father gathers himself up. 'They will require my services, I presume. Both mother and child, I expect.'

I look up at him. His face is flushed pink; if I were to be uncharitable I might believe it to be excitement. Certainly I do not see concern or sadness there. 'I hope not, Father. Perhaps it is a mistake, perhaps the wrong call?'

'Certainly not, child. Provost Jansz is the cousin of the Honourable Company Director Jansz. Mistakes are not in his blood.'

'I will pray for them, mother and child both. For their souls.'

'You are not a papist, Judith.' My father's face is as red as ever I have seen it, and his voice is as crisp as the sea. 'The souls shall be done with as the Good Lord has already chosen.' He marches off towards the Great Cabin, his back rigid.

Mother and daughter it is, indeed. Both wrapped in grey blankets, one bundle no bigger than my father's Holy Book. Two sailors find Jan Hendrickson, drag him out from the skipper's cabin with his gambling cronies, all of them tucking coins into their belts as they stagger, blinking, to the deck. They tell him that his wife and child are dead. Jan's face is bewildered; he stares around at the sailors who have laid down their work. Though he shakes his head, he makes no sound, offers no word of protest. Even when Father calls for the bundles to be carried to the high gunwale, Jan simply stands swaying, looking from face to face.

'From earth we came and to earth we shall return,' my father says, and a broad-chested soldier tips the blanket-wrapped bundles – one the body of Kaaren Hendrickson, the other of her stillborn girlchild – not into the earth, but into the sea. There is a distant splash, and then another, equal only to the sound of a fish jumping. Jan Hendrickson stops his stupefied swaying and begins to sob. I have never heard a man weep before in this way, have never heard weeping such as his even from a child. Two sailors gather close to him, hands on his back. One offers him a silver flask. The soldier who tipped the human bundles into the sea turns away from the gunwale and I see his flat face, his crooked mouth. There is no dimple when he looks up at me, not even a nod of recognition. Wiebbe Hayes. I know his name and he knows mine. This is all I know of him: his name, his plain face, and that my brothers love to be with him, though it is not proper.

Wiebbe Hayes steps to the back of the group gathered around the gunwale, his head bowed. He looks back at me and shakes his head, just slowly and so sadly. 'Poor, poor child,' I hear him whisper and for the first time I too wish to weep, wish to stand alongside Jan Hendrickson and weep with him for his poor, poor child and his poor, poor wife. Wiebbe turns away from me, and I see only the action of his arm, rising, lowering, and moving first to the left and then to the right. Crossing himself. Here then is one more thing I know about the ugly soldier with the soft heart. He is a papist, praying for the souls of the dead.

Chapter Eleven

For some days, there is a respectful distance kept from Jan Hendrickson, a silence observed in his presence. For these few days, Jan stays weeping by the rear mast. Father says prayers for him during the daily service and there is a muted tone on the poop. During the dinner hour at the commander's table there is little laughter, and when there is, it is quickly shushed, as though something indecent has been spoken. This lasts for less than one week, this sympathy, this concern for the dead and the dying. After some days, laughter is no longer frowned upon, prayers are no longer said for Jan, and silence is not held when he is near. Once again, Jan slips off to bet on dice, and nothing is spoken aloud. Though my father preaches several sermons on the evils of gambling, and though many nod their heads and tut-tut at the shame of the sport, nothing is spoken to the skipper or Jan. Soon Kaaren and the bundle which barely made a splash in the deep ocean are almost forgotten. When Jan weeps, we avoid his gaze. After such a half-breath of time, we are wearied by the effort of caring, of speaking our remembrance. Already weary, we are acquiring the habit of silence. None more so than me, for I am become full of curiosity, have forgotten already my wish to weep with Jan for the loss of his daughter. Instead I remember only the crossing of the hands, the bowing of the head.

I wish to see the beads in his hands, I wish to hear the Mary prayer. It is said that they carry incense and burn it when alone, also candles, so that a shrine will be created to their God wherever they shall be. Though I have little but soreness towards Wiebbe Hayes and his brusque manner towards me, I am full of hunger for the secrets he may hold. For many days, I hope to catch a glimpse of him, so that I may ask him about the incense, the candles, the priests, and what they believe on the matter of souls. For many days, he is nowhere. Soldiers eat below deck with the sailors, and do not take the daytime watches. What duties they carry out between the decks, in the dark quarters, I do not know, will not imagine.

We are moving closer and closer to the Cape, so the commander has told us, and the days are so hot that I have ceased wearing an under-dress. My hair is heavy on my head, even seated in the shade it feels wet and burning. At night, the heat stills and rots the air, so that our breath mixes each with the other's until I cannot sleep with the stench of it. Anna sleeps beside me so soundly that you would swear that our wooden ledge was a mattress of purest down. She snores loudly all the while. In the morning she denies this snoring, insisting that she is a silent sleeper; yet how would she know the sound of her own snores, if she sleeps through them?

Strangely, the ship tosses more at night as the heat rises, so that for the first time I feel the biliousness which troubled so many at the start of our journey. Five nights of lying awake next to Anna's snoring, the bile rising in my mouth with every tilt of the ship's walls, and I know that I must have air, must see the moon, walk upright. Deeper in me, the hope that I might see the papist on a night watch, might have the chance to ask of him this: are angels allowed in their chapels? And can we or can we not pray for the souls of the dead?

Anna does not move as I climb over her, merely lets out a startled snore and mutters something about butter and coffee: even in her sleep she thinks of food. No one wakes, though I stumble as I slip Myntgie's cape over myself. They sleep so easily and so well. I cannot see their faces in this deep dark, but I know the shape of my father's face when he sleeps, for he has often fallen asleep after lunch, his chin burying itself in his chest. His cheeks puff out and collapse, so that he seems like a flattened coat. Even his lips droop down and become thicker, sometimes with a spell of wetness on the edges. This is how he will be as I creep to the deck ladder, his face drooping and leaking spittle.

Even with the sun gone, the deck is damp and heavy with heat. Above the mainmast, the moon is round and clear, lighting the deck as well as any candle. There is a hot wind on my face which calms my unease. On the lower deck, shadowy figures gather round the wheel; there is no chanting now, only quiet chattering in a language which is not my own. French, perhaps, for it is said there are many French soldiers on board. When I listen intently, I know it to be French that I hear. Nor am I alone on the poop deck. At the far end, near the Great Cabin, there are two figures. Leaning, as I am, against the gunwale, both of them with skirts blowing. The moon slips behind a cloud, so I keep one hand on the gunwale and place my feet carefully.

The voice is sharp, startled. 'Who is it?'

The moon reappears, shining light on the deck, and on Lucretia's face peering at me.

'Lucretia, it's me, Judith Bastiaansz. I did not expect to find others about at such an hour. Could you not sleep either? This heat and the wind make it hard to be restful.'

'Oh, I can never sleep, not on land or sea. Poor Zwaanje – this is Zwaanje, my maid, though really she has been more like a sister this last year – has to make the best of it, for I need her to walk about with me when I am disturbed. You are braver than I, walking about on your own.'

'It did not occur to me that it was dangerous. Perhaps I am foolish. I did not think carefully about my actions; it was the need for air which drove me up here.'

'I do not know what it is that drives me. Only that I am so restless.'

Zwaanje is tall and broad next to Lucretia, and though she barely nods at me, even in the moonlight I notice that her eyes are as pallid as water. Around her neck, a gold chain.

'That's lovely.' I point at the chain.

'I gave it to Zwaanje before we started on the journey. She

truly is like a sister to me.' Lucretia strokes her white cap and I cannot help but notice that she speaks for her servant before her servant is able to open her own mouth; and also that Zwaanje almost bares her teeth. Like a savage dog rather than a smiling sister.

On the lower deck a sail is rising skyward; three men grunting and straining as if it is the anchor they are raising. None of them are recognisable in the dark: they could all be papists, or none. Beside me, more footsteps, heavy and hurried. They come close, and I jump as a man calls, cutting through the half-dark.

'Three ladies enjoying the midnight air, what joy to see it.' The voice is hoarse and thick with brandy. As he peers in closer, I recognise the skipper. 'Oh, look who it is: the high and mighty wife of van der Mijlen.'

'We were just about to return to our beds. Come, Zwaanje.' Lucretia turns towards the deck ladder.

The skipper puts his hand out, grabs Lucretia's wrist. 'Perhaps you will take me with you to your bed, this time. I have no doubt that you have shared your favours with others in command of this ship.'

My chest tightens, yet I am determined, this time, not to remain silent. 'You forget that you have an audience. Do not doubt that I will tell the commander of your crass words. I am sure he will deal with you accordingly.' Truly, I am sure of no such thing, for the commander has been ill in his cabin for a good many days of our journey and has shown little inclination towards disciplining the rowdy elements of his crew.

'Thank you for reminding me of the presence of our esteemed commander, he of the poorly chest and the elevated morals. I am sure her ladyship is grateful, I am sure her heart beats faster at the mere mention. Still, I am sure I would be as good a substitute as any. I am the one who makes the ship go where she will and my cock is as hard as any man's, and drives faster.'

'I am a married woman.' Lucretia seems taller, seems to draw herself up. 'And I do not require your assistance, or your admiration, or your obscenities.'

'Oh, I am sure you expect the admiration of every poor fool who passes your way. Yet I will see you fallen from your grand perch, madam.'

Lucretia, as far as I could tell, had done nothing to deserve his wrath other than refuse his advances. Yet he appeared enraged by her, even her white wrists seemed to drive him to the fury of a mad dog. That which he desired in her was also that which he despised. I have learnt that this is not unusual in a certain type of man. Nor in a certain type of woman.

Lucretia turns to leave. 'We will find no peace here, Zwaanje. Come. You should sleep as well, Judith.' Imperious as a noblewoman. Zwaanje follows, looks back for a moment, not at me but at the skipper, glancing down and then up, just as if she were looking at the sun, being careful of its dazzling light. When she turns to me, her lips pinch in and her eyes are so narrow that I think: *she hates me*. And then she smiles at me, says, 'After you, madam,' with lips full and head low; so that I am reeling, puzzled by my own imaginings. For surely these things must be, after all, no more than vain fancies, more tattered than the sails which fly above me, bearing me on to my new land.

Chapter Twelve

Father keeps count of the days very carefully, marking them in the side of his Holy Book. For many weeks, he greets us each morning with a loud proclamation of the day number: 'Blessed morning to you, Family Bastiaansz. This is the twenty-second day of our journey.'

My mother replies with her usual 'Thanks be to God for preserving us this far' or 'Glory be'. On what is perhaps day number forty-three of our journey, my mother slaps her head with her hands and says, 'Must we hear this infernal clock every morning?' Her voice is as loud as I have ever heard it. The next morning, my father does not proclaim the day, but simply says, 'Blessed morning, Family Bastiaansz,' very quietly, and then goes immediately out to the deck to join the morning call. Sometimes, a litany of the previous day's events: another storm blowing up, the sister ships disappearing out of sight.

Provost Jansz, too, marks off the days, counting them against the main mast each evening. His three children stand alongside him, hands behind their backs. The provost has a black beard reaching almost to his chest, and black eyes which seem often damp. When he bangs the baton against the mast, his face is as solemn as dough. Yet I have seen him laugh, at least four times, so hard that his waist and chest bounced together. He often pats his daughter on the head, sometimes leaving his hand resting there, and once he interrupted his speaking to hear her question. I have wondered how this must be, to have a father notice you so.

Oddly, in spite of the provost's daily count, I find myself able to forget which day we are, where we are. Somehow I have taught myself not to listen, or at least not to hear. My days are marked out by who spoke what to whom, by Roelant's slight achievements, by the quantity of the meat or biscuit we are given for lunch, and the quality of the dinner. In these ways, it is no different from my life in Dordrecht. Only that somehow I have gained the addition of a perpetual swaying, an ability to walk with softened knees. Also I have gained a strange condition of freedom for the first time ever; although I am not at first able to name it as this, not until much later. It is strange, strange indeed, that this condition should occur to me when I am unable to walk more than a narrow mile, and that only achieved through walking in a series of ever tightening circles. Here I cannot visit the market, nor run away, even if I wished. Yet in spite of the presence of my father, I feel that I have done exactly this: run away to a different life.

During one evening, Conraat van Hueson told Myntgie and me stories of women who run away to sea, dressed as men. This is true, he has sworn it. Not all of them young and straight-breasted, as you might imagine, either. Many are as round and curved as any woman might wish to be, and merely disguise themselves as the sort of youth who may partake in more than his share of beer. As strong as some boys, he said, and many of them harder workers, until they are found out. Myntgie shuddered as though there was a cold wind, and insisted that these women must be as ungodly as Lucifer himself. For myself, I am willing to believe them as godly as me, and much braver. Since I have heard of them, I sometimes imagine myself pretending to be a boy on a ship like this, so that I would be hoisting up the rigging, swinging from the stays and calling out to other men to watch their arses! For I am sure that to be convincing, such a girl must have to be as coarse as the sailors themselves.

Some days after Conraat told us these stories, I am watching the boys on the lower deck, wondering if any of them are women, though Conraat assures me that there is no need on the *Batavia*, with women allowed on board with barely a whisper. For the first time in many days, I am alone. And glad of it. Glad of the chance to watch the swinging and calling and the signs they each seem to know: here one boy passes the other and lifts his hand in the air; the first boy nods and runs to the bow side and begins wrenching at a pulley. When the work is fierce, there is little speaking. Words are passed between them, onc at a time: sweetbreads, to be used carefully. Now and then a song is started, and most join so that even the few words thrown across the deck disappear, yet the work continues. All of it is a mystery to me, how they make this enormous ship move, how they keep her upper deck clean and fresh and her sails neat and patched. Nor do I know how this happens: as I am standing alone, watching the work, wondering on the mystery of this great ship, a sailor on the main deck below me swings his arm back and punches a soldier. For what reason, I cannot tell. When his punch lands, the soldier hits back immediately, so that the sailor falls over onto the hard deck. Yet he gets up at once, only to be punched by another sailor, perhaps to avenge the soldier. This second sailor is in turn punched by a soldier. This soldier runs at the first sailor, runs at him with his head down, then another soldier leaps in, roaring gleefully, and then I cannot fathom who is punching who, nor why, only that it happens very quickly and all are yelling nonsense words at each other.

Why do men do this? For here is the greatest mystery: that in the midst of the punching and falling and throwing and bleeding, there is something resembling laughter. Something resembling joy. They have been waiting for this, they are all somehow agreed; they have been waiting since the commander first retired to his quarters, since the skipper first snapped a bird's neck, since they first heard the elegant undermerchant asking, 'Is he weak or weary?' I see this, somehow, in their grins disguised as snarls and it frightens me more than anything I have known.

'Where is the commander? Fetch the commander.' I trip over my own feet as I run the length of the upper deck, calling to anyone who will listen.

Lucretia seizes my arm. 'They have gone to get him, sit and be still, Judith.' She looks about the deck. 'It is not proper, running like this. Your father has gone.'

'The men are all fighting.' My tongue will not settle.

'Yes. How could I not hear them? It is a sailor's brawl. The commander will stop them.' Lucretia is calm and still. There are no words to tell her what it is that has frightened me, seeing men revel in the action of hand against face. Fighting only because they want to. Until this, I have always believed our wars, even the minor battles, to have a reason, and these reasons to be reasons of honour. How strange that it has never struck me before now that the reasons for war are twofold: greed and desire. We are told that the Spanish desired the Netherlands. But greater than their desire for power was their lust for war. Men wish to fight, they look for reasons.

My father emerges from the Great Cabin, his face flushed and red. 'Commander Pelseart is resting. He is unwell.' Father looks past me, lifting his chin at two men standing behind me. 'Again. It will have to be Undermerchant Cornelisz who deals with the men. Though it will be purely a matter of discipline now as the fighting appears to have settled.' It is true. Below us, on the deck, the men have stuttered to a stop, the punching and throwing and cursing ending as quickly and as pointlessly as it began. To me, my father says, 'You should be below, Judith.'

Behind my father, his long arms swinging, Conraat appears. And with his fair curls and lips which seem stained with wine, oh, and his nose as straight as a mast, he does indeed resemble the angels painted so seriously by the Italians. Already I am being won by this. For though his stories amuse me, I am being won by nothing more than the width of his palms, the whiteness of his hair, and the black-green sea in his eyes. It is true that he is a soldier, yet he is a nobleman for all that, and does not eat with the soldiers; it is easy to be won by him. As for him, what could he be won by? He tells me my innocence is appealing, and that my eyes delight him. He knows little of my thoughts, for when I open my mouth to speak, he presses his finger to my lips and shushes me, as he might shush a beloved pup.

'Honourable Predikant.' Conraat bows his head to Father, a tight smile curving beneath his beard. 'How fortunate for your lovely daughters, and,' he bows to Lucretia, 'for all the women on board, that the men have settled after all.'

'Did you speak to the soldiers, Lord van Hueson? For I notice that they calmed quickly.' Father folds his hands, appears to be in prayer.

'I did have a word, in the absence of Commander Pelseart.'

'Even now, in these feverish days, rank is able sometimes to still the beasts in men.' My father nods his head vigorously, so that his beard is like a dog's tail, wagging in the sun. How pleased I am to see you, it says, how pleased that you are my master.

Lucretia adjusts her hood. 'I must go and seek out my maidservant. My washing has not been done, I believe, for several days!'

'A firm hand with servants is always best.' Father speaks as though we have had twelve servants instead of merely Wylbrecht.

'Oh, really I treat Zwaanje more like a sister than a servant. Perhaps I am too soft.' Lucretia, it strikes me, says this often. She smiles at me. 'Will you accompany me, Judith?'

My father is a skin's width away from Conraat, though I do

not hear what he is saying. Across Conraat's face there lies a shadow, perhaps from the line of the centre mast, which cuts his face in two. One half bright in the sun, his skin pale, his hair gold; the other half clouded, deep and dark, his eyebrows heavy. His face is full of the deepest possibilities, the deepest promise.

'Judith?' Lucretia puts her hand on my elbow. 'Will you come?'

There is no reason, none that I can see, for her to want me to climb down to the cabins with her. And many reasons for me to stay here on deck, watching the shadows changing Conraat's face. Yet though I am wearing the green cap and collar given to me by Lucretia, Conraat appears immersed in conversation with my father. And I am happy for him to charm my father, for I have surely been charmed by Conraat van Hueson myself.

It is evening before I see Father again. Holding his blue prayer book, his elder's collar resting on his shirtdress, such a solemn face! He has become quite famous for his overlong graces, his long litany of requests to the Lord, and I know that many on the poop deck and in the Great Cabin believe he is a fool. No doubt the crew believe likewise. But my father is not a fool. Even now I do not believe this of him. Here he is, on this still-strange ship, seeking to be wise and strong for all on board. Wise he is not, nor strong. These things I know about my father. He wishes comfort for himself and for his family. 'Is that wrong?' he would say. 'Wishing the best for one's family?' He admires wealth, admires work, and is barely managing to survive my mother's desert of unhappiness.

Each morning, my mother stares at her feet, stares at Roelant, her last, bonny boy, and mutters that she cannot bear it, she does not believe she can bear it.

'Please, Maria.' Father kneels on the hard wood, his hands cold. 'Please, we are closer, nearly there, nearly there.'

She turns her head and her eyes are flat. 'Yes,' she says, 'nearly there.' Then she puts her feet on the floor, her head in her hands and says, 'I must go on, I simply must. Lord give me your strength.'

My father echoes her. 'Lord give us your peace.'

Each morning, before the morning watch is called, this is our recital. Silently, in my own thoughts, I finish: Lord give us your joy.

Yet Father shows nothing of this daily strain on deck, or in the Great Cabin, or in the ship's councils. He is puzzled, and hopeful and wishing to please, but this does not make him a fool.

During dinner of biscuit and white fish and grey peas with much rancid butter and sweet wine, Jeronimus Cornelisz engages Father in an argument of theology. Commander Pelseart is more and more unwell, rarely seen at dinner, and Jeronimus has become our chief raconteur. Indeed, though Father rarely understands a word he says, he claims to find the undermerchant extraordinarily stimulating, more so than the commander.

After dinner, Father whispers to me, 'The fine nobleman, my dear girl, from the Gelderland van Huesons, wishes to walk alone with you this evening. Of course I could not allow such a thing, but I did offer myself as a chaperone. Come.'

Tonight there is no music on the poop, although a group of sailors are singing a marching song on the main deck as they clean a sail, or are they stitching? Several of the men hold the sail and rub something back and forth, it is hard in the dim light to see exactly what. Never before has a man requested my company, never has my father been my chaperone. I cannot imagine why Conraat would desire me: I am eighteen, an innocent, my family have nothing. Perhaps I am being unfair on myself, for here, in these days on the *Batavia*, my lips are red, my waist is plump, my skin is soft and I am able to converse as well as any other of my age and experience. For these reasons – my newness at the game of courting and my bewilderment at being chosen for such entertainment – I am almost silent for our walk around the poop. Father walks behind Conraat and me, humming and ha-ing to himself, and I watch the sailors on the main deck. As we draw close again to the Great Cabin, two men emerge from the lower decks. A soldier, under escort. As I pass, the soldier looks up at me. Beside him, a torch is burning and I can see the plain face of the papist Wiebbe Hayes. He smiles up at me and bows his head. If he were closer I would ask him where they meet, what they speak of, where the candles are. He is not close enough, though, to call such disgraceful questions and Conraat's hand presses firmly on my back, steering me away.

Father trots closer to us, almost breathless with this tiny exertion, and says, 'Do not give any encouragement or acknowledgement to the common soldier, my Judith. They are not,' he looks at Conraat, 'our people.'

Conraat raises his fair eyebrows high on his head so that his forehead wrinkles into a prune rather than a peach. For a moment, something is clear: Conraat is somehow patronising not just my father, but me. We are a game of some sort. Then his forehead wrinkles into a cat's face: neat whiskers, eyes on the mouse. Then his face is smoothed and my mind is cloudy and gentle again. Cloudy and gentle and full of thoughts of Conraat, with his hand pressing firmly on my back in a moment which seems to last forever.

Chapter Thirteen

Tomorrow we will arrive in the Cape of Good Hope. Good hope! The name grows brightly coloured. What better name for a place could there be? Thinking of it fills me with a quiet joy, although I am often on the edge of joy, since Conraat's attentions to me have increased. All day, the sun beams brighter and rounder, I have never seen such a sun in my life. I can scarcely believe it to be the same sun which struggles to overcome the mist on our own Zuider Zee. So round and white that I cannot look at it, for fear of burning not just my eyes, but all that lies inside me. Burning my joy, my hope. For I cannot bear to look at this either, the hope I have. I imagine that if I do, if I glance at it directly, surely it will shock me, scold the very heart of me. In this, I cannot think of my wishes in relation to Conraat and must choose instead to look elsewhere. Briefly, I think again about the papists. Briefly, I seek out Wiebbe Hayes. Yet, when I find him, I am disappointed on every count.

From the waist of the main deck, I can see the steps down to the gun deck, a dark corridor with soldiers bent double over cannons and guns, shining with sweat. No chanting comes from this deck, only the thud of hammers and metal. Brief snatches of words, phrases. It is only through young Jan that I know the location of the gun deck, where the soldiers eke out their time in two cramped, dark spaces. For all their shame and noise, Jan seems besotted with soldiers, with their weapons. In the mornings, after breakfasting, he waves his tin knife, shouting, 'No evil ones shall get me or my family, for I can fight to the death.'

No, I say, you must not fight to the death, for I need you to stay with me and be my dear brother. Now and then I make him promise that when he is grown he shall seek his fortune as a clerk for the Company, or a predikant. Perhaps even a merchant. But never a common soldier, for they bring only heartbreak to their families and shame to their Lord. Yet here I am, seeking out the secret deck of the soldiers, with all its stink. And here is the truth: I cannot see the gun deck without straining, bending over almost double and peering down through a narrow door, half the width of a man. It is not through chance, or accident, that I see the rows of dark cannons edged against the portholes. No, it is entirely my desire, and my design. Below my feet, through the door, a ladder leans down to the deck. For the first time in the voyage, it occurs to me that I could step down, simply place my feet on the ladder and descend. There is nothing stopping me; no guard, no army. The very thought, the very possibility, shocks me so that my throat burns.

Where do these things come from, these sudden impulses? For I have no reason to seek out the soldier other than a mild curiosity. Yet the thought of climbing down into this forbidden place excites me. I am obedient Judith, I help my family, I am kind-hearted and reliable. This is what I know about myself, what I expect of myself. Yet now, standing with this ladder behind me, I think that after all I do not know myself so well, and I wish to be disobedient Judith: seeker of forbidden places.

One foot goes back and I feel the wooden ledge beneath my heel. If I am seen, if someone reports me to my father; I cannot imagine. As I step back, two women approach me, and then draw away to the gunwale. I will be seen, and this makes me even more determined! At the far end of the waist, four officers have gathered, speaking quietly and pointing at the edge of the sea. Nearer to me, a cluster of young women, giggling and walking in circles. Myntgie is amongst them and I hold my breath, waiting for them to pass. Myntgie turns her head as they approach the group of officers. She raises her hand in a cheerful wave, and I beckon her closer, putting my finger to my lips to bid her keep quiet.

'Who are you hiding from?' She creeps close to me, whispering in mock fear. 'Conraat? Conraat, whom you have been unable to see enough of, or speak enough of, these last weeks?'

'Hush. I am not hiding.' I give her a gentle push on the shoulder, so that she giggles.

'Well, it is a change to have you not hiding from me.'

'Myntgie! How could you think such a thing?'

'You have so little time to spend with me or Anna, or even the boys. You seem only interested in the corporal.'

Is it jealousy I hear in her voice, or anger? Or worry? 'He is –' I am suddenly halted by a picture in my mind, a picture of Conraat, with the sun around him, creating a halo against his hair.

A huge, lovely smile flashes across my sister's face. 'Yes, he is. Of course he is.' She hugs me.

'Myntgie. Watch for me.'

'What do you mean? Watch for what? And why?'

'See that no one comes near. Or distract them if they do.' I look around the deck, and feel suddenly shy with my sister. 'I am going to go down into the gun deck.'

Myntgie's face widens out; her mouth becomes a circle. 'What in the Lord's earth for? It is full of soldiers, Judith. It will do your reputation no good at all. Would Conraat approve? Anyway, what can you find to be interested in down there? A bunch of stinking cannons and soldiers who have not washed since we left Texel Island.'

'Conraat will have no opinion, as he will not hear a word. Because if any person comes close, you will distract them and indicate to me, by kicking your feet against the ladder, that I am unsafe.' I hesitate for a moment, unsure of how safe Myntgie is. 'I think they may have a Mass down there. No, please, stop scowling, Myntgie. I will not become one, I am simply –' I look down at my feet, notice that the buckles are in sore need of a polish – 'I am simply curious. Is that really wicked, to wish to see how they worship our Lord? Is it wicked to believe that they are not so different from ourselves and to wish to meet them? That is all, Myntgie, I wish to meet them, to observe the worship, to form an opinion.'

'It is hardly your place to form an opinion, Judith. The elders have already done that, and anyway, how could there be Catholics on board? The Company will not employ them. You will be disappointed, Judick.' Yet a smile has replaced her scowl and I know that she will keep her lips closed.

While Myntgie stands at the top of the ladder, looking about as though she is waiting to meet a friend, or perhaps her mother, I climb down into the gun deck. My palms are wet and my blood sounds fierce in my ears. New sounds: hammer on metal, something scraping against wood, a repeated heavy thud. And a tired babble of men's voices, which stops as soon as my feet touch the deck. The ship gives a lurch as my hands leave the ladder rails, so that my knees fold and my head flops forward, banging on the wood of the rail. Something wet is running down my face; I lift my hand, expecting blood. Water instead. Sweat, perhaps.

Behind me, someone calls: 'You seem to have made a mistake, miss. Come down to the gun deck. What was it you were looking for?'

The voice is not unkind, and I turn. Wiebbe Hayes is standing by a cannon, a cloth in his hand. Men fill the low deck, heavy bodies making the air itself thinner. Behind him, in the dim dark, hammocks hang like rotten meat. My hand covers my nose, for the stench is of ill flesh and waste.

'Yes,' I say, feeling suddenly filled with shame, 'I have come the wrong way. I was – I do not know, looking for something. Someone.'

Concern flicks across his face, or perhaps discomfort. 'Hello, Eldest Sister Judith. Surely you have not lost someone here. There are only soldiers here.' He smiles, a wash of pink travelling up his face. 'Soldiers who cannot appreciate fine things such as sunsets.'

I nod at his feet, feeling ashamed. 'I am sorry I offended you. I was rude.'

'No. I was discourteous and disrespectful.' He smiles again, his crooked teeth showing.

His shoulders stretch far across; his chest is the length of my arm. Wiebbe is a solid match for these cannons. I can imagine my fists enfolded by one of his ruddy hands.

'I am sorry, I am speaking out of turn again. You must be looking for your brothers, not for talk from soldiers.' He waves his arms about the corridor, almost hitting a tall, moustached, soldier on the face. The man's beard is long and matted, reaching almost to his chest. He stares at me for a long moment, his mouth turned down, until Wiebbe says, 'This is Gunner Jan van Bemmel.'

The soldier turns away as though I am of no more interest than a pea.

Wiebbe looks at the deck again. 'Your brothers have ventured down once or twice – remember the predikant's boys, Jan? – but we send them scurrying back up. A threat of being shot through the cannon usually does it, suddenly they are not so brave. Perhaps they are hiding in the gallery?'

'Yes. Yes, I am sure that is it. Thank you.'

Here I am, surrounded by forty, fifty, soldiers, some of them sleeping on their stained hammocks and stinking bed mats, and I know that I am ridiculous. Looking for the secret meetings when surely they are meant to be private. And why did I think he would tell me anyway? Strangest of all, I have no real knowledge of why I am here. No real knowledge of the reason for my desire to know about these people, the Mary worshippers, other than that it is forbidden by my father and it is a curiosity. No, I do not tell all of the truth here, for there is something greater than these simple reasons, and also harder to tell. My father's religion is one of order, of neatness. There is no room in it for the unexpected, for all is preordained. Sometimes, I am inclined to believe that the Company owns the Church, for they are certainly married and bearing fruit. And I am not entirely certain that I will ever be the Judith of neatness, of order. Here, on this ship, with the edge of the world constantly shifting and bobbing, and the platform beneath my feet always moving so that I am become used to swaying in my body as I stand and as I walk; here with all the creatures of the deep unknown and unseen beneath me; here, nothing is certain. I no longer know what sort of Judith I am, I am no longer sure of my father's religion with no room for angels. Yet with the sky unravelling above me, I am so certain of my Lord Himself that He and I stand still, perfectly still, together. Everything else is as unfathomable as the sea.

So I say nothing to Wiebbe Hayes. I do not ask him if he is, as I believe, a worshipper of Mary; I do not ask him where they meet, or if I could join them. I ask him nothing. I apologise for my mistake, thank him for his kindness and, with the soldiers watching me, I climb up the ladder again.

'Did you not go down after all? You took no time, I had barely a chance to perform my duties.' Myntgie is full of giggles.

'It was a fool's quest. I changed my mind.'

'I'm glad.'

We stand in quiet for a moment, swaying with the shift of the ship. Above us, all the sails are in full furl, white and glorious. From here, you cannot see the patches and passages of careful sailor's darning, the ragged greyness of the cloth. I tilt my head back and shade my eyes from the sun, although the sails do provide some shadow. Row after row of full whiteness, like gulls' breasts.

'Beautiful. They are simply beautiful.' I smile at Myntgie, somehow pleased with myself for keeping silence in the gun deck, for refraining from making a foolish display.

Myntgie lets out a snort of laughter. 'They are simply sails, my Judith. Sails full of wind, bearing us on. They are useful, that is all.'

'Can useful not be beautiful?'

She looks at me sharply. 'The two are rarely together, in my opinion. Useful, or beautiful. One or the other.'

'Yet goodness and beauty go so often together.'

'Perhaps they do.' But her lips are pulled into a frown. 'That is what is said.'

'Our Dordrecht house is beautiful and also useful.' I feel that I must show that she is mistaken.

'Yes.' Myntgie claps her hands together. 'Then I am wrong and you are right and I am sorry and you shall have my share of wine with your dinner. But remember the artist's words, Judith: early ripe, early rot.'

My mouth opens to ask her what these words have to do with me, but I am silenced by shouting from the mast boys, high on the centre and foremasts. One is swinging down the mast, his arms looping long, his mouth twisted in a loud cry so that he looks like a strange sort of animal. On the main deck, sailors are calling, backslapping, embracing. What is it he is calling? Myntgie pulls at my arm and points horizonward, as excited as a child.

'There,' she is saying. 'Look, look. There it is, the land of the Hottentots. Oh, Judith, solid ground at last, earth beneath our feet.' And she hugs me so fiercely that I can barely breathe.

Ahead of us is a grey haze, a solid shape rising out of the sea. No longer the endless line of the ocean. More than anything, I want to weep; but I shall not. All have taken up the boy's cry now; the sailors on the main deck, the officers here with us on the waist, the passengers on the poop: all joining in the exultant cry.

Land, we cry, until we become a leaping, hugging chorus. Land! Just ahead, look out, look forward. Good victuals. Good rest. Thanks be to the Lord, here we are, Good Hope!

Good Hope indeed. We are past halfway; from here, we cannot turn back. Here, the whole world changes. Glorious Good Hope.

Chapter Fourteen

The land of the Hottentots is not as I had expected. Not as I had hoped. Disappointing not in itself but in its distance. For some foolish reason, I had hoped that we would be able to step straight down from the *Batavia* onto dry land. Although quite where I would get this idea from, I do not know. When we left Texel, we were rowed far out, and why did I think it would be any different in a greener, warmer land? So, here we are, anchored in the balmy harbour of an exciting new continent, and I am still on the ever-moving deck. Anna says that she has no desire to set foot on the same land as savages, which is what she insists the Hottentots are, and is happy to know that the commander will be able to revictual. Happy to know that we are closer to Java then we are to Dordrecht. The journey will be easier from now on, she says; fresh food, warm breezes, an absence of storms. Both the *Assendelft* and the *Bueren* have anchored alongside us. The *Bueren* bumped fiercely into us as they tried to anchor; the bump was so sudden that Hilletje Haardens fell against the centre mast and had blood running from her nose. As for the *Assendelft*, we were anchored here for two nights before it arrived, with the crew calling out to us mockingly, 'All hail the high and mighty *Batavia*!' Father said he suspected that much ale had been drunk and perhaps this accounted for the slowness of the arrival.

Wylbrecht came to me yesterday, her long face drawn in and pale. Frightened, she said, for she heard Skipper Jacobsz muttering in the steerage with Jeronimus. Hunched together, whispering foul plans.

'Why surely it is reasonable for the skipper to talk with the undermerchant?' The sun was hot on my head, making me short of breath and of temper.

'No, no,' Wylbrecht shook her head, her grey cap slipping forward, 'he spoke the word mutiny. Said the *Assendelft* was already—' And there she stopped, for my father approached and Wylbrecht will not be seen to gossip by my father. He stood silent while Wylbrecht gathered herself up and hurried away to pound at our clothes with a quarter cake of dry yellow soap.

Father nodded at the *Bueren* and the *Assendelft*, said, 'Of all our fleet, this is what remains: three ships. It is sobering to remember that we are so easily lost.'

Yes, I said, yes; though my head was full of the one word Wylbrecht spoke. Mutiny. Surely, though, the skipper – and certainly, at least, Jeronimus – were speaking of ways to prevent any such plots from hatching. For Wylbrecht receives her gossip from others who have received it yet from someone else; I set no store, after all, in such rumours.

There are hills in the distance, and it is pleasing simply to see green land, and stretches of flatness. Conraat and several other officers are to be rowed ashore, to seek extra trade with the Hottentots. Commander Pelseart has been ashore two nights, trading pieces of metal for good fresh food. Father assures me that the natives are happy with what they receive. Though he has not been ashore himself, he has received this information directly from the commander. Tomorrow we shall have fresh fruit for our dinner, and new meat. For many, this is enough to provide cheer. But for myself, I want to walk on the earth. More than this: from the edge of the deck, I can see the shapes of people, though they are distant. Though I scarcely dare to say it even to myself, I wish to meet the Hottentots. Mama says that it would cause untold harm if the passengers were all to be rowed ashore, and although I have searched my mind I can think of no reason that harm would be caused. What should we do? Run away and live in a grass hut and eat dirt? We are still four months away from Java and I do not know that I will survive such a time without a touch, a tiny touch, of solid land.

As for the crew and soldiers, they are kept under careful watch; perhaps the rumours have met the commander's ears. Tonight, the skipper will visit our sister ships, bringing greetings and victuals, but his crew must be satisfied with waiting for new barrels of fresh water and news from the officers. Nor do they seem to have less work required of them. On the contrary, all day sailors have been scrubbing savagely at the lower decks, patching sails, mending and coiling rope. Always watched over by the high boatswain, a wide man who bellows so loudly that his face puffs out like the very sails he stands beneath. His beard and moustache are so black that his pale skin looks sickly green against the dark hair. I see some men cowering, as if he has a whip. Others gather round, drawing close. I am sure I would not wish to be serving beneath him. Sometimes, Undermerchant Cornelisz ventures out, arms folded, head nodding. These things make me more, not less, concerned about the whispers Wylbrecht brought to me. Mutinous whisperings from the *Assendelft*. On the matter of our own *Batavia*, Wylbrecht bites her lip, shakes her head and says nothing.

Lunch is served on the poop deck, and it is the younger crew and our own servants who attend us. For all my complaints, it is very pleasing to have the sound of still water lapping at the ship and to have the prettiness of the land in sight as a benevolent onlooker. The prospect of fresh fruit, and the kindness of the sun on my face, makes it difficult to maintain my mean spirits.

After lunch, Conraat approaches my father, bows slightly before him, and asks if he may have the pleasure of my company for the afternoon. Myntgie looks away, her lips tight together, but my father says that Conraat may indeed have the pleasure of my company. My body begins to sing.

Conraat steers me away from the poop, so that we are edged into the darkness of the gallery where the smell of rich broth is strong. He leans close to me, so that I can see the fine hairs on his cheeks, the crooked lines around his eyes. 'Judith, my Judith. You are so soft. So innocent. I think of you constantly. Do you think of me?'

My Judith! My body breaks into a victorious chorus. 'You know that I do.' I can barely answer for the sound of rushing wind in my ears.

'Would you do anything for me?'

I am unsure of his meaning, of what he could be asking, so I say nothing, merely lower my head.

He smiles and takes my hand. 'I am going ashore. Come with me.'

'Am I allowed?'

'It is allowed if I desire it to be so, and I do desire it to be so.' He lifts my fingers to his lips. 'Such tender new fruit.'

I pull my hand away. 'I shall go and ask my father.'

'No.' He holds a finger up to my lips. 'Ask no one. You have my permission.'

'No, I could not. Conraat, my father—'

'Do you not trust me? Your father will approve, I promise.'

'But I must ask him. It would be – I simply could not disobey him.'

He turns his face away. 'Then you must not come. We are leaving now, the sailors are waiting and if other passengers were to know that I planned to take you – surely you can imagine, Judith? Do not come with me. Or else come quickly.'

My legs shake beneath me as I climb down to the skiff bobbing on the swell. They shake so hard that I am sure I will slip and fall down to the bottom of the sea. Conraat assures me we are not in a strong tide here and I would be easily salvaged if I slipped. This is the word he uses: salvaged, as if I am a piece of gold. In the end, I do not slip. My feet are steady until I feel Conraat's hands on my waist, lowering me into the skiff. Both feet swing off the ship's ladder and into the boat, so that I feel as light as a gold ring and I barely notice his hands about me. It is only when he sets me down in the boat that I begin to tremble. Only slightly, but still it is a tremble. My father is above me, performing an afternoon reading for the family, wondering where I can have got to, and I am ducking my head down, staring at the boards beneath me.

There are four sailors in the boat. The two at the rear – the stern, I suppose – smile at me as I sit myself down on the bar. The two at the front show me only their broad backs. Three other officers climb in after me; all men I have seen on the main deck, none whom I have spoken to. And why would I? For Conraat fills my thoughts and time and words so that I barely notice another. When we are all settled, Conraat calls forward to the sailor ahead of him to row fast and well. The sailor turns his head and nods at Conraat. He does not look at me.

Seeing me look down at my hands, biting my lip, one officer leans forward and taps me on the back. 'I am Andries. Andries de Vries. Please, tell me if I can help you with anything.' He has a wound, a blood-brown knife mark, travelling from his lip to his nose.

Conraat pushes his hand away. 'She has everything she could need with me, de Vries. Get back to your place.' He laughs, mouth closed, as he says it. Andries nods his head curtly.

Although the sea seemed calm from the height of the ship, here in this tiny rowing boat it is as rough as a mother's slap.

Each crest of wave tosses us so that I bounce on my flat seat. Conraat smiles into the sun, the spray splashing his face so that he is even more beautiful. Another wave tosses us, and I slip sideways, letting out a cry.

'Are you not comfortable, little Judith? You are perfectly safe here with me.' His laugh breaks over me, leaves me breathless in its wake.

I cannot answer him, for all my mind and strength are engaged in clinging to the edge of the skiff, trying to smile or at least not look full of terror; and full of terror is not what I feel. Not quite, not exactly. I am exhilarated, pushed to the brim of myself with the waves and the sun. Yet certainly not unafraid; for I feel that with each wave I will tumble into the sea and be washed ashore as a dead thing. Conraat is here though, my protector, and I know I will not slip beneath the waves while his hand is near mine. This I believe, as I must. He is silent beside me, perhaps waiting for my answer.

'Yes,' I say, into the waves. 'I am safe with you. I trust you.'

If he hears me he does not show it, and soon there is the scrape of sand on the bottom of the boat. Three officers and both of the soldiers jump out, their hands slapping the water, and begin to drag the yawl up to the shore.

'Get out, you lazy lumps, cannot see why we should be dragging you.' A dark-haired officer slaps Conraat on the shoulder.

'And why should we all get wet, simply to please you? Anyway, I am accompanying the lady.'

Though I can see nothing funny in what Conraat has said, the officers dragging the boat let out loud hoots and yelps, laughing too loudly for my comfort.

And here we are, dragged up the tilt of sand so that Conraat can lift me out as though I am a delicate vase. One foot, and then the other, onto the flaky golden earth. Solid earth, not moving, not slipping. My joints go soft beneath me, and when I take my first steps, I almost fall to my knees. Five months of sea legs, and I have lost the use of my land legs! After such a long time wishing to feel the earth, it is strange indeed to suddenly find the earth alien. To find that I have, against my will, become a creature of the sea. A creature used to everything moving, always changing, always uncertain. Conraat puts his hand beneath my elbow and half carries me up the gentle slope to a grassy embankment. Here it is easier, the earth is at least resistant. Yet still, this swaying of the knees is almost comical. In front of me, a low tree. As I reach out my hand to hold onto it, the heavens open and I hear music, the music of God. Conraat points his finger to a line of people, dark as burnt bushes, swaying and clapping.

It is singing, yet it is unlike singing I have ever heard, or could ever imagine hearing. How could I describe it? Not at all like the boat chants, and yet with something of them in it. Also unlike the slow hymns sung in church, yet again so like. One woman starts, and another sings something completely different, and then the men join, their song brushing my shoulders, and my face. All of them melting together; not separate at all. A whole, complete sound. You see? I cannot tell it, I cannot make you hear it. How can I hope to make you hear any of this?

I edge closer to Conraat, suddenly frightened of the shiny

black skin, the smiles bright as coins. Hands stretch out, holding beads, pebbles, fruit. Pink finger ends wave at me.

'I will leave you with the children while we trade.' Conraat begins slipping away. Perhaps I look frightened, for he reaches out a hand to me. 'Don't you trust me?'

I look around me, at the black-skinned children, white teeth great moons in their faces; at the green earth and the pile of beads. The singing is still echoing in my secret parts. How could it be otherwise? I smile, shake my head.

'I will always trust you. I will.'

While the strange voices clack and click around us, Conraat takes a round purple fruit from a young boy and holds it to my mouth. Thick red juice runs down my chin, down my throat so that I am marked with its ripe sweetness. I wipe at it with my fingers and lick every last drop away.

Chapter Fifteen

When we row back to the ship, the sun is setting against the hills. The sky is a red flag, marked by a purple stripe. Conraat's face is covered in the glow of it, as I am sure mine must be. The summons for dinner is sounding, the evening watch chanting out their call. Father is standing by the provost, Holy Book in his hands, waiting to read the Word. As the chant ends, the provost strikes his baton and Father looks up at me. Wet skirts slap about my legs and I can feel my cap slipping sideways from my head. Also, I feel sure that sprinklings of sand drop where I walk, that grains of dirt are ground beneath my fingernails. Father stares at me for a moment, then hastily looks back to the Book and begins to read:

' "You began your race well; who came to obstruct you and stop you obeying the truth? It was certainly not any prompting from Him who called you. A pinch of yeast ferments the whole batch." '

He looks up at me again, and I bow my head. Though I should be thinking about the Lord and His ways, I find that I am thinking about bread. About the eating of it, not the making of it. Eating it warm and fresh and too good to waste. Conraat is breathing beside me, long slow breaths. This is odd, how I can hear his breath, how I imagine him breathing beside me at night. It is true, however foolish I may be, that I imagine being his wife. A pious wedding in Amsterdam. Bells ringing all morning. As for what comes later, the wedding bed, I cannot, must not, imagine that.

At dinner, Conraat is seated opposite my father. 'Thank you for the loan of your daughter, sir.' He passes the ale to Father.

Myntgie stares straight at me, mouth pursed, eyes hard; but though I hold my breath for Father's rebuke, he simply smiles at Conraat.

'It is an honour, my good sir.'

I look from Conraat to my father and back again. Does this mean Father knew all along? Or did Conraat tell him only after the visit to shore? In either case, I receive it as his blessing.

'You are not a slattern available for loan to any man who chooses.' Myntgie glares across at the flag of the *Bueren*, where scores of lamps shine along the decks. Lute music drifts across the bay with loud singing and truly I cannot tell whether Myntgie is angry with Father or with me. 'You must be more careful with yourself, Judith.'

'I am careful. It was a chaperoned trip to the shore. I should have asked Father's permission, I know, but he gave it afterwards anyway.'

'He had no choice. It does not look good, to have you

arriving on deck with a boat full of sailors. Truly, Judith, I am amazed that you are so blinded you cannot see this. You will have no husband if you have no reputation.' Her voice is thick with venom. Or perhaps with envy, though I have no wish to think this of her.

'Why do you dislike him so?'

She softens, turns her face to me. 'I do not know, truthfully. There is something in him I do not believe. Also, I heard Undermerchant Cornelisz telling the skipper that Conraat called Commander Pelseart a common worm of a man, worthy of insurrection. Please, Judith, do not open your mouth like that, I cannot help what I heard.'

I close my eyes for a moment, and draw my breath in deeply. Wishing for something solid, I put my hand out and grasp only air. Gleaming like knives, Myntgie's words gather up the moonlight. Worm. Insurrection. Conraat. I swallow air, turn to face my sister carefully. She is not right, she cannot be right.

'Then you must have misunderstood what you heard, or the undermerchant was lying. I am sorry, Myntgie, you are wrong to distrust him and I will not believe you.'

She shakes her head. 'You would disbelieve your sister?'

I say nothing, simply let the singing from the *Bueren* wash over me. Myntgie looks at me for a moment, then walks away.

On the main deck there is a party, as there is on the *Bueren*. Simply the knowledge that the land is there fills us with excitement. After so many months with only the waves and the line of the sea, the horizon endlessly distant, one begins to wonder if the land will ever exist again. Shouts fly up to the moon, calls for more wine, more songs, more dancing. Myntgie is perhaps below deck, reading the Lord's Book; I do not know. And Conraat, he is somewhere on the ship, though I do not know where.

Two sailors pass me, though they are not supposed to be on the poop at all. I can only assume that all rules are suspended whilst we are so close to the shore. They ask if I will be joining the party on deck. No, I reply, I am not sure that I will. Or at least, perhaps later. Over on the deck of the *Bueren*, I can see lanterns tossed into the air, candles thrown into the sea. Never before have I argued with Myntgie, nor with Anna. Sometimes I have snapped at the boys, even at Gisbert. Never at my sisters. Myntgie has always been the truest of sisters; I cannot bear to have her lying beneath the deck, on that harsh wooden ledge, thinking that I have gone to the Devil. Thinking at least that I do not care for her feelings. And though my mind is full of Conraat, it is not so full that there is no room for the love of my sister.

The waist of the main deck is dark, lit only by the remnants of light from the deck. I stumble along it until I find the deck ladder and back myself down, my feet feeling for each rung. From somewhere close to the officers' cabin, I can hear a woman crying. Gasping, rather than crying. Thinking that it is Myntgie, sorrowing for her rude sister, I grope my way down the corridor, away from our family cabin. Closer to the gallery, the gasping is louder, and I hear as well a man's voice. Not gasping, but speaking. No, not quite speaking: groaning out words which are unfamiliar to me and somehow shocking.

Something strange begins to run through my blood, something fierce. Perhaps fear, yet it is faster and larger than fear and I do not stop edging closer to the sound. The gallery door is ajar, and through it I can see two shapes, twisting. Shadows only. There is little light, and I strain to see, to discover if my Myntgie is being harmed, though what I will do I cannot tell. The grunting and gasping goes on, and somewhere along the corridor there are footsteps. Someone calls out a greeting, and a light appears beyond the end of the waist. I slide back against the wood, but it is a dim light, only enough to give the shadows form, enough for me to see my own hand but not the colour of it.

And this is the shape the shadows take: the woman is tall, broader than Myntgie, and rounder; the man is smaller. Her collar has been torn off, I can see it on the floor at her feet. Her dress and apron are both rolled down to her waist so that round white breasts shine in the quarter-light. His hand is on a breast, squeezing hard. Squeezing so hard, I imagine, that her nipple is thrust out, turns white. His head lowers to the breast and she cries out. She is pushed against the wall, head back. I should leave, find Myntgie, disappear from this immorality. Yet I cannot, for all my limbs seem to have turned to the softest, warmest liquid and my own breathing seems troubled. Perhaps I am sickening for something, for I am sure I am feverish. His hand slips down to her waist, to below her waist and she leans forward again, her head on his shoulder. Oh, she says, oh. She fiddles with his belts, his trousers, and he pushes her hand away, does something with his own hand and pushes himself towards her. She says, 'Yes,' but not like a word. And then there is rocking, her legs almost bare, lifted. Her breasts flattened against him. Her face turns to me and it is a face I recognise. It is Lucretia's servant, Zwaanje.

'Oh God, yes, yes, yes,' the man says, and even through the groaning, even through my own liquidness, I know that it is the skipper. It is the hoarseness I recognise; once I heard him calling to two sailors and I wondered if he was ailing, he spoke so full of coughs and croaks. I recall him throwing the bird to Lucretia, in an ill-mannered act which seems as far away as my days in Dordrecht.

My hands touch either side of the corridor and I lurch back towards the deck ladder, and down to the family cabin.

Myntgie is not lying weeping on the ledge, nor bowed down on the floor in prayer for me, though now I feel that I need it more than ever, for I close my eyes and I see Zwaanje's breast, white, squeezed by his hand. Even as I am overwrought by disgust, the bareness of her legs, lifted against him, appears before me. This is the Devil's work. As it is the Devil's work that right now I wish to go out onto the deck, look for Conraat, find him among the lanterns and have him bring me down here, to the darkness beneath the decks, and tear my collar away. The floor is cool beneath me, and I press hard on my knees. Push my hands into prayer. Begin to pray: 'Our Lord who chooses those who will be taken to Him, Our Lord who has chosen all things and all goodness before the dawn of time.' My words cease and I try to pray in the quietness of my mind. Our Lord. Her legs, bare, raised. Hear me, Father. His hand fumbling, her face crumpling on his shoulder. You answer those who are justified by your works. Conraat, biting my breast. Conraat touching my secret place. Oh.

I lie myself down on the lowest bunk, spread myself flat out so that the ledge is hard against my ribs and my hips. On my belly, my hands over my ears to stop the groaning I can hear inside my head, I lie very still, pushing harder and harder against the wood, until it hurts.

Chapter Sixteen

Deep and fierce voices, shouting. Something clanging loudly. They enter my sleep, these sounds, but I absorb them somehow, turn them into fuel for angry dreams. More clanging, and voices babbling, closer to my ears.

Myntgie shakes me awake. 'Do you not hear? There is an emergency, or must be, for there is shouting on deck, and they are ringing the bell.'

Father is pulling his collar on, Mama leans back, her eyes closed. 'You go and see to it, dear husband.' She pushes at my father's back. 'Off you go. You children go back to sleep.'

Above me, from the deck, I can hear a wooden sound, metal against wood. 'I will go with Father.' Myntgie has pulled her overskirt and apron on over her nightdress and Mama is too tired to argue.

Although my bones are worn down with tiredness, I gather myself up and wrap Mama's green coat round me. It is too warm for this night, but there is no time to wash and dress properly. Father is already stumbling towards the corridor, keeping himself low so as to move more quickly. Myntgie and I are both slight enough to walk upright beneath deck, a great blessing. Myntgie takes my hand and gratitude dances through my bones.

On deck, all is darkness except for one dot of light swinging wildly beneath the centre mast. Father holds his hand out for us. 'Stay here, girls. This is not for you.' His face clears, as if he has just woken properly. 'What are you doing here at all? Get back to your bunks.'

Myntgie and I say nothing, though Myntgie nods her head meekly. Father approaches the mast area with his arms held wide, the bearer of ominous or wonderful news. Myntgie and I wait a few moments, then creep behind him.

'Why have they woken us? Something terrible must be – Myntgie, what do you think?' I grasp her hand tightly.

'This is no emergency,' Myntgie whispers. 'This is too much ale.'

And so it appears. For while one man twirls a tin lantern about his head, crying out, 'Watch the moon spin around the world, hoo-hah,' quite as if he is a madman, two other men fight like savages. I do not recognise the man with the lantern, but I know the two men fighting by its light. One is Skipper Jacobsz, his square body taut with straining. I cannot be sure, but I think that the other man is the dark-haired soldier from the gun deck, Jan van Bemmel. Jacobsz holds the gunner's neck, so that his head is restrained and his body held back, and smashes punch after punch into his mouth. Blood covers both Jan's face and Jacobsz' hand. Jan kicks with his legs and flails his arms until he twists free. An officer bangs a metal gong with each punch struck, and counts them out for all the world as if it is a great game.

Several officers have come out on deck, Conraat amongst them. He does not see me, hidden in the shadows with Myntgie, but I watch him. He is in full uniform, and I would guess that his face is freshly washed, even now in the deep of the night. He says something to two sailors, and they begin to move towards the skipper. Father has stopped halfway, his arms have dropped to his sides and he is watching the fight, his mouth hanging idiot-open. As Conraat draws closer to the lantern light, Jacobsz picks Jan van Bemmel up, simply lifts him into the air. You would not believe that this man who is barely taller than me could lift the other so clean from the ground. And yet here it is, done, and before a word can be called, Jacobsz is throwing Jan against the side of the ship. Jan lurches forward and again Jacobsz lifts him.

My breath feels tight in my mouth, as though it cannot make it through the rest of my body. This is the skipper who should be leading our ship to safety, and here he is, blood-covered, spit on his face. Whichever way I look, there is no one to hang onto. Only Conraat seems solid to me. My amulet. Watching him will calm my spirit and ease my fear.

'Who is for the sea then, scum?' The skipper rushes forward to the gunwale, bearing the gunner with him.

'I cannot swim, Arian. Leave me go.' Jan's voice trembles.

Jacobsz slurs out something which sounds like 'all the better', though it is hard to tell, for the words run together and become one. There is a horrible pause, a shriek and then a splash. Father calls out 'Enough!' as if that is remotely useful, and Jacobsz holds his hands up in the air.

'Oh, Judith, look.' Myntgie squeezes my hand.

Conraat is pulling his boots off and climbing onto the gunwale. While the other officers hesitate, circling around Jacobsz carefully, Conraat jumps down, off the edge of the ship. Everything stops inside me. Surely he will die before he hits the water. Or drown when he does.

The pause before the splash is as hours. I cannot rush to the gunwale to see what has happened, I must stop myself imagining. Myntgie holds my hand, squeezing until it begins to hurt. After the splash: shouting, echoing. Then nothing, no noise for, oh how long? I cannot tell, even remembering it I cannot believe that it takes only minutes. Finally, Jan's face appears over the gunwale, his hands on the ship ladder, his skin reflecting white in the light.

Below Jan, out of sight, Conraat calls, 'Haul him up, for the sake of the Company. Quickly.'

Two officers rush forward and lean over the gunwale, pulling the gunner onto the deck. Water drips from his tunic and his beard hangs in two wet columns. Climbing up behind him, clothes clinging to his skin, Conraat picks up his discarded jacket and wraps it round Jan's shoulders. 'Predikant, please get the man a blanket, for the Company's sake.'

My father bows his head and hurries off, looking somehow pleased. I can only assume this is pleasure in finding that at last he is of some use.

'What kind of behaviour is this for a mixed ship? And for the skipper of that ship?' Conraat moves into the lantern light, his hands on his hips. 'Both of you, shameful. But you, Arian, surely you should force yourself into behaviour in keeping with your station, even if it is against your own nature. Throwing a man who cannot swim into the ocean, in the depths of the night—'

Jacobsz slumps against the mast. 'To the sea with you, van Hueson. You were not asked to be part of a private fight.' His words are tangled, bound together like string.

'We had no choice. You have woken almost the entire ship with your cat's yowling. And it was not necessary to sound the drum, we do not need to know of your childish games.'

Indeed, when I look around me on deck, there is quite an audience which has now gathered for the late-night show. Forty people at least. One or two passengers appear to be still in their nightdresses, not even bothering to cover with shawls or coats.

Jacobsz pulls himself upright again. 'So you have had to take over the job of captain, is that it? Do not believe for one moment that I am any more frightened of a bloody nobleman than I am of the fish Pelseart. Shame on you yourself, van Hueson, if you have taken over the job of one who is too useless to do it himself.'

'You will not speak of your captain like this.'

'Pelseart is a lazy worm and is not worthy to be my captain. He is shit beneath my heels. Or have you changed your tune?' Jacobsz spits on the deck. 'Pelseart is my spit.'

'Pelseart is your captain, and worth ten of you. This is not the moment, Arian.' Conraat looks around at the anxious crowd, huddled at the edges of the light. 'There is no emergency and you all should be in bed. Sleep is hard enough to find on this ship without an extra burden. And you,' he turns back to Jacobsz, 'will find yourself reported to the captain in the morning, and in turn to the Company. Now, to bed all.'

We turn to leave, just as Father climbs back onto the deck, waving a grey coverlet. 'Blanket, Corporal. I could not look in the cabins, for people are sleeping, so had to find one where I could; finally, here it was, covering a barrel in the waist.'

Conraat takes the cloth and does not ask my father why he could not have brought his own blanket. He merely thanks Father and advises him to return to the cabin.

Back in the heavy heat of the cabin, Myntgie whispers through the dark. 'I am sorry I doubted his loyalty, Judith. You are very blessed to have his attention.'

I stare into the darkness, still seeing Jacobsz' blood-covered hand. Beneath me, the wooden ledge feels too light for my body and I realise my legs are shaking.

Myntgie sighs deeply and for the first time I realise her own loneliness. I whisper up at her, 'You are the most wonderful sister, Myntgie.'

She does not answer and I cannot tell whether she even hears me. Roelant lets out a moan, and then there is silence again, all night, though sleep – at least for me – comes only with the dawn.

The morning is hot and harsh, the sun already beaming above us as we climb up to the captain's quarters. Provost Jansz, his milky, warm face creased by weariness, is calling the morning watch, and Father takes his place for the reading. Arian Jacobsz stands on the edge of the crowd. Every few moments he sways a little, and puts his hand to his head in the manner of a sick man. After Father's reading, from Leviticus, Commander Pelseart stands by the mast and takes the baton from the provost's hand.

The commander, too, is looking unwell. Each day of this journey he seems thinner, his skin more pale. Even his hair is weakening; the flat baldness at the front of his head grows larger, so that his forehead seems too big for his body.

He places one hand against the mast. 'I have heard that many of you were disturbed from your sleep last night, and I apologise on behalf of the Honourable Company. The culprits will be punished properly and the Company will be informed.'

Somewhere behind me, I hear the noise of spitting.

Pelseart continues. 'The men involved – and I know who they are – will receive no victuals for this day or the morrow, and will be assigned deck-scrubbing duties these same days. Trade is now completed with the Hottentots, and tomorrow we sail. A good day to you all.' Pelseart begins to move away.

'I'll not be going without any victuals, if that is what you are thinking, Captain.' Jacobsz steps forward, shielding his eyes from the sun.

'Oddly enough, Arian, that is what I am thinking. I am disappointed that I find it necessary—'

'We won't be sailing anywhere if I have no victuals.'

Pelseart looks at him for a moment and then hands the baton back to the provost. He leans for a moment more against the mast and then hobbles inside to his quarters.

Arian Jacobsz watches him go, and spits again. His face is creased, his mouth pulled back into his cheeks, as it was last night, pounding at the face of the gunner. Watching him, I feel again the cold shake of fear.

Chapter Seventeen

The storm blows up as soon as we leave the Cape; so sudden, it seems like a sign of sorts. Sails billowing, men hanging from the rigging calling out warnings, the creak of the anchor chain: we are beautiful, leaving the Cape. And the Cape is beautiful, being left. Blue-green clouds sit low on the flat-topped mountain, and as we creak and rock out to sea, I watch the solid edge of the land gradually soften and disappear. The *Bueren* and the *Assendelft*, the only ships still in sight from our fine fleet, flutter behind us; too far to see anyone swinging from the high rigging, too far to see any faces at all. What we do see is the trail of white sails, high and round. By the time we round the Cape, I have to strain to make out the sails in the distance. I stand on my tiptoes, watching the fine white shapes dotting about. Above them, grey shadows, blowing towards us. Grey clouds, black at the edges, and stretching with each moment, until they appear to cover the sky. The deck begins to bounce beneath my feet as the ship hits larger waves.

It is sudden indeed. One moment the calm viewing of a

disappearing land, sailors strolling from task to task, and the next: yelling, running, the call put out to get below. Even the water has turned to blackness, and thunder is pealing across the sky. Clouds ripple with a peculiar light, until there is a flash of bright whiteness, a lightning swipe across the entire arc. My back is rigid against the rough timber of the wheelhouse, and though I have no grip, I am steadied by the solid wall. It is almost a stampede, the rush to get below deck, but I have never seen such light and do not expect that I ever will again; just one more ripple, and then I will, I will go down to the stuffy darkness.

'What are you doing? Have you not heard the calls?' A strong, calloused hand pulls my wrist forward, so that I stumble towards the hatch. The flat-faced soldier Wiebbe Hayes yells close to my face, his voice battling against the wind.

I steady myself with one hand against the wheelhouse. 'Our cabin is up here, off the poop. And what of yourself? I do not see you disappearing down any hatch.'

'Would you prefer there were no one to sail the ship?'

'Soldiers do not sail the ship.'

I know that I have stung him somehow, for he takes my arm and lurches towards the hatch with his lips pressed together until they are white. He pushes me down the hatch as though I am a sack of chaff, then leans his head down. In the sudden dimness, his eyes look too wide for his face.

'Have you learnt nothing from all this time at sea? You are safer below, in the steerage, or the gallery if you must. Where were you during the last storm?' His voice is still raised against the wind, but with the storm shushed by the half-closed hatch, it sounds as though he is yelling at me, shrewishly.

'I expect I was climbing the rigging and swinging from the topmast.' Where does my own shrewishness come from, this desire to talk back?

'I expect you were making a nuisance of yourself with Corporal van Hueson. Good peace to you.'

Shame smacks itself into my belly, a sudden fist. Is this how I am seen on board? As a nuisance, chasing Conraat from his duties? Still, I swallow and push myself forward, calling, 'Wait!' I climb partway up the ladder again. 'Are you a papist?' Could there be a worse time to ask him? But, as always, my tongue has run away with itself.

He looks at me as if I am mad. 'No.'

'But—'

'Papists raised me. Goodnight.' The hatch bangs decisively behind him.

Lantern light shines in the steerage, and there is the mingle of many voices. Outside, the wind howls, yet it sounds muffled, distant. My feet slip as we tilt side to side and I collide with Jan Hendrickson, holding himself still on the edges of the steerage. Unsmiling, he nods at me but does not speak a greeting. Lucretia waves at me and I push my way over to her.

'Have you seen my family? I cannot see Myntgie here, though she was near me on deck.'

Lucretia appears distracted. 'I have not. Though there are folk in the Great Cabin.' She looks around, her arms crossed. 'And this is not the place I wish to be, not at all. Perhaps we should be there, in the Great Cabin. Will you come with me?' The ship gives a sudden lurch and Lucretia stumbles against me. 'Oh, my arm.'

'Perhaps this is not the moment to go wandering about the ship.' I step back, trying to recover my balance.

'As for Zwaanje,' Lucretia speaks as though in mid-sentence, as though I have interrupted a discussion. 'I have not seen her all the day. My washing is half done, my clothes unstitched. The girl is in a sulk and appears to have forgotten who is who and what is what.'

'A sulk?' I remember the face resting on Arian Jacobsz' shoulder, the lips pushed out, the eyes narrowed.

'Yesterday I gave her a very light slap. Zwaanje has become a slattern since we have been at sea, and I am afraid my temper frayed. It was a very light slap. My washing had not been done for days.'

I cannot believe anyone I know would ever slap a servant. Now, years later, I know that I can never tell what another person would do, how they would behave, given the right, or wrong, circumstances. I have seen good people, or people I believed to be good, destroy lives for no reason that I have ever been able to understand. If now, at the declining end of my life, I cannot understand these things, what hope had I of understanding at eighteen? Look at me: I am bright-eyed, impressed, desperate for happiness and pleasure, believing I have not had enough of either. Only the loss of these things can teach us gratitude for their existence.

Thank you, Lord, for all I have and for all I have lost.

Later, when the storm had ended, we trickled slowly away to our cabins, those who had not already tried to hold themselves to their bunks and sleep through the tossing and turning. Stumbling back along the gallery, with my arms spread wide, I tripped over someone's foot. It was a man who whispered an apology. There he was, waiting in the gallery, one could almost say hiding. Waiting to trip someone up. Yet I left him, and swayed the rest of the way to my bed. Harsh comfort at the start of the journey, this thin wooden ledge is now the sweetest of pleasures to me. My back is stronger and straighter for sleeping on it; I feel myself walk taller. True, too, that my skin is also harder. Mama has complained often enough of her own skin being turned to sow's hide, but I like my skin hard. I like feeling that my skin contains me, that it will not melt or bend so easily. Anyway, I am young enough that the hardness of my skin does not take away the smoothness, nor the bloom.

The cabin is dark, chorused by a cannon of snores, mutterings, deep sighs of sleep. They are all here: Father, his mouth loose, with the spit dribbling out; Mama, lying rigid on her side with Roelant tucked in beside her; Anna, curled into a ball; the two boys flat on their stomachs; and Myntgie, arms flung out on the bunk above mine. Light is not necessary for me to see them, I know the shape and the sound of each of them, I know the patterns of their sleep better than I know my own. Although I crash against the box by Father's bunk, no one stirs. Myntgie's hand dangles over the edge of the bunk, and I tread on it as I climb to my own bunk. She lets out no noise, not a murmur. You would almost think she was dead.

The boat is gentle after the storm, and I let the rock-rock-rock lull me to sleep.

Screaming. Perhaps it is a dream. I cannot tell if I am awake or asleep. Clambering to the surface, voices far away. Screaming. Once. No, twice. Shrill and desperate. My eyes open. Steady breath in the cabin, no one else moves. Slowly, my eyes close again.

Morning. The bell for the morning watch begins and before it has chimed its last, there is a shout. No dream this time, it is both a call and a scream. There is running outside, in the gallery. I pull on my gown and push my way out to the corridor, through a knot of passengers, peering forward.

'Get away, now. Just leave her be.' Gerrit Willemsz is pushing us back, towards the cabins. 'Where is the barber?'

Michel Fransz, the barber-surgeon, stumbles into the corridor, wiping his face with a towel.

'Madam van der Mijlen needs to be checked and cleaned and treated. And the villains must be found.'

'Villains are not my job, but the job of the captain. Here, let me at least give her a soothing solution.' Fransz edges himself closer and I push with him, following behind.

Against the edge of the waist, Lucretia van der Mijlen is wrapped in a ship's blanket. A woman I recognise as the cook's wife is wiping her cheeks. Dark muck covers Lucretia's face and also her hands, poking through the blanket. Her hair is tussled and her head down. Someone bumps me from behind and I am pushed even closer, so that I can see the thick red gashes on her cheeks. Her dress is torn at the waist.

Willemsz pushes us back and calls out, 'They shall be caught, mark my words, whoever you are.' He holds Lucretia by the hand; he and Fransz form a human guard, one on each side. As she steps away from the gallery edge, I see the ropes lying at her feet: long, thick ropes, and one torn sheet, presumably used to tie her mouth. She draws closer and I see the rope marks cut into her wrists. I see them and I do not cry out; I see them and I am curious before any other thing. And I believe that is true for all of us there in the gallery, we are curious, relieved that it is not us.

As Lucretia passes me, I draw in a breath, cover my nose and stumble back. Such a stench, sudden and sickly rich, so that I do not know how I did not notice before. And it is a stench I recognise; it is the smell of human shit. Lucretia raises her eyes, so that they meet mine, and I cannot look at her shit-covered face, or at the blood dried at her feet. It is clear to me, even an innocent, what that blood means, and I cannot look on her, for fear I may catch her shame. Though I try to hold her gaze, I do not. She looks at me, asking for some human touch, some human contact, when she needs it, now when she has been made less than human. She asks this of me and I do not give it. Instead I quickly step away, lower my glance so that you would think I had not seen her eyes raised to mine.

Each little mark we make, chipping away at our humanity,

chipping away at our own capacity for goodness. Not one great swipe; nor, as they have endlessly said, the fault of those born evil. No, no, no. It is these tiny moments that lead us there, into forgetting ourselves. It is the moments when we choose not to care, not to notice. And each moment tap-taps away until we are smaller and weaker, ready to crumble when faced with bleaker and darker and more murderous choices. Ready to become murderers ourselves.

Chapter Eighteen

Sometimes I remember my family as if they are one being: My Family. In these times, what I am remembering is the feeling of belonging with them. Never questioning them, not too much. Never especially expressing love. Simply belonging; knowing that they were my people. Now my daughter is my people and that is all. I have lost three husbands, all to the tropical disease; and my first love, who haunts me daily, in every possible way. But it is my family to whom I belong, even now. Perhaps this is why: they have never been able to grow truly wearisome to me, as I fear I shall to my daughter. Perhaps I am already wearing on her, for she has told me I am to have no part in the naming of her son when he is born. She has already chosen, she says, and I am to be surprised.

Oh, she is bright-cheeked, my lovely daughter. No sign of the wilting I had with her. Spots covered my skin when I carried her, fierce red welts, along my face and arms. Fransz, her father, would run his finger along the welts, crooning, 'Signs of love, my love.' And then he would kiss me, rich kisses full of joy and promise. He was unusual for a man: he held his daughter for hours at a time, staring into her little round face. Though I asked him often, he swore to no desire for a son. I do grieve, though, that he will not see his grandson. At night, he would hold me, stroking my hair while I wept.

My family haunt me in my dreams, sometimes alive, sometimes longing for something they cannot name. They are most often unhappy when they come to me in dreams, though sometimes they are gathered together, laughing. And sometimes, they come to me as I saw them last, when I failed them so poorly. In those times, I cannot bear to greet the new day.

Conraat, too, is halted in my memory. Always with a sheen, a bead of sweat on his cheek; as though he had been painted by, perhaps, the young painter Hals, with his way of capturing the fleeting moment. Yes, Hals would have caught Conraat leaning over me that first night, the night by breath first stopped, with the brazier shining a halo around him. Would have caught the gleam of mischief which bade me fall in love with him. There are others who would have painted him surrounded by darkness; even the old man Rubens could have given him a shadow of death. Not Hals, though. Only room for life in his paintings. I have lost touch with the new painters, I so rarely visit grand houses these days. My daughter tells me no one speaks of Rubens any more. He had a vase, lost with us on the ship, did you know that?

Perhaps if I had some idea of what was to follow, I would have been less entranced, more willing to pursue my less obviously attractive journeymates. But it is a fool's journey, to travel to the past intent on change. My father would say: think of Lot and his imprudent wife, turned to salt for looking over her shoulder. Do not look back: it was his banner call, even after all we lived through. Especially then. When the past has such horrors in it, too, all that can be done is to try to understand how. Why. And why me? Why did I survive? These are the questions the past brings to the present. Here is my sadness: that I cannot think of Conraat without thinking of my family. How could I? How could the image of one not give rise to the desperate longing for the other, followed by a cold, desperate fury. And then I try to settle myself, to pray, to find peace in my spirit. For I must.

When Fransz lay with the fever, his lips scorched white with the heat of it, he called me close and whispered this: 'You have touched me so deeply.'

No, I have failed you as I have failed all those I loved. I thought I spoke the words, but I did not; all was quiet but for the sharp tear of his breathing. Now, our daughter sits beside me, stroking the round swell of my grandson inside her. I watch her eyes close, one hand resting on her belly. The other rests in my roughened hand. Her breath deepens, and she twitches as the child kicks.

'Aaah,' she says. 'Mama.' Her sigh is as sweet as cinnamon.

I will not live a life of hate.

Chapter Nineteen

For weeks we sail closer to the sun. Word has it that we are drawing close to the Great Southern Land. Since the storm, we have been a lone ship, for the paltry remainder of our fleet was lost to us during the storm, and it must be said that Arian Jacobsz smirked as he announced this to the ship's table. There is an uneasy silence on the poop deck, and on the crew decks too. Commander Pelseart is locked in his cabin, too ill to speak, or to enforce the discipline which it is his bounden duty to do. Father has muttered beneath his breath about fools led by fools. Indeed, all about the ship it seems there are little pockets of discontented mutterings instead of the murmur of work and pleasure which was our accompanying music until we saw Good Hope. As for Lucretia, on the rare occasions that she is seen on deck, her eyes watch her feet, her shaved head hanging low, like a tulip.

It is the day of Anna's birthday, and we have spent the morning singing songs for her, and telling stories of her life. How strange to be celebrating such things so far from land, with such shadows lurking. There were no gifts for Anna and she declared it the worst birthday in the world, causing Father to lightly slap her hand and insist that she be grateful for the very life which the Lord has given her. Provost Jansz is chanting out the noon watch in his deep voice, and I wander along the poop, looking down onto the main deck, searching for the golden-haired glow of Conraat. Behind me and beside me, all along the deck, I hear snatches of conversation, all versions of the same questions. At the bow end of the poop, I stop and listen to the halfway familiar voices babbling behind me. 'He has barely been seen since embarking. Wylbrecht Claas said it was the fever, but I believe it to be sheer cowardice.'

'There was a cloud over his time in India, was there not? There, does that stitching look straight?'

'Even so, I am not sure I would call her above reproach, that woman.'

'I heard nothing of any clouds.'

'Oh, certainly she had something coming, but not that, my goodness, the poor woman. And has any man been so much as whipped for it? Not a sound, not a whimper. The bottom line is crooked, I think. Well, you should not ask for my opinion if you do not wish to know the answer.'

'She has named one of the attackers. Word is, many were involved in the planning. Even that skipper. Hoping for the chance to cause trouble with the commander. No, truly.'

'What cloud?'

'The skipper, though? He with the whore on his side?'

'Hush, you. Pass me that thread.'

For the first time, I long to be anywhere other than on board this swaying ship with her rotting food and her hordes of gossips. Surrounding me, there are more than one hundred strangers, some at least with grasping hands which will tie the mouth of a woman. Certainly before now I have missed home, have wished perhaps for the warmth of my soft bed, or the stillness of the outside paths, but never before have I hated this ship as I do now. And yet, even with the breath that hates the ship, I breathe a prayer of thanks for the ship which brought me to meet my Conraat, who will protect me. Conraat, whose very name makes me tremble in my secret places.

Below me, on the main deck, the skipper appears to be drawing lots. Three or four men have gathered around him, laughing, while he pulls small objects from a cloth bundle. Each time he draws his hand out, there is a cheer, and he passes the object to one of the men. Perhaps it is one of his magic tricks, for I have heard that he does them tolerably well. Wylbrecht told me that before being a sailor, Arian Jacobsz was a travelling hawker! Though this may be the gossip of servants and I should pay it no heed.

This is the first day in many that I have seen the skipper without Zwaanje, for it seems that she is now his public companion, whatever shame this may bring on the crew. Last night he even insisted that she eat with him at the commander's table. Lucretia did not look at either of them, only gazed at her plate, though the remainder of the company stared hungrily. And to my shame, I put myself in this latter category, for I was as full of curiosity as the rest.

Curiosity draws me now, too, edging closer to the skipper's group, hoping to hear the secret of the lots. If Myntgie were beside me, I would say to her, 'Perhaps it is Zwaanje that they are drawing lots for.' Myntgie would slap my hand for such wickedness and meanness, but still she would laugh and lay her hand upon my arm. My sister is not here with me though, so I whisper these thoughts only to myself.

The group around the skipper is breaking up, one of the men has his arm about another and is slapping him on the back. Two men have come across the waist, one of them holding a leather satchel. Light bounces off his hair; his beard is a corn-wash, soft yellow. Though I wish only to shout and to run to him, I hold myself for a moment so that I may watch him. Every movement is as clean as the moon; oh, truly, he is an instrument of the Lord! With him, thin and verbose, is Jeronimus Cornelisz, his bean of a mouth opening and closing, always delivering his little lectures. Even from above I can see the furrows in his brow. Beside Conraat, though, every man is led to looking plain and unfortunate. The red-haired soldier Wiebbe Hayes comes to my mind, and the image of him alongside Conraat is nearly shocking it is such a contrast. I do believe that our Lord Christ himself would have borne similar looks to Conraat: a similar build, surely, and an evenness of features. For of course the Lord could not inhabit a plain or ugly thing!

As I am about to call to Conraat, to wave my hand in greeting, he lowers his head to the skipper and nods towards the waist. Something in his look prevents me from calling out. Perhaps he is to reprimand the skipper for his behaviour with

Zwaanje? Arian Jacobsz immediately follows Conraat and Jeronimus to the waist door, peers behind him, then pulls the door shut after him.

'Judith.' A hand is on my arm and I leap backwards. My mother lets out a laugh. 'I startled you. Did you not hear me drawing near?'

'I heard nothing. My mind was elsewhere.'

'I need not ask where that may be.' Roelant is nestled on her hip, his dimpled hands clinging to her shoulder. 'Roelant was calling for you. He is restless, he needs some entertainment. Do you know where Myntgie is?'

'Not at all. I thought she was to organise some games for the older children. I would have expected her to be on the poop. Perhaps they are playing a hiding game.'

Roelant holds out his arms to me. 'Judick.'

I take him from Mama and put my face close to his. His cheeks are red and shining: freshly scrubbed fruit. Mama hands me his handkerchief and I wipe beneath his nose; it is permanently wet at the moment, though he has no cold. Mama says it is the sea air, though I believe it is simply the last of his teeth coming through.

In spite of Conraat and all her hopes for me, Mama is unhappy at sea. Some days, I am sure that she longs to be in Dordrecht, watching the summer storms take shape, or waiting for the white-gold light to pass across the sky. 'Keep him for a while, Judith. I am unwell again, I think I will lie below.'

'The air would be better for you, Mama. Being below without the light is not good for your spirit.'

Her eyes shut for a moment. 'It is the light which causes my head to ache so. It is better in the darkness.'

It is true that my mother misses terribly the shifting light of Dordrecht. She is inactive lately, staring at a far-off place, speaking slowly or not at all. Three days ago, Myntgie found her sitting on the deck of the poop, nursing Roelant and weeping silently, so that her tears rolled down onto his face. This has been slowly coming, drawing closer as we draw closer to the Southern Land. And yet I think she has been only half herself even before this, even before we left Dordrecht; she has been barely half herself since Roelant was born, suckling endlessly day and night.

'Of course I will take him, Mama. Go and rest.'

'Yes. Yes, I shall. Thank you, Judith.' She speaks almost in a whisper.

Roelant stays nestled in my arms for only a few moments; his face is pressed into my shoulder and his hair, sun-white and curled like Conraat's, tickles my nose. There is little time to enjoy him like this, for he wriggles free and begins to run towards the deck ladder. Rocking side to side and shrieking with laughter as he runs, he looks more like a wobbling wooden top than a boy. With his curls and his sweet-smelling skin and his roundness, he is more like a girl in some ways. Not just these things either, but his very temperament seems softer than a boy's. Perhaps it is that I was so much younger when Pieter and even Jan were young boys, but it seems to me that they were louder, rougher than Roelant. For all his joy and all his running, Roelant loves to be rocked and held close, to have the story of the woman who cooked the wicked man in her black pot whispered into his ear. He shivers and hides his face when he hears this story, and the one of the nobleman who had to swim all the way to the world's end, only to find that his heart's desire was back where he had started. It is not that he is a coward, only that his soul is open to such things. Fanciful Judith: I can hear my father mocking in my ear.

Roelant turns his head back to me. 'Chasing, Judick.'

When he is excited like this, Roelant's voice shrinks into a squeal, even his eyes become more shrill, screwed up tight. He turns again, before I can call yes or no, and waddles off towards the gangway door.

'Wait, Roelant, Judith will catch you.' Even as I call, he has disappeared behind the wooden door, slipping beneath the legs of Anneke Haardens, coming out from the gangway.

Anneke pats him on the head and nods at me. 'Are you his guardian this afternoon? You had better keep a close eye. He almost had his hand caught in a twisted rope yesterday. And he nearly knocked me then, you saw it. Your boys are too much trouble on this ship, running without care. You should look out for them.'

'Thank you, Anneke, I will.' Though I wish to swear silently at her as she passes, I force myself to say a prayer for her salvation.

Inside the gangway, I can hear the soft beat of Roelant's feet, but see nothing ahead of me. A tall sailor attempts to pass me, and I hold my hand out to stop him. 'Excuse me, have you seen a young boy running along? Just this minute?'

Without a word or a smile, the sailor points behind him,

towards the Great Cabin. I stumble in the direction he has pointed, calling out Roelant's name.

When I reach the Great Cabin, I am puffing hard and feel my hair slipping from beneath my cap. Roelant jumps out at me, letting a roar out of his mouth. I jump back and scream – for he has genuinely startled me – as the Great Cabin door swings slowly open. Commander Pelseart stands there, his hand on the door, and his face whiter than a fish.

'I am sorry for such noise, Commander—' I am unable to finish, for the good commander sways for a moment, and then slides to the floor, as still and as white as death.

Chapter Twenty

I have told no one of the Commander's fainting fit and I am not entirely sure of the reason for my silence. Only that when he came to he brushed himself down and was so kind and polite to Roelant and held him on his lap and yet was so clearly unwell – I think he is a good man and I do not wish to do him harm. He has ventured out to deck only once, and he was pale and shaking from the cold so much that he went immediately below. The cold comes as a surprise. Round and red, low in the sky, the sun seems to be drawing closer each day until it seems we will collide with it. Yet there is no new warmth, for this is a frigid sun.

Once again I am wearing the coat which Lucretia gave me, and at night I am wrapped in all the blankets, and still find myself curling catlike to get more warmth. Father says it is simply that we have become overused to the heat, that our skins have forgotten mild temperatures. Why, he says, in Dordrecht we were almost iced over last winter, and we barely felt the cold. Now this I know to be untrue, for I clearly recall Anna weeping from the cold. This Anna, here on board *Batavia*, is quite a new creature; virtuous, pious, and with a pleasing expression of contentment painted on her face, instead of the contempt which we so often used to witness there. It seems that Anna is a creature of the sun, for she unravels with its nearness, becomes softer and more pliable. Even this cold sun seems pleasing to her. She tells me that I am glowing as sweetly as the sun itself, that the attentions of a certain young nobleman are becoming to me. Anna is full of joy for my joy. More so than I am myself, perhaps, for I am as much bewildered as I am joyous. Conraat spins me about, so that my head is foggy, though I know he offers safe harbour. I cannot recall things. I have no opinion on goodness or piety; secretly, I know that if Conraat asked me to behave improperly, I would not hesitate. This disturbs me. Yet the Lord knew these thoughts before they passed into my mind, so why did He allow them there? Surely he could prevent them entering? Secretly also, I think this: that if the Lord has destined me to misbehave, I should help Him with his plan. And here is another thing which should add to my shame before my family and before the Lord: I have been kissed by Conraat, who has not so much as offered me a promise of betrothal, has barely even hinted at such a thing. Even so, I allowed myself to be kissed by him, gave myself back to him as though I were indeed a married woman. Or perhaps even married women do not give their kisses so freely and deeply to their husbands.

He came to me in the gangway, late after supper, after I had bid him goodnight. Myntgie and I were feeling our way along the gangway, for there was little light. He called from behind us.

'Wait, Judith, let me have a word.' Myntgie squeezed my hand and ran on, tripping with the effort of quietness. His hands touched my waist, turned me about so that all I could see was his face, large and solid. 'I did not bid you goodnight, young Judith.' His hands were still on my waist and I looked down at them, then back to his eyes, which I fancied were shining at me. Following my gaze, he slid his hands up from my waist up and round to my back.

I could not breathe, could not think a single thought. Yet still I said nothing, though he had already bade me goodnight and it would have been proper for me to tell him so, or to pull away, or even to remind him that we were not betrothed. But I did not do these things, not one of them. No, I tried to quieten my breath though it sounded louder than a storm and I let him pull me closer, his hands pressing on my back until there was nothing between our skins and I was so close I could no longer make out the shape of his face. His hand slid under my chin and tilted it up so that I could see his eyes. Still I spoke no word, did not cry out: we are not betrothed, you should not touch me this way. And when his mouth came closer and closer, I did not speak. His breath was so soft that I felt that I was made of the ocean. All the time, his hands on my back, on my waist, touching my gown. Then his lips, breathing across mine, until I needed to be caught by him, for my own limbs could no longer carry me. Finally, his lips closed, he held me out from him and sighed. 'Beautiful young Judith. Goodnight.' He turned and walked away, leaving me against the wall, shivering. All night I thought of him, and have longed since then to shout and sing.

Instead, I continue on my journey quietly and this morning I stitched an apron for a heathen girl.

Mama tells me that we are almost within sight of the Southern Land; she received this from Jan who received it from Wiebbe Hayes, with whom I have shared no word since the night of Lucretia's ordeal. Since then, with each of the men in the Great Cabin, I find myself turning my head away, swallowing my voice. With his pale fingers and his clever stories, even the undermerchant Jeronimus Cornelisz seems huge to me, capable of pushing a woman to the floor. Mama's voice is still empty. She touches Roelant and Jan as if they are cases of old fabric: heavy, unwieldy, unnecessary. She does no stitching, and little praying. Everything about her is dulled. During lunch I hear her whispering to Father, 'Why did you bring me here? Why?'

Father looks at his hands, then at the table, and after some moments says quietly, 'It is the Lord's will and it is the Lord's work.'

Mama stares at her tin plate, pushes the dried meat aside, breaks a piece of biscuit, lifts it to her mouth and puts it back on the plate. Her wine goblet is still full. Father takes another mouthful of white peas and crunches loudly on some biscuit. Finally, Mama wipes her hands on her apron and says, 'Yes. It is the Lord's will.' I have never seen my mother so unhappy, though she wept often after Jan's birth, for no reason that we could see.

Commander Pelseart is no longer present at the evening

meal. As for Lucretia, she has taken to wearing the plainest of gowns, never a frill collar. She eats quietly and with her head bowed and disappears to her cabin after the meal. Although I try to speak to her, I stumble over my words and can only think of the stench that came from her that night, so I stop trying and remain silent. Even the wine feels dry in my throat. There is relief at our table when she leaves.

The ocean is quiet and the moon is round. I am full of thoughts of Conraat, but since his kiss, he has been distant, like the sun. On the poop, there is a merry party gathered around a brazier. Myntgie holds my hand and laughs. Someone on the main deck is singing a song about a cheap woman from Haarlem; there is laughter and some applause when he finishes but I do not like it, neither the words nor the tune. I cannot help but think of the woman in the song as someone who may have been my sister, or my friend. You see? Already, my mind is going far from the places it should go. By the brazier, the talk is quieter, though I can see shadow-shaped men on the edges, drinking from flasks and swaying gently. One of the shadow shapes is Arian Jacobsz, I am sure of it, though I will not edge close enough to know for sure. There is a woman clinging to his side, and I am sure that it is Zwaanje. The two shapes meet briefly in a kiss; they become one shadow and for a moment I lose my breath.

Later, I am awake on my wooden ledge, counting the breaths of my family. Myntgie lies awake above me, praying silently, her eyes open. Further above, on the deck, Arian

Jacobsz is awake, on skipper's watch, steering our ship to promise. His hands are steady on the wheel, his feet steady on the deck. He is the best seaman in the world and he is concentrating all his force on guiding the *Batavia* to the fair island and soon we shall be there, our new home, beginning all things again, making all things new. Except this is not what is happening on deck.

All my life, all the long years that I have spent remembering, imagining, wishing. Turning it over and over, like Fransz's rosary beads, in this cursed imagination of mine.

Arian Jacobsz is on deck, and he does not think of me and of the way he may shape my life. No, he thinks only of two things. One hand holds his silver flask, and he tilts it to his lips, eyes closed. Sweet ale, rich and good. The other arm squeezes Zwaanje's breasts: sweeter, more rich, better than the sweetest ale. Oh indeed. The ship is a beauty, the best of Holland's best fleet and she can steer herself, and Zwaanje rubs her hands along his breeches, slips one hand inside and Arian says, 'That's it, girl, that's it.' Sometimes when I imagine it, she does not do this, but stands mute beside him, waiting for disaster. But always this, I always see this:

In the crow's nest Mattys Beer is hanging, watching out for who knows what? Mattys clambers down, his arms aching, and creeps along the deck. 'Ha!' he calls, slapping Arian on the back. 'Got you!'

Zwaanje jumps and squeals, knocking Mattys's hand away. Laughter circles the wheel quietly. 'Tonight,' says Arian, 'we shall throw him over. The crew are ready and even officers are tired of his absence. There are plenty willing to take part, even those under his very nose. He does not know who commands this ship. Commander indeed!'

Mattys takes the silver flask. 'We are waiting.'

'Go on then, get away and wait, I have business with my woman. Go on, away! And give me the flask, you dirty thief.'

I imagine Mattys laughing, returning the flask, climbing back to his perch. He is halfway there, can see his nest above him, when he turns his head and looks down. Below him, on the deck, Arian and Zwaanje are wrestling by the wheel. Her skirt begins to be hitched; Mattys wants badly to go down, to get a closer look. He leans far out, so that he is hanging by one arm. He is used to this; though slight, he is strong and horse-like. On the water ahead of the ship the moon reflects in lines of white patterns, shining on the ripples from the bow. The white shapes dance in and out, back and forth and for a moment he wonders if they could be flecks of surf.

'Skipper.' Mattys lowers his voice carefully. 'Ahead – surf?'

Arian steps away from Zwaanje for a moment, his hand still on her breast, and peers ahead to the lines of white. He takes another gulp of ale. White ripples moving in and out. But there is no land here, they are not near land, and besides, his mind is full of rich plans. He does not bother calling back to Mattys, but waves his hand up in dismissal. Keeps one hand on the wheel, holding it steady, right where it is, sails up and full and flying on ahead. Pulls Zwaanje back to him with the other hand and whispers, 'Only the moon, bright enough for me to get a better look at you, girl.'

Below him, the surf from the reef hisses and dances, cool as sirens. The reef spreads, flat and solid as it has always been. The *Batavia* sails on, straight ahead. When the ship hits, there is a cannon-like thud, loud enough to echo all the way back to Dordrecht.

Chapter Twenty-One

The first crack knocks me from my bed. The cabin deck is cold beneath me and my head hits the box in the middle of the cabin. Father falls to the floor as well. He sits up and reaches for me, touches my forehead. Blood is on his hand when he pulls it away.

We are all awake, but for a moment all silent. Shaking sleep from our skins, looking into the darkness. For a moment, barely a fragment, we are ready to sink back into sleep. And then there is the second bump, and a scraping which feels as though my belly is being torn. There is no sleep then, only the terror of holding out for hands, feeling for faces, calling to each other: are you there, Anna? Are you safe, Pieter? Who has Roelant?

Father lights the lantern and I see that his hands are shaking.

'What is it, Gisbert? Is it another ship? A whale?' Mama's speech is sharp, her shadow swelling on the cabin walls.

Father's voice shakes as much as his hands. 'No, I am sure it is nothing.' He reaches for the Lord's Book. 'We shall take a word from the Lord. Come, sit. Sit, Judith, there is no need to hover as if awaiting an announcement. We shall be called if—'

Myntgie leans over to him, interrupts. 'But surely, Father, we should go up to the deck? If we are sinking, then we need to be with the crew. There, what was that? Another cracking – it sounds as though we are losing bits of the ship.'

'I will go up.' Jan bounces to his feet, full of excitement.

'And I will go with him. Let me.'

Mama holds her hand out, restrains Pieter. 'No, Pieter you will stay here. Jan as well. We will stay together until we are instructed to go to the deck, and there shall be no more talk of sinking. We are safe in the Lord's hands.'

'Then we shall be fools. Can you not hear? We are the only ones waiting.'

'Myntgie is right, Mama. I can hear footsteps.'

'Myntgie will not speak to her mother like that. We wait here. The Lord will instruct us, as is his wont. And the watch will call us up if need be.' Fear is my father's watchword. ' "And today the Lord has obtained this declaration from you: that you will be his own people, but only if you keep all his commandments; then for praise and renown and honour, he will raise you higher than any nation he has made and you will be a people consecrated to the Lord, as he has promised." We give thanks to the Lord for our nation, for she is a chosen nation—'

'Out! Out! Everyone on deck!' There is a sharp pounding on the door. Footsteps run past, voices are calling out, a woman is crying. We hear the frantic ringing of the bell and dress quickly, the lantern in our midst making grotesque dancing demons of our shadows.

Myntgie leans close to my mother and says quietly, 'I am sorry, Mama. Fear made me speak sharply, but I should not have done so to you and I will not again.'

My mother nods and hands Myntgie her coat. 'You may need extra warmth. It will be cold on deck. Take your blankets.'

There is another pounding on the door. We can barely hear it for the insistent tolling of the bell.

Father pulls open the cabin door and calls, 'Quickly, on to the deck!' as though he has been calling us on for hours and we have been resisting. He leads us up to the deck holding one hand out before him to prevent the bumping, for the ship is still shuddering.

We blink into the moonlight, and everything seems still again. Still and – for a moment – quiet, except for the sound of Claudine Patoys, sobbing into her handkerchief. Even she seems far away. Though her daughter is clinging to her hips, her husband, Claas, is nowhere that I can see. In between her sobs, she calls out his name. In my ears there is a great whistling, as though my very spirit has disappeared, so that all I hear is the wind. Though the ship rocks with each hurl of the waves, the dreadful cracking has stopped and the entire ship's company is crowded on the main deck, as close as neat stitches. We squeeze our way through the crowd, Father muttering to people that he needs to be near the skipper. I would be happy to be a child, quivering at the back, though I am anxious to know that Conraat is safe, for I do not see him in the crowd. People part for Father, as though they believe he will call down the Lord's saving grace. As if he has the power. I know that this is why

Father pushes himself forward, for he wishes to believe this of himself. No, not simply of himself, but of his role. He wishes to believe in the particular power of the Church. Even though this is one of the points on which he damns the papists, that they believe in the power of their Church. Ah, my father. And there he is, scuttling about like a terrified mouse, yet waiting for the word of the Lord. And why not? For the Lord loves the terrified and the lost, as I will come to learn.

A cloud shifts above us, letting the moon shine on the deck, tilted like a wave. We shrink against each other once more, for the moon shows us the stern mast, cracked and hanging drunkenly. Mattys Beer is clinging to the base of it, weeping.

The dark-haired high boatswain pushes past us and kicks at Mattys. 'Off with your girlish weeping, you child. Come on, up! There is rigging to be cast off – move your arse or I'll whip you.'

Mattys pulls himself up and, still weeping, runs towards the centre mast.

Father looks from side to side, birdlike. He edges close to Arian Jacobsz, who is a storm on deck. I have never seen the skipper so full of movement. 'Cannons off – get down and cut them away – rigging too. Everything off, for we are too heavy to cast off. Move fast.' He is even more hoarse than usual and his shoulders heave.

Father cups his hands round his mouth and leans towards the skipper. 'I cannot see the commander.'

Below us, on the gun deck, several voices cry, 'Now!' and a

huge cannon, shining black in the night light, crashes into the sea.

Father jumps back, clutching his coat. 'What is it? Are we losing pieces of the ship?'

He shouts the question to me, but it is the skipper who answers.

'We are too heavy. Must lighten her in order to get off. Damn!'

The sea lifts the ship from the reef, and we are hurled back down with such force that those standing fall back. Arian grabs the gunwale and calls over his shoulder, 'Passengers, sit. Hold to each other and be well away from masts and rigging.'

The *Batavia* shudders again, a terrible grating echoing up from the hull. We are tilted so sharply that waves are beginning to spray over the port side. Sharp winds accompany every spray and I rub my arms with my cold hands. With every shudder of the ship, a violent wave of my own rushes up from my stomach, threatening to fill the whole of me with puke and terror.

Father has managed to stay standing, and he calls again to Arian, 'Where is the commander?'

The skipper spits onto the deck, and hurls a chest overboard. 'I have not seen him. The man is a sickly coward, I expect you will find him huddling with his riches in his chamber. Go and look for him there if you will, I myself would rather try and save the ship and her passengers. If you wish to be helpful, Predikant, gather rope, boxes, rigging, and throw. Or sit with mouth closed.'

'Shall I offer a prayer for the passengers?'

'Do as you wish. If you think prayer is of more benefit than useful work.'

'The Lord requires us to—'

Arian turns to face Father, and raises his voice to a shout. 'I do not wish to discuss your filthy fucking religion.'

Another wave lifts the ship and grinds it back down; my teeth snap onto my lower lip and I feel sweet salty blood fill my mouth. Though I try to swallow it back, it mixes with the violence in my gut and the stabbing of the skipper's words; I hold my hands to my mouth and catch the puke as it dribbles out. Shamed, I rub my hands on the wave-wet deck.

Father stumbles backwards, falling onto Roelant, who is tucked in Mama's arms. Roelant begins to cry and then, when no one responds, to scream. Finally, Myntgie takes him from Mama's arms and rocks him back and forth until he buries his face in her shoulder, whimpering occasionally.

The crowd, who have until now been stilled by fear and confusion, begin to stir. Several people are shouting, 'Are we sinking?' and 'Where is Pelseart?'

Father stands up on a rope coil and clears his throat. The shouting continues and even the people closest to him continue to look about for some sign of the commander. There is splash after splash as sailors throw rigging, chests and barrels into the waves. Father closes his mouth; his hands twitch at his side. Around him, all are shouting, 'Pelseart! Pelseart!'

Someone nudges me aside, such a gentle nudge that it feels like the touch of a young girl. 'Please, let me through.' Even his voice has become thin and wasted.

We step back from him, and Father holds his hand out to support the commander as he climbs onto the rope. 'We have hit a reef. We are perfectly safe. It is best for all to be on deck.' He turns his back to the crowd and steps down from the coil as the *Batavia* pounds once more against the reef.

'Arian, what state is the ship in?'

'She has hit a reef, what state do you expect her to be in?' The skipper's face is tight, with each breath his eyes widen so that he resembles a rolled fish.

'Can she be mended from here?' There is no answer, and Pelseart, his voice thickening, repeats the question.

Arian Jacobsz spits at the commander's feet. 'How the hell should I know in an instant? Bloody fools, putting a frigging salesman in charge of a ship.'

Pelseart is pale, his face a mirror for the moon. Though still trembling, his shoulders are square. 'I did not ground the ship, Arian. I warned you that we could be nearing the Houtman Islands.'

The commander climbs back to the coil.

'We will stay on deck until Skipper Jacobsz has overseen the reparation of the ship, or until we know otherwise. Cook! Bring the biscuit and the brandy. Everyone may have one measure, for warmth. All crew are to be with the skipper. Step back, allow the crew room to work. There is nothing to fear, the Lord is our fortress.'

Father does not mention to the commander the vile talk he has had from Arian Jacobsz, but I watch the skipper's shoulders flex as the commander calls us all to prayer. Myntgie hugs Roelant to her more tightly, as a frightened silence falls on the deck.

Behind me, Claudine Patoys is whispering, 'I do not trust him, that man, he will kill us all, yes he will.' She begins to weep again, even during the prayers. I cannot turn to see who she is addressing, and do not ask her which man she is referring to. For all except Conraat seem to be unworthy of trust: my father, waving his prayers about like a torn flag; Pelseart with his girl's voice and offers of brandy; and this hard-skinned skipper, blaspheming to my father's face as the ship he has grounded thuds and thuds against the solid rocks below. Wind groans through me, but I keep my eyes shut and say my own prayer, a private prayer to my own Lord, who sometimes seems to me to be a different Lord from the God of my Father and the provost and the elders. I pray for Conraat.

Two officers push us back, towards the waist, while the cook and his servers carry a jug of brandy to each of us, one by one. Each person is allowed one sip only. When I take mine, I close my eyes and let the sharp warmth travel through me. It is soft, and if I keep my eyes closed, perhaps I will believe that I am not on the cold, sloping deck, waiting for Arian Jacobsz and his men to stop tap-tapping at the side of the boat and tell us we are safe. The tiny sip does not last long enough for me to believe this, and when I open my eyes, I am leaning against my sister, with two hundred frightened faces glowing pale in the beautiful, beautiful moonlight. Surely the moon should not shine amid so much worry. But there it is, white and perfect, lighting the crippled mast and the huddle of anxious sailors as clearly as it might light a lovely dance.

Arian ties a rope round his waist and climbs over the gunwale while three sailors hold the rope. One of the sailors leans over the gunwale, calling down. Minutes and minutes later – I am not sure how many, but certainly long enough for my father to ask Pieter to run to the cabin to collect the Bible, and for my mother to say that no one is going anywhere, not unless the commander decrees it himself – they haul Arian back up to the deck. There is some shuffling and scuffling and then they lower the yawl and Arian climbs down into it. Mattys, holding a lantern, is lowered down too, held by two men. I can hear them shouting as they go, their voices getting dimmer and dimmer. Beside me, Jan slips his hand into mine. I turn and look at him; he is so neat and brown, like a leaf, and his eyes are wide. His wood-hard fingers press against mine, and I squeeze his hand in return. Pulling him close, I whisper, 'When we get to Batavia, you will have rum every day. And never eat pickled fish.'

He nods back at me, and adds, 'And you will be a married lady, pious and good.'

'Yes,' I say, hope still floating in my heart, 'that is what I shall be.'

We wait in the cold white night for the word from the skipper.

There is a commotion near the bow, and we edge forward. Three sailors pull Arian back to the deck, the rope still wrapped round his waist. Beside him, Mattys shivers, making his lantern shake. Pelseart steps close to Arian and asks something. I do not hear what, but in response, the skipper sharply shakes his head. They talk to each other quietly for a moment, in urgent whispers, and then Pelseart strikes the mast.

'*Batavia* has a substantial hole in her bow. She is on a dry reef and is not taking water at the moment. However, the skipper assures me that the reef is low and that when the tide changes, the water may begin to enter. There appears to be a cluster of islets to our east, and the skipper will be sending four men to assess the situation now. If they are indeed islands – please calm down, I cannot speak if you are yelling – then we shall find temporary refuge there until the ship can be repaired. Until the men return, Cook, please take the brandy barrel around again. And the biscuit.' The commander puts his hand out to steady himself on the mast.

The darkness is beginning to shrink away from us, the moon has sunk and although I cannot see the sun, a grey light is spreading over the *Batavia*.

Mama reaches out for Myntgie's hand and stares up at my father. She says nothing, but a tear runs down her face and my father turns away.

Chapter Twenty-Two

Across the sky, a gold streak spreads, and then a red band. The sun appears, round and red and low in the sky. Five sailors leave in the sloop to look for the land; I can see no soldiers and cannot tell where Conraat might be. He seems rarely to be counted among the soldiers, yet does not do the work of a sailor. My place is with my family. This is what Mama tells me when I whisper to her that I would like to look for Conraat. She puts her hand on my wrist as she says it, and her nails dig into my skin.

Gisbert pushes his way through the crowd and joins us, slipping his hand onto Mama's arm. His hair is damp, clinging to his face, and his eyes desperate as a preacher's. Father calls Commander Pelseart over and asks him if one of the sailors could go below and collect his Holy Book. The commander stares at my father, as at a madman, and then very slowly says, 'The sailors are trying to repair the ship, Predikant. Property will be salvaged, please do not fear.' His skin is leaf-like, thin, fluttery. When my father puts his hand to grab at the commander, Pelseart almost topples over. He pulls himself straight and says, 'Perhaps the provost may have a copy of the Lord's Book he would be willing to offer.'

Father thanks the commander but does not rise to seek out the provost.

Mama folds her hands in her lap and taps one finger against another, then say, 'Oh, then I will go and ask him, Gisbert. Truly.'

She is up in one motion, with Roelant balanced on her hip. Strangely, in the midst of this grounded ship, my mother seems to have life flowing back to her. It is her fear, coming to meet her; it is what she has waited for from the day we left Dordrecht, and now that it is here she is relieved and ready. She is fierce and alive in the face of it. My mother, who seems to have forgotten that her place, like mine, ought to be with the family, disappears into the crowd and is still invisible to us when the boat is raised to the deck again. The sailors are wet but jump from the skiff to the deck.

A sailor who looks no older than Pieter cries out, 'There is land! Three small islands, all flat, with water or not we could not tell. There appear to be others nearby and all are raised from the sea and dry enough to provide protection until the ship is herself again.'

The skipper looks away, biting his lip.

Commander Pelseart steps onto the gunwale of the skiff. 'Company officials and women will be carried to the near island.' Pelseart's voice is beginning to crack and the cook carries the brandy to him. The commander takes a sip and continues.

'Officers of the Company and women to the boat first.'

The sun begins to blaze above us. Maria, the cook's wife, steps forward alongside two sailors' wives. Maria's belly is round, the child due any moment. There are four young children with them.

'Officers, then passengers, then crew. Servants last, though you may always dare the waves yourself.' The commander looks down at Maria, blinks, and then looks away.

Behind us, her husband continues pouring out brandy for cold passengers, his face drawn and weary. Maria and the other two women step back. One of them, a young, dark-skinned woman, holds her hand to her face as though she has been slapped. She looks at me and Anna and Myntgie as we start to move forward with Jan and Pieter, and tilts her chin upwards. I could be mistaken, but I am sure I hear a hiss coming from her mouth. Behind us, people begin to push against each other, so that I stumble as I move forward.

Commander Pelseart holds out his hand for us. 'In the middle, here.'

'Wait. Mama?' Myntgie puts her arm out in front of us, fencing us off from the boat. She calls again. 'Mama?'

Lucretia climbs into the boat, her grey coat wrapped tightly about her. She looks up at me and does not smile, simply inclines her head. I feel myself burn, and nod back. Urgent hands help three other women in, and a cluster of children: Hilletje and Anneke Haardens, Cornelisz Aldersz, and three children I do not recognise. The commander calls to us, tells us the sloop is filling.

Mama pushes towards us, her arms flailing left and right, swimming through the crowd. Indeed, she is gasping when she gets to us. Gasping so that words can barely escape. 'Roelant. I do not have him. Someone took him for a moment while I looked for the provost, and now – where is he? Roelant!' She shrieks his name sharply enough to slice meat.

The commander's hand is still stretched out to us.

I shake my head and call to him. 'My brother – someone has him.'

The commander calls out, 'Who has the predikant's young son? Quickly, we are waiting.'

Someone pushes forward, I recognise him as Jan Pelgrom, one of the boys who has served our dinners. Roelant is sitting on his shoulders, waving happily at us. When he sees my mother he calls, 'My mama.'

Mama snatches him from Pelgrom's shoulders and does not say thank you. She is so rough that Roelant begins to cry again, and holds his arms out for the boy. Mama keeps hold of him and climbs into the bow of the sloop, not looking at Lucretia. Myntgie climbs in behind her. Jan Pelgrom stands still, his arms empty of Roelant, watching us. Not one of us speaks a word to him. I wish to, but Mama has been so fierce that I can think of no words to say. So I say none, and the boy stands, watching. Anna squeezes close to Mama, and Myntgie is on the other side. Pieter and Jan are towards the bow and I am to be with them.

As I am about to step in, my arm stretched to take the Commander's hand, I turn my head and see the straight nose, the fine cheek of the one who makes my whole self full. He lifts his head and raises his hand to me. Behind me, my family and the commander are calling, insisting that I climb into the skiff, and truly, they are strangers to me, for all I can see is Conraat; his brown hands, his curled beard. I cannot run to him, as I wish to, cannot call out to him, for even with – what? Who knows what? Even with whatever the next hours hold hammering at my door, I still have a reputation to think of, and the reputation of my family. I do. So I stand on the deck, not in the skiff and not running into the arms of my love, stand with my hand held in the air. He calls my name and several sailors turn and stare at me. His mouth is opening and closing, making a round circle, an o. He makes a pushing motion with his hand and my head clears. Go, he is saying. Go, Judith.

My father wraps his arms round my waist, lifts me into the skiff and sits me on his lap. 'You are holding up the entire ship, Judith. What are you thinking of?'

He takes his hands from me, so that I am able to shift alongside him, but he does not move. He looks up at Pelseart. 'Should I stay with them? To offer prayer for each arrival?'

Pelseart is not thinking about my father. He nods, but as though he has not heard.

My father taps me on the arms and repeats, 'What are you thinking of, wasting valuable time like that?' He looks up at Gisbert, standing alone on the deck. 'Quickly, Gisbert, come.'

Gisbert shakes his head. 'I am neither a child nor a woman, but a lowly servant of the Company.'

Mama is as strong as fire. 'You are a member of this family. And if we perish, we shall perish together.'

As Gisbert climbs in, Mama stands again, scanning the deck.

'Where is Wylbrecht Claas? Surely she should be with us.'

Staring past her, at Conraat lining up his soldiers and giving them instructions for something or other, I reply that I do not know. The seawater has rushed to my head and filled it. Though I can feel Anna trembling beside me, my head is so full of brine that I have no room even for fear.

Four soldiers get in the boat with us, and three sailors. They will stay with us in case there are natives who might attack, and to help us find shelter. Several soldiers gather round the boat – there must be twenty of them – and begin tying ropes to each hook. One of them carefully places two barrels of water in with us, along with two boxes which he points to and says, 'Biscuit and peas.' Wiebbe Hayes is among the soldiers, and, as is usual with him, he does not look at me, does not smile or nod or even growl like the ill-mannered bear he is. On the other side of the deck, the larger double-masted yawl is being uncovered. People are pushing forward to get to it, scratching at each other, thrusting elbows in faces.

The soldiers grunt together and count to three. Our boat lifts into the air, swinging on the ropes and on the strength of the sweating, grunting soldiers. Two of them call to each other, something in French, and Wiebbe Hayes tells them to concentrate. I hold my breath, waiting for the drop while four men guide the boat over the gunwale. We bang against the edge and my father grips the wooden bench, his teeth biting into his lip. Pieter leans his head over the side and Mama slaps him. Above us, the soldiers grunt and call instructions to each other: 'Hold tight. Pull it in a little. Step back.' Below us, the black eye of the sea. Halfway down, one of the soldiers slips and the boat bangs into the ship. We tilt and swing so that several people fall onto one another, scrambling back when the rope is balanced out again. Mama holds Roelant so tightly that I am concerned that he will turn blue. We hear the water before we feel it. A deep roar, a shush of the wavelets on the reef, then a bang which seems as loud as the crash which woke us, and half of the ocean rises up to meet us, rises up to cover our already shivering faces. The sailors row fast and hard and silently. No one speaks, not even when a grey fish jumps out of the wave beside us and makes a squealing noise. When the waves get larger, so that we are tossed and sprayed, so that we may as well be fish ourselves we are so wet and salty and thrown about, even then we are silent, clinging to the boat with everything we have left.

Ahead of us, the island. The sailors grunt more, pushing towards the patch of rock and sand. There are no trees, not as far as I can see, and certainly no mountains. But we are not coming to live here, so we do not require a pleasing island. No, we are coming to seek shelter while the ship is repaired, which will take the shortest of time, one or two days perhaps. Those two days will be difficult, it would be foolish not to anticipate this, for we have no shelter; but they will not be impossible. The

Lord will be with us and it will be the briefest of times. I look back at the ship, teetering on the reef. Hanging spider-like from the stern, the yawl appears empty, lowering down to the waves. There is the sound of wood splitting and I could swear I see someone jump into the ocean. On the deck of the *Batavia*, I can see people running. Several boxes soar overboard. I think I hear a scream, although it could be the sea.

The boat begins to scrape on the rocks and the soldiers jump out, pull us in. Myntgie starts to climb out while the boat is still moving, and begins dragging it with the soldiers. They try to slap her away, but she is strong and it is clear they are glad of one less body to haul, so I climb out as well. The water is cold and makes my dress cling around my knees so that I trip as I try to walk onto the dry ground, this strange unwelcoming surface of rock. One of the soldiers picks me up, carries me to the dry ground and places me carefully down on a flat rock. He nods at me and says, 'Corporal van Hueson told us we are to look after you, on pain of death.' I watch his back as he stalks back down the beach where my mother is still struggling out of the boat.

It will be fine, it must be. The land is safe, the ship will be fixed. Even now, it must be fixed. We have food, and two water barrels, which will surely last the day or two required. Mama's face is set with fear and determination equally; I have seen her with such a countenance only once before, when Roelant was being born. And inside my own skin, amongst all of this, I blow on a flame of pleasure. On pain of death, they are to look after me. On Conraat's instructions.

With a strange flush of madness, I allow only this to have meaning: that Conraat has ordered my protection; that Conraat thought lastly of me. If I concentrate on this, as with prayer, then the cracking ship, the wet legs, the arms flailing in the waves – all of this will disappear.

Chapter Twenty-Three

Pieces of the ship begin floating to shore almost as soon as the sloop makes its second trip. The sun is high, directly above us, but gives off little heat. I lay my coat out on the rocks to dry. Thick with sand and salt, my skirt scrapes at my legs. We gather by the large, low rocks and wait, the whole Bastiaansz family, except for Father, who feels it is his bounden duty to explore the island and bring back news for the commander about the whereabouts of water, food, shelter. There is no point to that, I tell him, we will not be here long enough to require food. Mama looks sideways at me when I say this, and asks me when I learnt to be such an optimist.

We wait on the rocks, as flat as palm prints, listening to the barking of the seals nearby, and when the yawl arrives we gather at the water's edge, ready to offer hands if needed. We let out a cheer when they draw near, for they carry precious cargo. Mattys Beer calls out a litany as he stands on the gunwale: two water barrels, one biscuit barrel, several of pickled vegetable and one of wine. Enough for several days, should we need it.

A thin-boned sailor, his arms and chest wet, sits firmly on a bulky casket. When he climbs onto the rocks, he holds the casket to his chest and smiles at me. A brown scar joins his nose to his lip and I recognise him from Good Hope: Andries de Vries, the only officer who thought to speak a word to me.

He leans near my ear and whispers, 'Company jewels. Must be careful,' and sits on his haunches, nursing the casket as he would a sick child.

On the fourth trip, the yawl carries more soldiers, a pale box marked 'FRANCISCO PELSEART, BAT. JAVA', and a crowd of servants. Though Wylbrecht is among them, she does not return my mother's embrace, or my smile. The boat is buoyant with barrels: more wine, ale, bread and also some grey sailcloth, with which the soldiers offer to make shelters. They have done it before, they say, having been taught the method. Wiebbe Hayes is with the soldiers, his wide face salt-marked and red. Lowering his head, he smiles at me and I smile back. We are all one and equal on this island, surely.

Five sailors turn the yawl back out to sea, calling that they will be taking it to the islet to the south, to gather instructions from the commander, who has landed there with the skipper. As we watch them turn into the wind, Wiebbe runs from the cat-sized mound at the peak of the island back to the shore, waving his arms, calling out for us to look to the *Batavia*. There are perhaps ninety of us already ashore; lone women, families, some crew, and the few soldiers.

We gather on the shore and watch in silence as the huge waves rise up and beat the ship down onto the reef again. It is hard to see clearly, but it seems that people fall into the waves, which are as high as the ship itself; I have never seen such a thing, the spray flying up as high as the topmast. Mama holds my hand as the side planks of the honourable and unbreakable ship *Batavia* split away. We cannot hear the sound of the splitting, but even in my imagining, my own fanciful mind, the sound is loud enough to scare my hope into hiding. We stay together, standing in a long line on the beach, holding a terrible silence. Another section of the ship breaks away and we can see the water beginning to rush into the hold. Myntgie presses her hand to her mouth and moves closer to me. The planks which have broken off the ship bob on the waves, which are now becoming smaller.

'Look! There are people on the planks!' It is Myntgie who cries out, bouncing on her feet. 'Can you see? On the bit there, you cannot see it now because of the wave, oh, there it is again. Three people. No, four.'

It seems that each piece of flotsam has a person holding onto it, floating grimly. One section becomes a makeshift raft, holding a small society of men. We call our encouragement, hoping foolishly that they can hear us. One of them tumbles off the plank and tries to swim back to it. The waves force him away and though the men on the raft try to cut through the water, his hands stop waving. His head goes under, or at any rate is no longer visible. We wait for him to come up again, but he does not. A cold ball of fear fills my body.

When the men on the raft arrive, they stagger immediately to one of the water barrels and begin pouring it over themselves, mouths open. Though Father cries out, 'We must save the water,' a crowd of men join them, breaking open the barrels, gulping desperately.

Mattys Beer is among them, his puny body covered with red-raised welts. He guzzles at the water, then, rubbing furiously at the marks on his arms, he turns to Father. 'Predikant, we have waited all this day on board, and can see no reason to wait for water. Not after all this.'

Father slices the air with his hands, one precise stroke. 'You drink, we shall all die, boy. Yourself included, do you see?'

Mattys stares at him, then pours wine so that it drizzles down his body. 'Perhaps we have plans other than yours, Predikant. Besides, there is more to come. Plenty to last, for we have barrels and barrels on the ship.'

Though Father calls more and more for order, for calm, and for prayer, several of the men – I do not know them – seize the last water barrel and throw it onto a rock so that it splits open. Liquid runs into the sand and some of the men lie on the ground, licking at the rock like dogs.

Mattys and his gang of sailors shove at Father's back, calling for water and for wine until there is little of either left. Someone, I do not know who, drags a wine barrel down to the shore and men begin swigging the wine at length, throwing themselves down on the sand with drunken groans.

Father pushes each of us forward, so that we too will have some water, calling, 'If it is to be finished, it is at least to be shared.' He stops suddenly, and points out to sea. 'There must be equal desperation there.'

We stare out to the ship as four men, all in a line, jump into the waves. Turning away before their arms stop thrashing against the foam, I take Myntgie's hand and whisper, 'The Lord is with us, surely He is, and we will prosper after this testing.' With her hand cold and damp in mine, I will it to be true.

When the sun begins to dip into the ocean, Father gathers us, and bids us lie knitted together on the raised rock. Myntgie takes Wylbrecht's hand, calling her to lie with us, sharing what little warmth we have. I call to Lucretia, standing alone on the thin stretch of sand, and invite her to bed down with us. She holds her hand up in a wave, but shakes her head.

Aching with cold, I lie curled like a lamp, and push close to Myntgie. Her shoulders are sharp beneath her dress, and her neck is covered with neat red bite marks, similar perhaps to the bites of bedmites, though this rocky shelf would provide scarce comfort for any as choosy as a mite. Roelant cries all night, a constant low keening. After some hours, when the moon is high overhead, I turn to face him, to smell his salt-skin, and tear my sleeve on the rock below me. Trying to free the cloth from the rock, I pull my arm sharply up and graze the flesh of my wrist. The pain is pleasing, a satisfying shred, and I push the wrist into my mouth. Blood seeps in, salt-sweet and thick.

Once, when I was quite young, the butcher in Dordrecht gave me a leather pocket, folded and stitched. Inside was a brown tooth, pointed at one end. For a whole year, it was one of my pleasures to rub the tooth between my fingers, feeling the point press into the round flesh of my finger, sometimes until I drew blood. I have always been a creature of strange desires.

Closing my eyes, I bite harder at my wrist, pulling at the flesh and letting the pain still my mind. Beneath my tongue, the skin tears a little more. I imagine biting away at myself like this until I am bones, nothing but bones. Beside me, Roelant hits his arms out at the air, slapping off the hungry black insects, and cries again. We lie like this, biting and hitting and fearing, until a flat light spreads over the island with a morning chorus of drunken sailors calling, 'Hail dawn! The barrels are empty and we are free!'

Myntgie shakes her thin shoulders and picks three trumpets of coral from her hair. 'Free of what? Wine can make such fools of men.'

Wylbrecht raises her head but looks away from Myntgie. 'They are free of the Company. I am convinced it is their desire. Free to drink wine, free to steal the Company's goods.'

Father blows through his nose, a habit made no more pleasant by our surroundings. 'Servants' gossip, Wylbrecht. Chests of jewels would do them no good here. And how should they carry them away?' He strokes Myntgie's hair. 'As you say, girl, it is wine which makes such fools.'

Mother is as quiet as the clouds. 'If the barrels are empty, Gisbert, what are we to drink?'

'Water,' Father answers, with barely a tremble, 'for the commander shall bring us supplies, as we have many, and if the ship is not mended we will have enough to last until rescue.'

My brother Gisbert scratches at his face. 'And for food, there is fish, seals and surely birds and other meat.' He prods Pieter, still huddled into the rock as though it is a warm bed. 'Come, we can surely find fish willing to be caught even by town boys.'

All day they float to shore: men on barrels, planks, rafts made from bits of the stern mast. Barrels float to shore on their own, too. One of brandy, which raises a song and a prayer, and one of grey peas, greeted with less joy. When rolled to safety, the brandy proves to have split, leaking into the sea, though the peas are unharmed. Lucretia has spent the night, as far as I can see, standing in the same position on the sand. Wiebbe Hayes tells us that they will be able to create beds from the sailcloth, if there is enough, with branches from the island. He looks around as he says it, at the barren mound rising half-heartedly from the ocean, and then corrects himself. If they can get to the ship to gather wood, he says, they will be able to build hammocks, beds, proper tents, anything we could wish for. No one says that what we wish for is to be back on the *Batavia*, in full sail, on our way to a land of riches.

Late in the day, when the sun is high above us, Conraat comes. He arrives like a hero, his hair a tight helmet of curls. He has made a raft from some planks, tied together with a stretch of thick rope. Five men are with him, all well. Conraat pulls the raft to shore almost entirely on his own (only two other men helping, and only he putting in a proper effort), and I run to him as soon as his feet are on dry ground. He embraces me right there, on the shore, with all the men watching. And I do not care, not at all, for surely on this island the rules may be a little different. Surely here we may be a little free. None of this is thought clearly by me at all, only that I must have my arms on him, must kiss his cheek. For Conraat is alive, he is well, and the Lord is surely good.

Father calls to Conraat, 'What news of the commander?' and Conraat replies that he has none. There are no water kegs on his flimsy raft, and when we look to the sky we see only high white clouds, as fine as lace.

The wine and water are all gone; Mattys Beer is mottled red and pale from the effects of such guzzling under this cheese-white sun, and three men are lying in their own puke, all mixed with the gravelly sand.

Father says the commander will come to us, with food and water, and he will bring with him news of our salvation. Surely salvation will come, for the Lord has chosen us as his people.

When the sun begins to slide again across the red sky, Conraat calls Gisbert and Pieter to him, and they begin to snap driftwood into kindling. Though Conraat speaks to my brothers, he watches me, his eyes slow upon my body.

It is Pieter who looks up first, drops his armload, begins to yell with the mad joy of a gull. 'Here,' he cries, running to the shore, 'the sloop!'

Shadow-dark against the deepening light, the sloop chops across the twilight swell. Pieter's call is louder, hopeful. 'The commander is with her!'

Even against the red brightness, I can see him. Standing now, his thin arms waving a piece of cloth, and he is calling something, but only the sound of the words carry, not the meaning. There are perhaps twelve others in the sloop with him; I cannot tell who they are. As the boat draws further in, others pick up Pieter's cry, so that it becomes a cheer, 'The commander!'

The thirsty and the tired have pushed their way to the shore, so that we are a good crowd, though marked with salt and dirt, applauding the arrival of our leader. Conraat stands still and quiet beside me, neither calling nor applauding as he watches the sloop come near. She draws up, almost to the shallows, and we are like children, looking out to the waves, holding our arms out to Papa. And Papa stands in the sloop, calls to us, his children, holds his arms out, and begins to climb out of the boat, begins to jump into the water to come to us, to bring us our salvation; and in his arms is a barrel, surely filled with water; and as his leg arcs over the gunwale, the ball of fear in my belly begins to roll away, away down the flat beach; and as he touches the water, for the first time in three days I believe my own words of hope; and at exactly that moment four men pull him back, snatch the barrel from him, and I see a fist fly and, I swear, also the flash of a knife; and it is then, as the sloop turns again towards the sunset, that hope leaves me, snaking away into the waves with the battered craft.

We watch the boat disappear, each of us holding our breath, unwilling to speak of what we have just seen. Conraat puts his rough-skinned hand on the back of my neck, and I know this: he is all I can believe in now.

Chapter Twenty-Four

The next day, more men, and some women, come to shore on planks and barrels. Those who are able swim alone, arriving half dead of thirst and cold. Provost Jansz comes to shore on a flat piece of timber, his lips milky white as he calls for the water we do not have. There are some still on board, he says, too frightened to leave. And some who have not survived. His round face folds in on itself. 'I am not a young man. I did not think I would live for this.' On board, the wine has been guzzled, papers thrown overboard, drunken men, mad on fear, have begun rioting. He tells of one man thrown into the sea by his own brother, in a fight over the last mouthful of ale. For two days, the provost's family have huddled under a sailcloth shelter, believing him dead.

Sara, his tall and fine-skinned wife, says, 'Those on board did not require your presence: your family did.' His children, though, throw themselves onto him with the enthusiasm of mongrel dogs.

'Water,' he says again, a thin line of blood creeping from his nose. 'Please, water.'

We do not sleep the night, but call instead to the Lord to deliver us, as he has delivered our people before. My father says that this is the Lord's will, for we are a chosen nation, and I look up to the stars, wondering why it was not the Lord's will to keep the *Batavia* safe at sea.

Staring up at the white slice of moon, Mama says, 'Why did they not let him land? Did they think we would cause him harm?'

Wylbrecht, sitting next to her, says quietly, 'I have heard talk that there are those who wished to commandeer the ship, to live off her riches and the riches of other ships. I do not know of its truth, only that this has been spoken. It may be that they wish to attack a rescue ship, should one arrive, and to use the commander as a decoy. Or perhaps they simply plan on sailing to Java for rescue.'

'Surely not, Judith? Surely not the skipper?'

But I have no answer for my mother, for I know nothing now except the hard scrape of the rocks beneath my feet and hands.

There is no rain the next day, nor the next. Sand is caked thick on my skin, even beneath my tongue, so that it feels I can barely breathe. We lie in a row, like Bastiaansz fish ready for pickling. Roelant sucks and sucks at Mama's breast, sometimes scratching at her face, or pulling at her hair. She says it is because there is so little milk for him, poor child. And then we do not speak, none of us, for the effort is too great. My mouth dries together, and the sun begins to dance slowly behind my eyes. Beneath my head, the harsh stone softens, moves, becomes a rocking sea holding me. Birds scream above me, even speak words. I hear them call to each other, I think it is in French, but their voices are too shrill, they spit blood as they speak. When I try to open my mouth to catch the spit, or to make some of my own, I find I cannot. Nor can I open my eyes to see them; I am too weary and find I will lie here on this rocking gentle surface of sea-rock, lie here rocking until I disappear.

A shadow leans over me, presses his weight against me, calls me back to him. Conraat holds a shell full of seal blood. 'Drink it,' he says, lifting my head and holding the shell against my lips. 'It will keep you well, bring you back. You must not be lost.' He holds his head close to mine, so that I hear him.

Raising my head, I sip at the red mucus. It is barely liquid, as thick as bread and as bitter as vinegar.

'Drink more. Please, Judith. I care for no one except you. All others may die, I care nothing. But you must not. Please, drink.'

His breath is sour, as fetid as rotting meat, and his eyes shot through with red, yet he is my saviour, the only one I have, and I will drink the blood he brings.

We hobble down to the shore, each of us holding the other so that we make a line so long we spread out almost the width of this tiny plot of desolation. The water is a siren before us, wet and endless. Perhaps it is me who starts it, perhaps Father: I am never truly sure. Kneeling in the shallows, I lower my head to the sea, let the brine trickle in and take one, two gulps. It shall be the end of us, surely, but better to have such salty relief than none at all.

Something bumps gently against my legs and then drifts away. Wood, perhaps. It bumps again and I look down at the shallows. It is face down, and the hands are swollen and pale. One foot is bare, and it too is swollen, though the skin is shrivelled. Around the head, his hair floats out in brown waves. Anna is behind me with the boys, so I do not scream. Staring at the body floating at my feet, bloated beyond recognition, I step back until I feel the ridge of the island shelf behind me. My brothers trip through the water after me, stumbling weak-legged so that they fall every third step. When I reach the flat, I drop down onto my knees and begin to scrape and scrabble at the sand, groping desperately for the well I know I will not find. Grit and sand mixes with the seawater on my hands and face, chafing at my skin.

Wiebbe Hayes kneels beside me, puts a hand on me and stills my digging. Says, 'There is no water here, Judith.'

Unstuck by the water from the sea, words come from my mouth again, but they are unformed, unclear. 'You – it bumped – there – hair – the hands, I could not tell – why are you here? It was – I will not – not die –'

'No. You will not.' He stands, looks around at the swarm of survivors, wracked by thirst, covering the stretch of sand. There must be forty of us here on the beach, and easily one hundred more scrabbling about the island for drops of water. Wiebbe grabs quickly at a piece of mast timber and wades into the ocean.

Holding the timber with one hand, his arms flash in and out of the water, yet he appears to cover no distance. The waves grow larger and the timber rises up, appears to be no sort of raft at all. We stand on the shore and call to him, some thirty of us, with bird-weak cries, but we are not enough against the waves. Barely halfway to the ship, he turns and kicks again to shore.

'I cannot get close enough – the waves – . . .' Wiebbe drags the timber up to the beach. 'We must wait for it to calm.' He looks down at me. 'It will calm, Judith.'

By the shore, men lie on their backs, mouths open, or curled on the rock like snails. One boy lies on his back, arms spread out in an empty embrace. Father begins to pray. I peer at the boy's face, open to the sun, his eyes shut but his lids flickering constantly. His tongue hangs from his mouth, and he is pretty with the sun dappling his skin. I do not know his face. With prone men and boys scattered across its face, the shore looks like a strange battlefield.

Out to sea, the *Batavia* is still lying half on its side, with most of the hold torn away. The ship teeters with each blast of wind, and the topmast sticks out to the side like a broken finger. It is sudden; a gust of wind and there it is, yet another terrible crack, and the topmast splits and drops. Though we see a thin figure floating on the mast as it drifts ashore, this time there is no cheer from the company assembled on the island edge. And how we have increased in number, with many folk drawn to this beach by our miserable shouts of hope; there must now be more than one hundred of us here on the shore, half of that number lying as dead men. We wait in silence, watching the *Batavia*'s mast float ashore with the last survivor.

It is Undermerchant Cornelisz who floats in to the shallows, his arms wrapped round the mast, his face pressed into the wood. Even when the water is shallow enough to wade through, he does not climb off the mast, but stays with his face pressed to it, as though it is his betrothed, rescued from the waves. Three soldiers go to him and prise him off. He leans on them as he staggers ashore and then collapses on the sand, breathing heavily. Eyes shut, he leans back, takes gulps of air. When his eyes open, they are almost yellow.

'I am the last,' he says. 'I waited for the ship.' He looks over at the provost. 'I tried to save the ship.'

The provost says nothing, only stares back at Jeronimus as though he has remembered something important, something he had forgotten to say. He stares like this for heartbeat upon heartbeat, and then says, 'The commander tried to take you in the yawl, did he not, Jeronimus?'

Jeronimus shakes his head. 'He asked me to stay with the ship, as he was seeking water. Where is he? Survived?'

'We do not know. Taken on the sloop. To look for water, we presume. Or to seek rescue.' Father folds his arms, a petulant child.

'I am to take charge as next in command to the skipper and commander. We have a council? Where is the water?'

Provost Jansz points to the prone men. 'All gone. We have had no order, Jeronimus, and no council.'

'I am here now. No water?' Jeronimus swallows. 'We will organise a party to the ship. There is enough driftwood, surely, to build a skiff. If not, we will build one from the mast here. Gather more barrels, if there are some. Otherwise we must wait for rain, and who can tell how long that may be?' The yellow has gone from Jeronimus's eyes, though his voice is cracked.

Praise God! The next morning, as we pile up driftwood and the few salvaged nails, fat drops of rain begin to fall. Slowly at first, and then faster and thicker, so that I long to be like the drunken boys, taking my clothes off, dancing! The barrels are lined up, their wide hungry mouths pointing up at the sky, and the sweet, sweet rain pours down into them. Even Father claps his hands, shouts out loud, 'Rain! The Lord has saved us!' While Mama and I stand with our faces pointing up, as though we are barrels, waiting to be filled. And filled we will be, for the Lord has brought rain and forgiven me my lack of faith. Truly, it is as if He has sent it as a sign, a blessing on the arrival of Jeronimus Cornelisz, who will bring order and goodness out of chaos. Jeronimus, who will be the Lord's representative. Standing with the cool water pouring over me, I can believe that if I long for it enough, it shall be so. Dear Lord, let it be so. Jeronimus will bring us home to safety and we shall not thirst again.

Chapter Twenty-Five

I took little notice of Jeronimus Cornelisz on the ship *Batavia*. It is strange how people who are not noticed seem to wait their moment. Perhaps this is true for all of us, that we wait our moment, though for some of us it never arrives. Or perhaps it is true, and this was certainly suggested at the time, that there are certain people who await disaster, knowing that opportunities will be found there. Some animals are like this, maggots for instance, thriving on putrefaction. Or crows, who survive on death. Animals should not be judged by it, certainly not, for they do not have souls. As for us, turning our heads away when we should have yelled and demanded and insisted, where did our souls go then? And as for me, blinding myself with desire, destroying that which I loved, this is not the behaviour of a creature with a good soul, but one who has lost her way between good and evil. I want to believe that in spite of our failings, we were not the ones who invited the terrible wrath of God. In the midst of our loss and bewilderment, Jeronimus flourished. Like the crow and the maggot, he was made for disaster.

When I met Fransz, I was no longer famous. The desperate interest had subsided, and I lived quietly in Amsterdam, lying awake at night, counting the mistakes I had made. Sometimes I would write them down, compile lists of all those I had wounded, all those I could have saved. Other nights, especially in the midst of winter, I would wake in the early morning while the cold dark still covered the city, and walk alone by the canals, tarrying close to the edge of the water, hurrying on icy paths; but I never did slip. When Fransz declared himself, I told him I caused harm to all who loved me, told him that I would wake him each night with my weeping and my misery, told him my worst secret, too: that I was a creature who had lost my faith. He was a large man, Fransz, big enough to enfold me. Enormous hands, and a way of walking so that his body rocked. Watching him move, my breath would slow, become steady. Even his voice was slow; our daughter says that he was the incense to her prayer. You see, she has inherited my edge of heresy.

We left Amsterdam together and wed here, in Friesland, quietly. The first time we lay together, he was so large and soft that I felt myself slide into him, felt all my skin peel away, so that even as he rode me, I wept great tears of relief. When I close my eyes now, I smell the wool of his skin, the musk of him. For nineteen years he lay beside me, my wellspring, placing his hands upon me when I wept. Our daughter would sometimes find me coiled on the floor. It has not been easy for her. Yesterday we watched the child move within her, saw his legs lift the cloth of her dress as he turned. She took my hand and rested it on him, and he grew calm again.

'Thank you, Mama,' she said, 'you always could bring peace.' She pauses for a moment, then adds, 'I would like to know more, to know everything. When you are ready to tell me.'

I sit for a moment, hand upon my grandson, then say, 'I failed, that is all.'

She speaks as slowly as her father used to. 'I have been with you for almost half of your life, Mama. And you never failed me.'

Like her father, she brings me such relief.

Chapter Twenty-Six

Once the topmast has split from the *Batavia*, the wreck is fairly safe. After the storm, the sea settles, and Provost Jansz insists that the officers form a Company council: Provost Jansz himself, Father, and the clerk Salman Deschamps, the scar on his forehead gleaming red in the sharp sun. Jeronimus is elected chief, as is fitting. We have little hope of the commander returning; I believe he has gone to seek rescue, that he will yet provide salvation for us. The team of carpenters build two skiffs. 'Batavia's ribs' we call them, for each is made of driftwood from the *Batavia*, like Eve from Adam's rib. When the clouds are high, the *Batavia* can be seen, tilted like a cat's tail, swaying on the far reef. Wooden planks stick out, and at the side a rough wound, a great gaping hole where wood has been stolen by the waves.

Each day sailors take the skiffs back against the waves and return with what they have salvaged. As the boats approach the island, we gather on the rocky shore, waving and calling them on, each of us hoping that they will be carrying our own box. One of Lucretia's chests is recovered, and she opens it there on the shore, pulls out brine-ruined gowns, weeping. Wiebbe helps her drag the box away from the crowd and she digs deeper and deeper until she pulls out a dry lace collar. A man's collar, so it must be a gift for her husband, yet she puts it about her own neck and strokes it as she would a child. There are at least two boxes recovered each day and, more importantly, canvas, blankets, water, food barrels. Jeronimus waits on the beach and calls to the sailors when they arrive, 'The Company boxes?' When the sailors nod yes, he splashes out to the skiff, letting his breeches get wet, and helps pull the boxes out. He notes down the entire contents, then has them taken to his tent for safety. One of the chests is full of guilders! Not that money is much good here, as Anneke Haardens says. Another chest is packed with muskets, their points stabbing at the soaked wood. Lucretia lends me a gown from her box. It is a solid black, and it feels ridiculous for this island: thick, heavy fabric, salt-marked and rippled from the sea, not at all for working in. I wear it without stockings, for bare legs dry with more ease than stockinged ones.

The Bastiaansz boxes do not appear, though Father prays for this every morning, every noontime and every evening. Three cases come for the commander, full of rich breeches, and a Company box full of fine red cloth. Jeronimus claims these as his own, as he is the commander's replacement. We are lent clothes by those who have their boxes, and the women are set sewing with odd bits of salvaged cloth, so that we become a brightly and strangely dressed society. The Company cloth is left in the box. The soldiers have been put to work making tents from the canvas and sailcloth, the north corner kept for

Jeronimus, Conraat, the ugly clerk David Zevanck, and the soldiers Jacob Pieterz and Olivier van Weldren. The swords and muskets are kept in their tents, too, lest anyone should partake of excess wine again and fall into madness.

None of us speaks of the loss of the ship, not properly. When the sail is torn to make tents, we look away and do not speak, for what is there to say? The soldiers make beds by stitching canvas to four columns of wood. The canvas hangs like a low hammock, and it is more comfortable than the wooden beds on board the *Batavia*.

Jeronimus is our bandage-cloth, gathering us tightly in so that we are held safely. Morning and night he gathers us together on the narrow shore, assigns tasks, counts our number. Almost two hundred of us are now safe, with the rains filling our water barrels daily. Council is held nightly; my father returns from each meeting breathless with importance. Water is to be hoarded, he says, though only Jeronimus decreed that this was wise. Also, an expedition is to go to the other islands, there to seek more seal meat and water.

My brothers are bright in the sun and wind: they gather shellfish and help skin the fat seals caught on the rocks. The soldiers, too, busy with hammers and nails, wood and canvas, seem to glow more than I ever saw them on the *Batavia*. In the evenings, they light a fire and the fish caught during the day is cooked with seal meat and peas. Some diners tried grass as an accompaniment but even fried in oil it was found severely wanting. When all the tents are made we have turned this barren island into quite a village. The women's tent, in the middle of the island, is the largest, and it seems that even Lucretia will sleep there, sharing a sailcloth roof with servants. The sailors' tent is near it, for reasons of defence, though I am unclear what we need protecting from; we have already been attacked by storm and thirst, and there appear to be no wild animals on this island except for the rather docile seals.

It is into the sailors' tent that Jeronimus calls the councillors. He rings a salvaged bell against the skiff, dragged up onto the reef, so that many of us – perhaps seventy – run to the island edge, expecting what? A ship? Some sign of promise? We wait until the sun begins to sink, looking out to sea, waiting for the council to carry us tidings of new plans, new hope.

Hope we do receive. The sun is sinking by the time the council meeting is done, and the members march down the beach in a line. Jeronimus rings the bell as he walks, calling those who are not already on the shore. Lucretia sits alone, indeed it seems that she has not moved from this beach, for she seems always here, alone, looking up at the clouds. We wait in silence until the undermerchant reaches us on the beach, and then we stand, for it seems to be expected. Jeronimus waves us back to sitting though, and says, 'We shall wait until the entire company is here.' He rings the bell again, and Pieter calls out, 'There are some people hunting shellfish in the next bay, shall I run and call them?' Jeronimus nods his head indifferently and rings the bell again. A cluster of women come from the women's tent, smoothing down their dresses though they are encrusted beyond redemption with salt and sand. When Pieter returns with young Allert Jansze and the boy Jan Pelgrom,

Jeronimus claps his hands together. 'The council has news for all.'

Father, flustered, steps forward, wiping at his forehead. 'With respect, Undermerchant, it is normal to begin with a prayer. To give thanks for our deliverance. Perhaps a word from the Lord's Book first. Provost Jansz?'

The provost hands Father a salvaged copy of the Lord's Book. The cover is torn away. Father riffles through the pages, his hand shaking slightly. He does not like to be unprepared, my father. Does not like to leave the Lord wanting. Several pages drop to the ground and flutter around his feet. Illustrations, the pages not bound in. I catch only glimpses of the pages: a hand, a staff, a tent. No one dares pick them up and the papers fall over themselves, rolling towards the sea.

Father watches them being gathered by the wind and clears his throat. 'Ah, yes. A word from the Lord: "Out of the deep I cry to you, Oh Lord. Oh Lord, hear my voice. Let your ears be attentive to my cry for mercy. I wait for the Lord, my soul waits, and in His word I put my hope." ' Father closes his eyes, and says, 'Oh Lord, we thank you for making us part of the elect, and for your protection of the Honourable Company. Protect now all her goods, that the Honourable Members may be well pleased when we are rescued. Amen.' He does not mention the servants of the Honourable Company gathered about him, who may also require some of the Lord's protection.

'Thank you, Predikant.' Jeronimus nods at my father, his lips pressed together. Father stays standing. Jeronimus glares at him. 'You may sit. The council has met and decisions have been taken. Lieutenant Zevanck and his men have returned from the two near islands to the north, and have found water and seal colonies. Also a note from those who abandoned you here to your fate. Your previous commander has gone, he says, in the yawl to Java with Skipper Jacobsz and others, there to seek rescue, or to perish on the journey.'

Someone behind me calls, 'He shall not perish!'

Mattys Beer adds: 'Foul deserter, Pelseart!'

Jeronimus holds one hand up. 'This second is most likely, so, as we have not yet found water here, and have only enough to last a little longer, we must reduce our numbers. This island cannot support us all. We have agreed, therefore, that a group will go to the other islands. Forty will be chosen or will volunteer to go to the northernmost land. We call it Seal's Island, for the colony there is large, enough to feed easily that number. Three barrels will be sent with them, and canvas. Likewise a lesser number to go to the nearer south island—'

'Which should be named Traitor's Island, for those who have abandoned us.' Mattys is loud again behind me and Conraat, standing close by Jeronimus, shakes his head.

Once again Jeronimus raises his hand and continues as though uninterrupted. 'Also tools for raft-making will be provided, so that each party will be well equipped and ready to join us if a ship comes for rescue.'

Provost Jansz leans close to his wife, his long beard flapping against his throat, then stands abruptly, calling, 'Undermerchant, please.'

Jeronimus turns slowly, his brows raised.

'We will go. My family, and servant Pieter too. We will all go.'

'Good.' Jeronimus looks around. 'Are there others who would choose, now?'

Many people stand, pushing forward; certainly there are twenty folk calling out, 'I will go.'

Yet Jeronimus walks through the crowd, pulling people aside, whispering all the while, until he has a party of fifty or more standing far from the water's edge. At last he stands and, arms out in benediction, calls, 'Give thanks to those who will enrich our means, until the rescue ship comes.'

Squashed tight against each other, we call, 'Hurrah,' and those standing look nervously past us, out to sea. When Jeronimus finishes speaking, and those choosing to leave have sat down again or drifted off to their tents, the Bastiaansz family sits quietly. We have nothing to do but wait and endure. I pull Roelant onto my lap and kiss his soft head.

In the morning, Jeronimus is by the water, checking the skiffs, as soon as the sun is up. There is barely room for all of us who gather on the scrubby beach, our hands folded in prayer, our heads full of wishes. Two pregnant servant women are amongst the number elected to leave. One of them almost trips on the gunwale as she climbs in. In the larger skiff, Sara Jansz, tall and still, waits for her husband. The children nestle into her sides, eyes ahead. Provost Jansz hurries down to the skiff, calling, 'I was just collecting shellfish, to keep us a moment on the island.'

Jeronimus hands in two barrels of water and one of pickled vegetables and declares, 'We wish them well,' and all on the shore cry, 'Aye!' Yet I do not, for as he is speaking, I am staring around me at my island mates, now fewer and no less sure of survival, shuffling on the sand. Something cold is lodging in my belly as I send my own prayers heavenwards, barely believing any more that they will be answered. Wiebbe Hayes and three other soldiers push the two boats out, grunting with the weight of them. We all cry out, 'Good cheer! Water on the morrow!' and the company in the boats call back, 'Water indeed,' though Jeronimus's face is hard-set and he does not smile or wave.

The fire glows warm at my feet and the sun glows on my shoulders. I wave until the boats are specks in the distance, the sails blending with the dotting of the waves. Even then I stand on the shore, watching, feeling the absence of God. I stand there until the sun begins to burn my arms, and then I pull my skirt to my knees and wade to the south bay. I am thirsty and hot when I reach the other side, for I have brought no water. There is a low rock creating something of a shadow; I look around me carefully, and call out, 'Hello?' before I sit in its shade. When I am sure that I am alone, I take my apron off, bury my head in it, and cry.

Chapter Twenty-Seven

The island is stubble, suiting the name we have given it: Batavia's Graveyard. Yet there are some patches of life even here. From the shade of my rock, I can see a tiny clump of yellow flowers – weeds with no scent, yet with a brightness which shines against my skin, like fine sand. It is quiet here, the voices from the east side not carrying past the wind. The water is blue-green and bright. Further out, there are dark shadows forming a curved pattern. Another reef, I suppose waiting to trap ships or fish. Beyond that, close enough to see the rocks, Seal's Island and Traitor's Island rise out of the sea, looking somehow like flat hats. There seem to be five islands here, clumped like ringworm. The two great islands to the west are further away, so that I see merely their silhouettes. I sit still, letting my tears dry. There is a lovely emptiness in my body: I am poured out of every single thing, every thought, every desire. My apron is crumpled and marked, and my hands are red from the sand. Though it hurts me to do it, I pick a handful of pebbles up and rub them in my palms. I keep rubbing until the skin is ready to burst.

I am desperately thirsty; my tears have made me more so, and the sight of endless wet ocean makes me long for water. I pull at the tough grass by the rock and suck at the stems. There is little liquid to be had, and the taste is unpleasant, but there is at least saliva damping my mouth. Overhead, the sun burns, even as the wind whips through me. I stand up and shake my apron out, trying my best to smooth the creases, then put it on over my dress. Fortunately, I have no looking glass, for I will not imagine the sight that I must be in my borrowed dress and my worn apron. Facing the wind, I take off my cap and smooth my hair with my hands. Rubbing at my face, I walk down to the water's edge, splash my red hands in the cool water, then tie my cap on. With the sun burning into my cap and my mouth as dry as biscuit, I walk back across the flat island, back towards my family.

When I get to the centre of the island, closer to the village of tents clustered around each other, I see someone is coming towards me, waving arms. Closer, I can see the white beard, the curls. A flask in his hand, which he waves at me. I run towards him, but stumble and fall.

'Here. Silly girl, where did you go to? Drink.' He gathers me up and folds me across his knee, as though I am a baby, looking up at him.

I gulp at the water, fresh and cool.

'Where did you go?' He pulls the flask from my lips.

I shake my head and reach for the water again. 'Looking. More water.'

'Only when you tell me.'

'Tell what?'

'Where you went, who you went with.'

My mouth is too dry to talk, but I try. 'Across the island. On my own. Looking for—' I pause, wondering what I have been looking for, and why I am afraid to tell him that I have been looking for a place to weep, '—looking for food. And water.' I reach again for the flask and this time he hands it to me.

'You must not wander off on your own, Judith. I am here to watch over you.'

I smile, grateful for his attention, for he has been gone from me these last few days, gone in his thoughts at least. Staying close to Jeronimus, guarding the weapons and the wine. 'Thank you, Conraat. But there are no fierce animals to be protected from, not that I can see.'

'It is not the animals that I am concerned about.'

'Then what?'

He takes a drink from the flask and then puts his hand on mine. 'Just stay with me. I have seen men without authority and they can become beasts. I have been part of –' he stops, raises my hand to his lips and kisses it. 'You are precious. You must trust only me.'

I nod in gratitude. With Conraat here I am as soft and pliable as cheese.

'Only promise me you will let me guard you. With me, you are safe.'

There is a strange catch in his voice; his hands are clenched into fists and he seems not to notice me, to be looking elsewhere, thinking of another Judith. Please, I think, please turn, look, see me. Speak gentle again. Still the quavering uncertainty tap-tapping at my back.

I speak slowly, trying to keep my voice steady. 'Yes. I will.'

'It may mean that you will need to stay with me at all times. Day and night.'

I want to say yes. I want to say I will stay with him day and night: what more have I wanted these last months but this? Yet instead: 'I must be with my family.'

He looks away from me then, fists colliding with each other so that I pull back, calling breath like a knife into my throat.

Conraat stands and holds his hand out to me. 'Come then. We shall get back to your family.' He says 'your family' with a flourish, as if it is a foreign phrase needing explanation. Though he holds my hand on the way back to the camp, I stare at my shadow, noticing the cool air between our palms.

When we get back to the camp, Lucretia is standing by Jeronimus's tent, her hair, beginning to grow again, is free of cap or band and shrieking in tufts around her head. Jeronimus is leaning into the wind surrounding her. 'It would be best for you, Lucretia, surely you see that?'

'I do not see that, no. It is best for me to stay in the women's tent, where my safety and reputation will be kept intact.' She swats him away, her hand a pale windsock flipping left, right.

'It is your reputation, precisely that, which I am thinking of. There are women who are free with their attentions and I have no wish—'

'Nor I, Jeronimus. Thank you.' She nods at me as she passes, though she will not look at Conraat.

'Hail, General.' Conraat releases my hand without turning his face to me and steps closer to Jeronimus. They form a neat point, sharp and precise, facing away from me. Scraping my feet in the dirt, I wait for the point to turn, become expansive and inviting. Instead, therc is whispering, muttering like thieves.

'Judith.' Conraat turns to me, his skin shining. 'There is an important matter here. You should return to your family.' There is none of the former flourish in his voice, and no whisper; he has turned away, into the tent, before I am able to answer.

The Bastiaansz tent is stitched from the topsail of the *Batavia*, and held underneath with two poles hewn from her decks. The sailcloth droops sadly on one side so that it seems our tent is leaning towards the sea, straining to reach the *Batavia*'s remains. Grey dirt forms a line around the bottom, clinging in an even hem. Inside, crouching in the grey light, the Lord's Book closed in his hands: my father. As I push the flaps aside, my shadow steps across him, painting him the colour of the dirt. He looks up, drops the book on the floor as though it is a tin cup. He beckons me over, finger to his lips, bidding me be silent. When I am seated at his feet, pebbles catching my skin, he whispers, 'They had a plan to mutiny. On the ship.'

'Yes,' I nod. 'So Wylbrecht has said, though I chose not to hear it.'

'Yet it is surely true, for word has been spread by one in the plan. Swears the skipper was involved, and many more besides.'

'Arian Jacobsz wished to harm the commander?'

'This is what is whispered.'

'By whom, Father? Who makes such claims?'

'I received it from the sailor Andries de Vries. Says he has it from one who spoke close with Jacobsz and those others. Watch ourselves, he says, for all authority should not be trusted. It may be that there are those who planned mutiny who are here with us, still waiting their moment.'

'We must tell Jeronimus, have him call them out.'

'They would not confess. No, best to be on guard, for they may wish to harm Jeronimus also.'

I remember Wylbrecht whispering beneath the moon, words of Company goods, and theft, and plans for piracy on the seas. Take care, she whispered then, her face flat in the moonlight; we must all take care.

I lift myself onto my hammock and sit watching my father. 'Yes,' I say, 'we must take care. I will speak to Conraat.'

'We must protect ourselves. Do what is necessary.' For the first time in my entire life, my father leans forward and kisses me on the cheek. 'I am uneasy, that is all.'

I touch the place he kissed, but he has turned his face back to the Lord's Book.

That night, Jeronimus announces that a group of soldiers is to search for water on the High Island, one of the sizeable atolls to the west, where they are sure to find meat and water for all. Cheered by the hope of more rations, the entire company feasts on seal meat caught by Conraat and Andries de Vries. They drag back three of the creatures, blood seeping through the canvas bag. The seals have more meat on them than a turkey, yet even so, there is only enough for an unsatisfying morsel each. Jeronimus, as acting commander, has the greatest portion, which he takes back to his tent to eat. The meat is tender and sweet and I would eat a good deal more of it if there were more. I suck my bone dry and take my sip of wine. Each day the boat comes back with more goods salvaged from the ship: goblets, plates, bayonets, hammocks, odd assortments of wet clothes and fabric. Even a table was carried back on one trip, teetering in the stern of the skiff while those rowing crouched down to make room for it. The Company flag was carried back on an early salvage trip, and planted in the sand by Salman Deschamps, with the declaration, 'This land we claim for the good of the Company. May we do her honour.' Today, when I returned to the camp with Conraat, I noticed that the flag had been taken down. I did not see where it had been taken to and no one gave it mention.

Mama gives her wine ration to Roelant, and Father requests an extra ration, though I am not sure on what grounds. He says that he requires liquid if he is to continue to preach the Word and lead the flock, but I do not see him preaching or leading. Each day it seems to me that he disappears as soon as he is able, coming back once the fires have been tended, the tents repaired, the food hunted. I do not wish to call my father lazy, but he does not enjoy the nature of hard labour. He is a man of the mind. He prays constantly for the return of the commander with the promised rescue ship, and sometimes returns from his prayer walks with posies of seaweed to eat.

When we have eaten and washed in the salty water, we lay

out our blankets on the canvas beds. We are all in a row, pushed close together to keep the warmth in amongst us. Myntgie spreads her arms out and mutters and sighs until she is asleep, and does not stop when Pieter kicks at her. Outside, the surf whistles and whispers, storming the beach. At night, it seems louder than anything I have known.

The moon is high and round tonight, though not quite full. If I sit up, I can see the shadows of the other tents, grown wide and long. For hours, I lie staring at the moon and its shadows, thinking of Conraat and my family. I do not know why he loves me, for it is clear he does not love my family. It is possible he thinks them common, for Father does sniff and rub his hands together in a common fashion. And Conraat comes from a noble family; I cannot think why he would choose me. More than anything, I feel extraordinary, perfect, chosen indeed. I will myself to notice only this, to concentrate carefully on his desire to shield me, to care for me. For I am all caught up in fear, it is everywhere on the island, tripping us up as we try to speak of rescue, of Java, of days back in our homeland.

My family are snoring and breathing deeply beside me when I hear the scuffling outside and see the shadows pass over me. I sit up in my hammock and peer forward. Above the sound of the welcome rain, I hear a man singing, a low mournful tune. The shapes of three men run past the tent flap. They pause and whisper something to each other.

The whispering gets louder until one voice says, 'Do you wish to wake the dead as well as the living? NO? Then keep your stupid mouth shut. We do not need to discuss this here.'

I know the voice as well as I know my own, for I dream of it when it is not near me, yet now it is rasping, metal-hard. Though I wish to, I do not climb out of my dismal bunk and run into the moonlight, calling, 'Conraat!' For surely he knows that I am nearby, and does not wish to wake me. Besides this, he is obviously busy, mending something perhaps, or hunting. A few moments later, there is lantern light from Jeronimus's tent, making the shadows shine across the camp. The light flickers and then is darkened quickly.

I lie back down, watching the patterns of the raindrops against the moon. Though it is many hours before I sleep, I do not hear the footsteps or see the shadow of my love again.

In the early daylight, Roelant begins scratching at the dirt, forming it into neat piles. The soil is his plaything now. Mama watches him with half-moon eyes. When Salman Deschamps pokes his head into the tent to call Father for a council meeting, she raises herself up and says, 'Are our numbers shrunken enough now to please the council, Salman?'

He rubs nervously at his scar, pressing his lips together like a woman.

Again Mama says, 'We are sixty less, now. Are our rations safe?' Sitting up properly, she says, 'I will do whatever is needed to keep my children in rations.'

Salman looks away from my mother and says, 'For now, with so much rain, we are well enough. Yet more will go to High Island today. You should not worry, Maria, we will tell you if worry is called for. Shall we go, Predikant? Council is waiting.'

Father does not look at any of us as he leaves. Gisbert follows, saying he will catch seal, or at least some miserable bird.

After breakfasting on ship's biscuit, which still seems plentiful, I neaten Anna's hair with my fingers. She asks if she can smooth my stained cap, and I let her pull at my locks though her fingers are cold. Rubbing at my face with a blanket, I tell the boys to gather some shellfish if they are able, then, cold under the morning sun, I search out Conraat.

He is by the shore, gathering together the entire group of soldiers. Beneath his sleeves his arms ripple like wine. When at last he looks up, he pulls me away from the soldiers. 'What are you doing here, lovely Judith?'

I turn to leave. 'I am interrupting, I will go.'

He pulls me back, his fingers tight on my skin so that I feel weak with the strength of him. 'I am sorting the soldiers, they will leave before breakfast.' I notice Wiebbe Hayes gathering the men together, and notice too that there is no water barrel and only one blanket in the boat. Wiebbe stands behind Conraat and coughs lightly.

Conraat turns. 'Ready, Hayes?'

Wiebbe bows his head. 'Ready, Corporal.'

'Did you choose the men who would go?' I need to extend every possible moment with Conraat, however prosaic.

Conraat looks around at them. 'They chose themselves. They are the most trustworthy of the corps.' He tosses one more blanket into the skiff. 'The most loyal to the Company. If there is water to be found, they will find it.'

Wiebbe bows at me and smiles. 'When you see smoke, Judith Bastiaansz, you will know that water is on its way; and I promise, we will find it.'

I offer him my hand and he kisses the palm. I pull my hand away and clasp my fingers together.

'God speed.'

We stand together, Conraat and I, and watch the soldiers row out to sea. The tide is with them and they are far beyond the reach of the island before the sun is properly risen. Wiebbe Hayes lifts his hand up in a half-wave as they swing the boat about and disappear around the point. Conraat takes my hand, wipes the palm. 'This is not a hand for other men to kiss.'

I smile up at him. 'Why did you not whisper sweet things in my ear last night?'

He laughs and tickles my waist. 'What sort of an invitation is this? What do you mean?'

'You were outside my tent, whispering. You could have called to me and stolen a kiss.' I am shocked at my own self, at how daring I have become. 'What is it you were doing?'

He steps back from me, letting his hand drop. 'You are mistaken, my love. I was asleep in my tent all night. Perhaps I shall steal that kiss tonight.' He kisses my cheek softly. 'But last night, you must have been dreaming.'

He begins to walk towards the store tent, and irresolute, I turn back to the Bastiaansz tent.

Father is praying. Kneeling, blanketless, on the pebbled dirt, his face pushed to the ground, his Bible left open on his hammock. Grey-brown dirt streaks his cheeks when he raises himself to look at me. His mouth twists and untwists; I can see his tongue, a thin pink thread coated with white, flicking in and out, hungry for water or words. His hands, too, are hungry, pulling at something, pulling at the air while his face turns as pink as his tongue.

'Father?' I kneel beside him, hand on his back. 'Are you unwell? Where is Mama?'

Finally, words. 'The council – terrible things, my Judick.'

'You must slow down, Father. Wait, where is Mama?'

'Gone with the children. Collecting rations. Wylbrecht Claas with her.' He wipes the streaks of dirt further into the creases of his skin. 'We are dissolved, destroyed.'

'Dissolved, how?'

'Last night, late, the gunner Hendrix sneaked into the supplies tent, thieved wine, rations for several days. Was discovered in the night – shared wine, he confesses, with the gunner Ariansz. Council agree execution on Hendrix, for he has taken the rations of many people.'

Dust is drying my throat, I feel it rising, blocking my breath. Hand on chest, I open my mouth, force air in. It is cool and sharp, but does not cut away the word still echoing: execution.

My father repeats himself, as if I have not heard, or need reminding. 'Council agree execution on Hendrix. It is the law, Judith, and should be honoured. Yet for the young gunner, Ariansz, merely drinking wine given – we are not agreed. Jeronimus insists execution on him too. Entire council says no, should not be done, and Jeronimus,' his mouth contorts again, 'Jeronimus says council is dissolved, as we are not for leading in these times, says example must be made and we lack the courage to do so. As chief he is able, it is the law. He is to call a new council this morning.'

'Yet who would serve on the council now? Even Provost Jansz is gone.'

'He has chosen already, so he says: David Zevanck, he with the red pig's eyes, Jacob Pieterz, and Conraat van Hueson. Executions of both men will take place at noon.'

The dust rises again, until I am suffocating, struggling to catch my breath at all. Dizzy with the weight of my father's words: execution, new council, Conraat. *Keep your stupid mouth shut*. His voice, moon-hard in the night. Three shadows, running past. And a council elected to approve execution. Yet Conraat spoke nothing of this, and swore to nothing but sleep last night, and it is possible – is it? – that it was not him at all, but the drunken gunner. It will be made clear, it must; for I will stay sure of this, that Conraat would not lie to me. If I could not believe this one thing, then all my certainty, all my safety, would be washed out beyond the reef, and I would surely drown.

Chapter Twenty-Eight

Conraat's hands are mud-brown, as wide as a solid branch. He holds them out to me, and I follow. 'I have found a place I want to show you.' He puts his hand on my waist and lifts me over a bracken mound. Holding myself still, I pull back from him, keep my body stiff.

'What is it? Why do you resist like that?' There is hurt in his voice, and in his dark eyes, too.

'Why did you not tell me of the council, nor of the execution? Have you lied to me, Conraat? Why would you lie?'

One brown finger moves to his lips as he whispers, 'Wait, please, Judith. Please trust me.' The finger moves to the soft base of my throat, traces its way up to my chin. 'Judith,' his voice jumps as though snagged on a hiccup, or a cry, 'you are all I have, now.'

'Then speak to me. For I will not be deceived, Conraat. You must not make me a fool.'

'Not here.' He holds his hand out again. 'Please, come.'

We walk in silence, my palm small in his. Though my hands

are brown and tough, they are still as tiny as a child's. They are pleasing hands, I have always loved them.

We stop near the middle of the island and look back at the camp. The fire is forlorn on the ledge. Behind us, there is a man-sized hollow. Conraat lifts me down to it, sweat prickling his upper lip. Lichen and moss fill the hollow, so that it is as smooth as a bed. He lies down beside me and pulls me down to him, so that our faces are almost touching.

'Here,' he says, 'this is where we can speak. I do not wish to be heard.'

Lying beside him, my skin feels bruised. If his leg grazes mine again, if the breath lifting his chest brushes me once, if his hand should stray – I pull myself taut, tucking my skin away from him. Everything in me is softening in the most extraordinary way, even my eyes are blurring. When I open my mouth to speak, I am astonished by the sound of my voice, astonished that I can speak at all, though it is barely a whisper. 'Tell me. Tell me the truth.'

He speaks so soft that his murmur brushes my eyelids; his lips rustle my cheeks. 'I was out last night, you heard my voice. There were noises which woke me, I woke Zevanck and took him with me, caught them right there, did not need confession. Treating their own greed at the risk of all our lives. We have been fortunate with rain, but any moment it could end. Wine must be reserved. It was needed that both should be punished to stop it happening again. I am sad for it, Judith, I am. Yet we can take no risks here, we have only each other. Survival is all, you know that.'

He moves his mouth close to mine as I open my lips to speak, to challenge, to demand more answers. Closer his lips come, burning with the salt and the early morning sun, burning so that when they touch mine, I cook: I sizzle like seal fat. He pulls me to him, so that our whole bodies are touching and I can feel all the edges of him, even where he is rubbing against me, that hardness, I can feel it. His hand moves up my dress and settles on the outside, where my breast is. He kisses and kisses and his hand is left lying there, doing nothing, until I cannot help it and I know I will destroy myself but I am not thinking with my own mind only with my body, and there you have it, you may judge me as harshly as you wish, for I lift my hand and place it on top of his, making his hand knead my breast. Is it his voice or mine which is moaning? And is it me, pressing myself to him and rubbing myself as much as he is rubbing against me? What will become of me? Conraat's hand slips down to the edge of my dress and slides up to my knees, pushing them apart so that I have one leg lifted on to his waist and the other on the ground. His breath is loud in my ear. His hand slides further up to the top of my thighs and oh, I want him there, for I have never imagined such a feeling and long to know where it will lead; still, though water is ready to gush from my body with wanting him, I push his hand away and pull my legs together. Rolling away from him, I cover my face with my hands.

He strokes my back. 'I am sorry. I have offended you.'

Offended? I have become as low as a whore in Amsterdam, opening my legs to him and without a marriage or even a betrothal.

'Judith?' He rolls me over to face him, wipes my eyes. 'I think only good of you. You must remember this, however things appear. It is different here, all the rules, everything.'

'Not so different for me to become a whore, Conraat.'

'Whores do not usually have the love of their suitor.' He pulls me to him and kisses the top of my head gently. 'As you have mine.'

He stands and offers his hand. When we get back to camp, my legs are still shaking and I am wishing I had never started, or else that I had never stopped, and all my questions are forgotten.

The bell is ringing as we approach the bay, and we scramble faster on the hard ground. My entire family is huddled in a circle, seated on a piece of torn cloth, and Myntgie calls me over. Roelant toddles up to Father's feet, puts out his arms and calls, 'Up,' though I cannot recall a time when it has been Father who lifted him. Clapping my hands, I call Roelant to me and swing him high onto my hip. As soon as I have lifted him, he wants to climb down, and runs to the edge of the water, the shelf of this island, squealing. Jan Pelgrom rings the bell again and calls out, 'Are all here?' which seems to me a foolish question, as those who are not here will not be able to answer. Jan is simple-minded though, as though he had been dropped in water as a child, and full of pleasure at his bell-ringing task. No one calls out their absence, and it seems that, even with our reduced numbers, there is no room on the beach for any more.

Jan rings the bell again, four times slowly, and calls out, 'The

Honourable Merchant and Commander of our island.' Mattys Beer and Jan Hendrickson climb over the dune, followed by Jeronimus.

Myntgie whispers to me, 'I thought he was an undermerchant.' The skin on Father's cheek jumps in a sudden tic, but he hushes Myntgie and says that we should be obedient to authority, that it is best for us that way, is it not?

There is no answer to this, so both Myntgie and I remain silent, which we must do, anyway, as Jan is ringing the bell and calling out in a puffed-up version of a man's voice (truly, he is speaking down in his chest in the way that young children do when they are playing at being judges or elders; Myntgie and I have our hands over our faces, for it would be cruel to laugh outright), 'Quiet! Listen to the words from the Honourable Merchant.' He places a wooden box in front of Jeronimus who climbs up onto it. He wears a long red cape, unlike any garment I have seen, and his hat is covered with lace. I have never seen a cape, or coat, or any other garment made from such colours. He bows so low that he almost topples from the box and the hat drops to the ground. Jan picks it up and hands it back to Jeronimus, who tucks it under his arm.

'It is a matter of grave disappointment to us that there have been found men among us who have stolen from us all, stolen from the ration store. In keeping with the law, they will be executed. It has also come to our attention that the carpenters Roeloffsz and Dircx have attempted to maroon all our company here by stealing the skiffs.'

Wylbrecht, sitting close to Myntgie, looks over at me, her

thin brows drawn together. The tic in Father's cheek jumps faster.

'These men, too, will face the sword one hour from now, on the rocky beach. The new council, legally appointed by me, Jeronimus Cornelisz, and by the right of God, will watch over the executions. God is with our righteous rage.' He lowers himself from the box and is gone in a swirl of red. One hundred people sitting on this hard sand, and the only sound is the shivering of breath. At the edge of the shore, I see Lucretia raise her hands to her face.

Take care, Wylbrecht said. We must all take care. The council is protecting us from theft, from marooning, giving warning to those who would leave us boatless or rationless; surely that is the case. Yet across my chest and back, violent shivers are erupting. My body shakes the way Mama shook in labour; sudden, furious, and born from no cold. Roelant snuggles between Gisbert and me, one fat hand on each of our laps. His lashes are so dark that his skin against them looks bruised, and he taps his hand on my leg, singing a tuneless la-la-la. Four men are to go to their deaths one hour from now, and my brother wants to play, wants to sing.

I smile down at him, my talisman, and grip his hand tighter.

Chapter Twenty-Nine

No one wants to wrap the bodies, no one wants to see the slit throats and dried blood. In the end it is Father and Conraat who wrap them and carry them on their shoulders to the centre of the island. There is the sparsest gathering for the burial. Father sprinkles sand onto the cloth-wrapped bodies, reads nervously from the Word and offers up to a prayer for their sins. Says, 'For their sins they died, may such theft continue no more.' Two soldiers cover the bodies with more sand, Father brushes his hands together, scrubbing at them with the dusty air, and we walk back to the camp. Myntgie holds my hand as tightly as if she is an infant and I am her mother. No one asks about the burial.

Myntgie pulls me through the camp, Jeronimus's tent, with a flag of red brocade hung from its pole. Jeronimus is standing outside, his head bent, murmuring quietly to Jan Pelgrom. Myntgie stands opposite them, outside Jan Hendrickson's family tent, waiting, keeping hold of my hand, though I try to squeeze it free. Jeronimus raises his head and smiles his brown-toothed smile at us. He wears the commander's brooch on his jacket, and two lace collars, faintly ridiculous. Some sort of green cloth seems to have been stitched together to make his breeches, also edged with gold brocade. Breeches is perhaps not the word for them, for they are long and flowing, improper for a man. He holds his hand up for Jan to stop his babbling, and waves us over.

'Yes, Predikant's daughtcrs?'

'The executed men have been buried. Yet I have heard no proof that the carpenters planned to steal the skiff, and there was no trial.' Myntgie lets go of my hand as she speaks, and steps forward. I do not know where she has discovered such bravery, such intolerance for silence.

Jan Pelgrom looks down at her feet, and then slowly up her body, stopping at her chest. When she folds her arms across her breasts he grins and lets out a breathy snort. 'Proof is in the pudding, daughter Bastiaansz.'

Myntgie snaps round to look at him.

I grab for her hand and whisper, 'Myntgie, leave it be now,' but she shakes me off. Stepping closer to Jan, she says, 'Must you be so simple-minded, Jan Pelgrom? Are you the stupidest boy in the world or is this something that you pretend?'

'I am not the stupid Jan Pelgrom, Predikant's daughter who will be sorry; I am the Honourable Merchant's Chief Assistant.'

Jeronimus smiles, showing his top and bottom teeth. 'Indeed you are, Jan. And would you go now and serve my supper? Good boy.'

Jan trots off towards the kitchen tent, and Jeronimus smiles again at Myntgie. 'My apologies for the simple boy. Indeed, I do understand your concerns, girl. And it is pleasing that you bring them to me, though perhaps too late for the thieves.' His lips slide across his teeth again. 'The men confessed to their crime, you may be sure. We do not want our people concerned like this. Trust us.'

Myntgie nods, says, 'If they confessed, then all is well enough,' and turns back to our tent. Bobbing my head at Jeronimus, I run after her. When I look back, he is standing outside the tent, his foot tapping, watching us go.

When Jan Pelgrom rings the bell for the evening gathering and Jeronimus climbs again onto the wooden box, Myntgie whispers to me, 'I wish only that I had heard the confessions, Judith, for though he is our leader, I am finding trust hard to find.' Hush, I say, looking quickly over each shoulder. We are a much shrunken crowd now. Almost half our number have gone: some drowned; some, like the provost, left for the two near islands; and the soldiers, gone to seek water on High Island. For the first time, I feel exposed, cracked raw like an egg. The kind, solid faces are absent now: Provost Jansz; his wife Sara; the commander; even Wiebbe Hayes, with his crooked mouth and way of making me feel wormlike, even he provided some surety. Sometimes, when the light is high, I can see figures moving about on Traitor's Island, and on Seal's Island, too. High Island is further, and there are some days when I see only the haze surrounding it. Many nights have passed, yet we have no news of how they fare, and I wonder if they are as unsure, as anxious, as we are here on Batavia's Graveyard.

Jeronimus claps twice as his gown flaps in the breeze: 'We are three days without water and with rations running low. Council has decided, therefore, that more men are to join the soldiers on High Island, to help in the search for water and meat. Men will be chosen by council and taken by skiff there to stay until water is found. Four men will be rowed to High Island at dawn tomorrow.'

Father stares down at the dirt, as he always does when Jeronimus mentions the council. Later, he says, 'It is a good plan, though. To seek more water, yes, a good plan.'

There is no cheering and farewelling this time, when David Zevanck and Mattys Beer row the skiff out, with eight other men turning their faces to High Island. Four have been ordered to stay and seek water, the others to return, bringing news perhaps of how they fare. The yawl is lighter on its return, moves faster with only the four men weighing it down. The following dawn, it loads up again: two cadets, and the warm-faced Andries de Vries. He waves at me as I pass, and calls, 'I am to seek water for us all; we have great promise, I am sure!' His smile is so broad that his scar disappears into his creased cheeks.

It is almost dusk when the skiff returns, and I am sitting on the pebbled shore, plucking wet feathers from a white seagull. The skin of the gull is pimply smooth, more grey than pink, and blood has dotted the entire body. Gisbert, though not neat with the slingshot, is at least efficient enough to provide some meat for our camp table. David Zevanck and Mattys Beer jump from the boat and begin to pull it up the shore. Mattys has a blue thread of skin tracing up his arm. Perhaps it has always been there, but it has surely not always been throbbing as it is now. David says no word to me, nor indeed does Mattys, and I bend towards my half-plucked gull, pulling at his puny flesh. When the skiff is well settled, and both men standing by her side, I glance up again. Andries de Vries looks down at me, his shadow long in the twilight. His clothes cling wetly to his skin, he appears drenched through. Perhaps that is why he is shivering so, although I feel no coolness in the air.

'Andries,' I squint into the sun, speaking to his shadow, 'have you found water already? I thought we would not see you for days or even weeks now, not until water had been found. I see the cadets have stayed behind; so what became of you? Did you swim rather than row, or did you take a dunking?'

Five faces turn towards me then, each one painted blank, and Andries gapes at me, fishlike. His mouth opens and shuts, and it seems he is trying to speak but is unable. David Zevanck comes close to him, stands so close that his breath would rustle Andries's hair, and whispers something which I do not hear. Only these words travel to me: *promise, lucky, forget, your turn, you saw, remember*. Snatches which mean nothing. David steps over me as he walks up the beach, as if I am a shadow myself. Andries kneels beside me and says, 'Stay clear, Judith. It is best for you. Please.' Sweat lines his forehead, trickles down his throat.

Mattys calls to Andries, 'What do you say to the girl Bastiaansz?' and Andries begins to cough, until he doubles over, hands on his knees, and opens his mouth. A long line of puke falls out, as though it has been waiting there, beneath his tongue, ready. My bird and my legs are splashed with creamy white vomit and I wipe at it with my hand while Andries dabs at his mouth. Finally he looks up at me, and I see that his eyes are wet as well. It seems to me that he is dissolving, becoming liquid himself and disappearing into the sea. He lifts his hand up, as though in prayer, and says, 'Oh, Judith, I am a child of the Devil. Just stay away from us all.' Then, wiping at his eyes, he stands and stumbles up the beach. Mattys spits near my feet, then follows Andries towards the camp.

On my lap, the grey skin of the gull looks pimpled and flaccid. My skirt is marked with its blood, and beside me I have traces of feathers, puke and spit. Yet I cannot move, for all around me the shadows begin to stretch. Holding the mottled bird in my hands, I sit alone until my own skin begins to dimple with the cold, wondering about those who sailed off to the island yesterday. When the moon rises, I carry the gull to my mother for supper. But though she presses me to eat, I find my appetite has left. I give my tiny portion of breast to Gisbert, and sit until sunset, listening to the sea.

Chapter Thirty

Andries de Vries comes into our tent when the sun goes down. He sits silently on the ground, letting pebbles drop through his fingers. He sits for minutes and minutes before he whispers, 'We are on an island with devils, I swear it. Can the good Lord not save us?' He looks at my Father, bowed over the Holy Book. 'Can you not save us, Predikant?'

My father closes the book and shakes his head. 'There are no devils here, Andries. And the Lord will protect us.'

Andries stands up and wipes his hands on his breeches. 'So I will have to save myself.' He ties the tent carefully behind him.

Deep in the night, something presses onto my chest, and I wake with a sharp knife-cut of fear. A hand is flattened against my mouth, and Conraat's voice is whispering in my ear: 'Come with me.'

Anna is lying beside me, her breath as calm as the sun.

He breathes in my ear again. 'This is the only time we can talk. Please. Come with me.'

Outside, the rocks are sharp on my bare feet. Conraat whispers, 'Let me lift you, hold you. We might be heard here.' He steps close to me, folds me into him and carries me across through the dark camp to the sandy beach. Sure-footed in the dark, he makes barely a crunch on the stones. He puts me down on the damp sand and I dig my toes into the wet grains. Lit by the thin moon, the two skiffs are nestled alongside each other, curved like the waves. Conraat takes a blanket from one, and lays it on the ground. He kneels on the cloth, and pats the space next to him. 'Sit. Come.'

Kneeling beside him like this, in the darkness, I could be his wife. We could be anywhere. 'Why have you woken me and brought me here in the cold? Do you have something to ask me?' Thinking: *Now, this is the moment to speak of betrothal.*

But instead he points to the boats. 'I am on guard. We want no one stealing them now. I thought company would suit me.'

'You woke me for that?' Already I speak as his wife, discourteous, impatient.

'There is no other time to talk.' In the blue light, his eyes are black, dwarfing his face. 'I need you to understand things. To understand at least that which it is possible to – there may be moments when you will think badly of me.'

'That is not possible.'

'But there may be, Judith. You must trust me. Trust at least that I am full of love for you. Whatever else you would think of me, you must trust –' He breaks off again and grabs at my hand. 'I am different when I am with you. But it is too late, my lot is already cast.'

I stroke his palm, pressing my fingers against his. Then I say, 'Why did Andries de Vries come back?'

He pulls his hand from mine. 'Why do you ask me that? Why is it something that I should know?' He sounds older, angry, and his tone confuses me so that my own words come out in a childlike stutter.

'No. Nothing. No one. But.' I press my fingers to my eyes; I can feel stabs at the back of them, and my face starting to flush. 'I thought the council would know.'

'No. I did not speak with him today. Perhaps he simply changed his mind. Give me your hand again.'

I place my hand, palm up, on his lap, and he lifts it to his mouth. He holds my wrist, takes my middle finger and slides it into the warmth of his mouth, then holds the same finger to my own lips. 'We are bound, Judith. Somehow. You know that we are, and will always be.' He follows the line of my arm, presses his lips to my neck. With my face pointed up at the sky, the moon is a benign eye, watching. He mutters into my throat, 'I want all of you, so badly,' and then his tongue is thick in my mouth, his spit filling my throat. The moon disappears, everything does; there is only the dampness of the sand grinding beneath the blanket, and Conraat's hands shifting over my legs, under my skirt, and, surely, surely, the rules are changed here, surely that's true, and when I feel his hand sliding close to me, close to my inside place, I do not push away but sigh and let my thighs fall apart, and then there is his hand, rubbing at me, and there is my body pushing back, and his hand pushing harder at me, and I am sighing so that I am drowning out the sea and wanting to scream in his ear: now, please, take me now, I want you; but I hold my tongue and sigh in his ear and push against his hand and I have turned into the sea, sighing and wet and unable to stop, and then I am frightened, for my body shakes, swallows itself, and the water is running up my body so that I think this must be how it is to die, this must be me dying. Then it stops, and the sea is too loud in my ears. My breath is overloud, my body still shaking. I say, 'I am sorry.'

Conraat takes his hand from beneath my skirt, and says, 'There is no shame in your own pleasure, Judith. All is good, for all is from God.'

I remember Jeronimus saying that, and my mother pursing her lips. But here, on the beach, I begin to understand.

Conraat carries me back to my tent, and I wrap myself in shame so deep that it makes the memory of those shudders seem even more like death. Bitter though the aftertaste is, I cannot wipe the honey warmth from my body, and I find that I am longing for yet another taste of shame.

The first screams wake us just after dawn. While I struggle to sit up, to understand where I am, it is Myntgie who climbs from her bed. Father pulls her back to the hammock. 'It is nothing,' he says, 'stay asleep.'

Myntgie sits up fierce, but whispers nonetheless. 'Father, it clearly is something. It was a scream.'

As she speaks, another sharp cry knifes the morning air. Other cries seem to carry across the water, twisting across the waves. We are all awake now, how could we not be? We sit and listen; for a moment, there is no other sound.

'There.' Father has a tremble in his voice. 'Someone dreaming of demons.'

'Or seeing real ones.' Myntgie will not lie down.

'Myntgie, please.' Father pushes her down, his hand firm on her chest. He speaks through his closed lips. 'I do not want to lose my family. Do not speak. Do not question. Obey.'

'And what good is a life not speaking? Surely if there is evil—'

'It is just a dream, Myntgie. Someone's dream. Please. A life lived is better than none.'

Myntgie lies still on her back, but I can hear her crying. We lie, waiting, until more screams come. Three, one after the other, and a woman yelling. I cannot hear the words. Myntgie sits up straight on her hammock and grabs at her gown. Father pulls his breeches on, his eyebrows pushed together. When Mama puts her hand out for him, he swipes it away. Myntgie and I get up and dress over our nightgowns.

Mama puts her hand out to stop Anna and the boys from moving. 'Stay with me. We do not all need to know.'

As I dress I am thinking that surely Mama meant to say 'go': we do not all need to go. Yet 'we do not need to know' is what she means, deep in her, deep in all of us.

On the sandy beach, fifteen or twenty people are huddled together. Fair-haired Susie Fredericks has her hands over her face, her broad shoulders hunched, shaking. 'They were in the boats, little ones, little boats, I could see them. Here I was for early shellfish, and there was the sun across the sky and who would expect such a thing, now?' She tucks her dimpled chin in towards her body and such a storm of wails come from her that I fear she has been taken by the Devil. 'Ohohohoh. All of them, children too – could see – no, do not want to see, please – no. Throats cut. Just like that. Chased in the boats. Provost Jansz, the children, all, all, all done. And two there, in the shallows, look, there you see them. Two who sought help from the Honourable Devil Jeronimus Cornelisz.' She rubs her face on her sleeve, takes a breath and looks up at me. 'Throats cut.'

I step forward and hold my hands out, but Father pushes me back. 'Do not touch, Judith. Even in such circumstances, we are expected to speak as the Lord's chosen.'

Susie waves her hands towards the shallows. 'There they are, the Lord's chosen. You speak to them, Predikant, if you wish for proper language. They are beyond using the words of the gutter.'

Beyond the shore, in the mudflats, blood smears amongst the wave froth, washing over two bodies, both face down. From the beach, we see only their shape: two men, arms out, life cut away.

'A Christian burial. They need a Christian burial.' My father speaks as if he is in a trance, repeating his words. 'The council will deal with it, as is proper.' His eyes look past the bodies, past everything, and the shake in his hands is worse. I do not believe he could light a lantern. His eyes are flat, as flat as this island, as he repeats, 'A Christian burial.' It is all he knows how to do. His hand shakes more as he turns back to Susie and asks, 'The provost?'

'All dead. All done. Drowned, bodies under, gone. Children too.'

Provost Jansz, with his round face gleaming; Sara, fine-boned and calm-voiced; and the boys, little older than Jan and Pieter. Cold stone fills my body, my mouth; I am turning to rock, heavy, ready to be smashed. 'Are you sure, Susie, sure that it was Provost Jansz? How could it be?'

Susie points towards Traitor's Island. There are no shadows dotting back and forth. One driftwood raft, blood smeared across its planks, has been dragged up to our beach.

'Jeronimus says they are traitors, fitting for the island. Were planning to steal the yawl, he says, to take it and plot mutiny with those on High Island, who are pirates, so is his word. These two ran up the beach, calling to him for help, trusting him, calling that the provost was killed in the water of Traitor's Island. Jeronimus calls: "They are traitors indeed, planning to thieve our boats and water too." And then he gives the order: kill.' Susie is speaking louder, her voice carrying across the beach.

'Provost Jansz was no traitor. It could not be. Nor would Wiebbe Hayes be a pirate, I cannot hear that. Father? What are we to do?'

Trancelike, he repeats, 'A Christian burial. That is what we must do.'

Trying to lay my hand on his arm, I say, 'I could help, Father.'

He pulls himself back from wherever he is, notices me standing on my toes, waiting. 'Help what?'

'Help. With the bodies. Wrapping.' It is an unwilling offer.

He puts his hands on my shoulders. 'What are you thinking, Judith? Go back to the tent. You are a woman, not an elder. And in the absence of elders we must have council.'

'I thought perhaps things might be different in these circumstances. Here.'

'Things are not different. Go.'

Before I turn away, I take Susie's hand and ask. 'Who did this, Susie? Who killed the provost?'

She spits on the ground before she replies. 'His council. Jeronimus's council: David Zevanck, Jacob Pieterz, and your own Conraat van Hueson. What say you to that, Judith Bastiaansz?'

With her words hammering at me, I run back to the tent, my arms held tight against myself. Mama is kneeling in prayer, Roelant scratching at her feet. I curl myself into her arms, as a newborn, and stay there, rocking, until the bell begins to ring.

Chapter Thirty-One

Jan Pelgrom is standing on the box, calling, 'Gather now, come gather now.' Bedraggled and bewildered, we answer the call, and gather awkwardly by Jeronimus's tent. We are careful to look at the ground or the sky, to avoid meeting the gaze of another. Jeronimus does not bother to climb onto the box, but stands next to it, holding his arms out like banners. 'We have discovered more thievery. Those on the apt-named Traitor's Island had planned just this morning to steal our yawl and, like the treacherous carpenters, leave us stranded with no new driftwood to build another skiff. Their plans were clear, and they have been executed for their scheming. As representatives of the Company, this is our duty.'

Mama draws me so close that her skin breathes on mine. Her face is sickly pale but there is no space here for whispers. Jeronimus keeps speaking, preaching his word, yet I hear only droning. Mama holds me up and I hold her, trying to keep Roelant close to my legs. When I lift him to me he feels weighty, and his skin smells of yeast. I draw in his scent, thinking: *I will keep you safe, whatever I must do.*

Conraat is beside Jeronimus, his face pointed to the sun. He looks over to me and smiles thinly. I hold Roelant closer to me, lowering my head.

There is no talk of burial or remembrance, and when Jeronimus finishes speaking, none of us speaks or looks at each other. We are all infected with shame now; for how can we speak? Wylbrecht whispers, 'The provost would never steal. He was no traitor. We are here with the traitors, Judith, and they have their own plans.'

Mama hushes her. Quietly, keeping her eyes on Roelant, my mother says, 'We will keep ourselves safe from harm. That is the Lord's will.'

Conraat is beside me, his hand on my waist, speaking softly to the nape of my neck. 'We must talk.'

I shake my head free of him, and his hand tightens against my waist.

Again he says, 'We must talk.'

Father is standing beside my mother, clinging to her arm. Beside her, he seems shrunken, and it is she who waves me away.

Conraat keeps his hand on my waist, pushing me along, until we reach the rocky shelf on the far side of the island. There, he pulls me to the ground beside him. Though I do not wish to sit, I let myself be pulled.

'You must understand.' He picks up a piece of coral, rolls it in his hand.

'Must I?'

'They were stealing the yawl. This was the plan. It is our duty to protect all here.'

'This is not protection, drowning boys. Children, Conraat.' I can barely hear my words, for the sound of my blood pulsing, louder than drums, through my head.

He turns quickly, snapping the coral in two. 'I did no drowning, Judith. Though I do not deny it was done.' Leaning over to me, he rubs one rough hand against my cheek. 'It is my duty to guard the boats. It is true that I called David and Jacob to me when I saw the movements. And that I rowed the boat, too. It was David and Jacob who slaughtered, and it was not pleasant, no. Yet what choice was there?'

I am remembering his voice in the night, outside my tent. Shaking my head, I say, 'Yes, I see now.' Though I see nothing except darkness.

He turns my face to him, looks at my cheeks, my hands, my eyes. Says, 'You do not see.'

I think of Roelant's fine skin. Of Pieter and Jan, gathering shellfish. I let him take my hand, and I nod my head. 'Tell me, then.'

'They were traitors. It is hard to believe, I know. Yet in these last few days Mattys and others have lurked on Traitor's Island after carrying barrels of biscuit to them. Have heard Jansz, yes, planning methods for stealing our skiff and food, hoarding them for themselves.' He snaps another arm from the coral. 'It is a terrible thing when a man such as Provost Jansz is driven to these things. I will keep you safe, that is all I want to do.'

'And my family.'

Smoothing his hand on my cheek again, he says, 'Please do not abandon me.'

I keep my hand in his as we walk back to the camp. Weakened by this island, my shoes are beginning to let the rocks slice through.

When the sun is setting, Gisbert calls to me, tells me he wants to try to catch a bird for breakfast. There are few gulls left now and they have started to nest further out, on the rocky islets. I say I do not wish to eat, cannot understand how it can be his concern.

He holds his hand out to me. 'Please, Judick, come with me, please.' He knows I cannot resist when he calls me Judick. And we do have to eat, in site of everything.

The day is hazy, clouds pouring in from all directions, and the wind blasting about our legs so that the tents sag and whistle. Salt sticks in our ears and mouths.

'I do not think they will be out today,' I call to Gisbert across the wind. 'They are protecting themselves.' I think of Conraat's hand pushing against my waist. Spit bubbles in my mouth.

Gisbert keeps clambering over the scrub, as if I have not spoken. He is almost running, breathing hard.

I run after him. 'Gisbert?'

He takes my hand. 'Keep going, Judick. We will find them, really.'

It is only when we reach the far side of the island that he stops, his chest rising and failing. 'Here.' He points across the water. I peer out, seeing only waves and cloud and haze. Gisbert laughs – a laugh! – and points again. 'You have to look. Look.'

I do look, almost toppling into the sea with my efforts. I am doubled over, squinting at the waves. And then I see it, rising up from High Island in a defiant, hopeful prayer. Bright orange beacons of fire, brighter than the disappearing sun.

I stand to run, calling, 'Smoke! Water is found!' but Gisbert pulls me back.

Snapping me close, he says, 'They will see it themselves. There is no need. And they will not call it good tidings, Judith. There is evil about, and we must take care.' He takes my hand and whispers, 'We should make a raft. Get to High Island.'

I look at him. 'Why? When we have a skiff here? And we would be punished for disobeying. Would it not be mutiny?'

'You can be a fool sometimes for such a grown sister. The mutiny is here. I believe what Wylbrecht said, that there are pirates here with us.' He breathes in deep, moving closer to me. 'You cannot believe the provost was a traitor. We should go. Build a raft and go in the night. All of us. It is the only way we will be safe.'

'It is hard to believe, I know, but Conraat swears, Gisbert, that it is so. Desperation may make pirates of good men. Anyway, Father is needed here. Who would be predikant if not him? Who will carry out –' I stop myself saying 'burial services' for surely the executions will stop, any moment now. I gather myself. 'Who will carry out the morning services?'

'The services are to be banned. I heard tell today.'

'Still, he would not go.'

'You mean that you would not go.'

'I could not. I could not leave Father.'

'You mean you would not leave Conraat. He who has not so much as proposed to you, yet steals your kisses shamelessly and takes your good name so that you should never be pure again in Dordrecht. He who sat fit to row a boat for murderers.'

In the deepening half-light, I feel my face burn and want to slap him, hard.

He is silent for a moment, then, 'I am sorry, Judick. I do not mean to insult you. It is only that it is necessary that we go. For what can we do here? Zevanck or idiot-boy Jan guard the weapons, the skiffs also. We must build a raft, there is no other way.'

'Roelant could not stay on a raft, he would climb off.'

'Then you would hold him, for Roelant will not live if we do not go. Please, Judick.' I can hear the crying in his voice. 'I know it to be true.'

'How do you know such a thing?' Because he is frightening me so, I make my voice full of dismissals.

There is silence for a moment, and then in a clear voice, he says, 'The Lord told me.'

His words swim past me, dance through me, yet I can make no sense of them. For the Lord does not speak, except through the Holy Word, though I have never known Gisbert to lie. I cannot believe such a thing, and besides, I cannot leave this island now.

Beside me, in the twilight, I can hear my brother crying. When I put my hand out to him, he takes it and rests his head against my own. Still weeping, he says, 'The Lord told me in a dream that I was going to die.'

His tears run down onto my own face, until my cheeks are wet, as wet and as salty as the sea which has become our prison gates.

Chapter Thirty-Two

Wylbrecht says she has no wish to attend the morning gathering. Red marks cover her cheeks, as if she has rubbed sand on her face. The rash deepens as she says, 'I know what they will say. We cannot respond to the signals, cannot go to High Island because they have become traitors. Or they are pirates. Something of that nature. And what choice have we? There is no place for argument here, is there? I cannot bear to listen to that man's lies another day.'

Gisbert, wiping at his face with a piece of blanket, looks over at me. 'Do we have a choice, Judith?'

Father pulls at his beard with his fingers. 'Our choice is to keep ourselves safe, that is all. It must surely be possible to do that.' He stops tugging at his beard and adds, 'Perhaps the provost was a traitor, after all. We have no evidence to believe that Jeronimus speaks lies. Only the Lord can truly know a man's heart.' He does not look at any of us.

Jan Pelgrom runs to the edge of the shore, carrying his infernal box. He pulls out the bell and rings it wildly, swinging it in a circle and banging it against his hand. When the entire camp is gathered, Jan rings the bell again and calls out his customary, foolish question: 'Is every person here?'

Mama has plopped Roelant on my lap, where he climbs between me, Anna and Myntgie. Jan and Pieter run in and out of the water, while Gisbert sits alongside Father, his legs tucked up to his chin. He stares at the dirt beneath his feet.

Jan Pelgrom makes a loud and artificial cough and claps his hand. I believe this is the greatest pleasure the poor boy has ever had in his miserable little life. 'Attention, each person. An announcement from the Honourable High Commander Cornelisz.'

Myntgie looks at me, eyebrows raised high.

Jan is jiggling on one foot, so that it looks as if he will topple from his box. 'Firstly. On the matter of smoke from High Island, the High Commander has explored and discovered that they on High Island have become traitors and pirates. The smoke is a trick. Second: for the safety of all, a law has been instituted to shelter the women who could themselves be harmed in the night without knowledge or consent of the island leaders. For their own security, it is now decreed that all women are to be the property of all men. In this way, if a woman is alone or even not alone, any man may take her to his tent and thus provide protection of her during the night.'

My mother cries out, 'No!' and then claps her hand across her mouth.

In front of me, Susie Fredericks shouts, 'This is not protection, but whoring, and we will not have it.'

David Zevanck, puckering his squinty eyes, says, 'You have little choice, Susie. Disobedience is treachery.'

There is a long silence, then several men begin cheering. I am breathless from the announcement. It is for our safety, yet we are to sleep in any man's tent who would fancy. How, then is this protection? Though I long to stand and call questions to the stupid Jan Pelgrom, I know that silence will shield me and words will not.

Myntgie stands up and cups her hands around her mouth. 'Jan Pelgrom,' she calls. I grab at her hand and try to pull her back to sit beside me, for what is the point in making an argument? She will not be pulled. All her life, this has been her downfall and her salvation, that she will not leave silence alone.

'Jan Pelgrom,' she calls again, pushing me away, 'and what if the woman will not go to the tent? What if the woman has already protection enough, or feels that she has?'

'Where would this protection come from, if not from the leaders?'

'From the Lord.'

Jan spits on the ground. 'I would not wait for it, young Bastiaansz girl. No, this is the best way – it is decreed by the Honourable High Commander.'

'But I do not see how it will provide security. For surely it is a danger to us to be taken into the tent of any man?'

Father stands up and puts his hand on Myntgie's arm. 'My daughter will obey any command set by the Honourable High Commander, though of course it must be pointed out that as a family, we do provide some safety. Sit down, Myntgie.'

Myntgie kicks at the ground, but sits, glaring at Jan Pelgrom.

Lennert van Os, a wide-shouldered sailor, stands up surrounded by a league of cheering. 'And is this the case for all women?'

Jan rubs his hands on his breeches, as if wiping chicken fat away. 'Certainly. Any woman you feel to be in danger, who you feel could be shielded by staying with you for a period, then it is your duty to safeguard her by taking her to your tent.'

'Any woman at all?'

Jan moves his head from side to side, as if counting each of us. 'No. There are these exceptions: women who are with child, and Lucretia van der Mijlen who, because of all she has suffered, will be under the direct patronage of the High Commander. Any man discovered bothering her will immediately be executed, by order of the Honourable High Commander.'

I turn my head, looking for Lucretia. She is at the back of the crowd, near the south bay. Her head is down and she does not look up. Her shoulders appear to be shaking.

The sun spreads out above us, and Jan rings the bell again, calling an end to the gathering. Women are wrapping themselves in blankets and shawls, looking about nervously. Father stands up, straightening his hat. He holds his hand out for my mother, who takes it and stands. Rising, she whispers to me, 'Wylbrecht was right. We have evil here with us, and we have let them in. How do we stop them now, Judick?' She clings to my father, huddling close.

When Father offers his hand to Myntgie, she looks away, to the sea, and stands alone. Jan Pelgrom places his bell in his box and walks through the crowd to face Myntgie.

'You should be glad of the safety offered by the leaders.'

'I do not require protection which compels me to stay in a man's tent who is not my husband.' She curtseys slightly to him, though her face is cold.

'Yet you will be glad, I promise you, of the chance to stay in my tent, girl Bastiaansz.'

'I would be glad of no such thing. I would rather die, Jan Pelgrom, than stay with you.'

He shows his teeth, rotting and half broken. 'We shall see, girl Bastiaansz.'

When he leaves, she turns to me, full of fury. 'And this is approved by the council. Approved by your pretty nobleman, Judick.'

'No, not by him, Myntgie.'

'He is on the council.'

'He is trying to protect us.'

'He could protect us by not guarding the weapons tent so well, nor the boats or supplies.'

'They are doing their best, Myntgie, that is all.' I call the words after her, though barely loud enough to be heard.

All morning I sit on the hard sand. When the sun is high above me, a trail of women and men and children appear at the end of the beach. Six women and four men, each of them empty-handed and clustering close.

Tritje Willemsz smiles through closed lips at me as she passes, patting her rounded belly. 'They are splitting us up so that there will be more water. Have spent all morning gathering us, look.' Her eyes are grey, as grey as her skin. 'I hope it is the truth they tell us. Still,' she wraps her shawl about herself, though the sun is burning overhead, 'what can we do, eh?'

David Zevanck pulls the skiffs to the water's edge as I draw close. He looks up and laughs. It sounds empty of breath, as though he is choking. 'Here comes the young Bastiaansz. You need not worry, girl, your honourable nobleman will keep you from harm.' He looks up towards the camp, then back at me.

Stepping away from him, I point to Tritje. 'Where are they going? Why have we not been told?'

'Not all things need be told, nosey girl. These ones will have water on the western island.'

'With the soldiers?'

'Pirates.' He gives another of his breathless laughs. 'Surely not. We are not fools. The High Commander especially not. No, these will go to the greater island to the north of High Island. Do you see it there? We cannot continue to rely on rain and as these ones—'

'Are with child,' I say, looking at the women climbing into the skiffs.

David squints up at me. 'Exactly. They are little use. Their men can care for them there, we are not concerned.'

A wash of dizziness travels down my body, so that I must put my arms out to be steady. There is a single high note humming in my head, drowning out David's words.

Four of the young sailors run down from the camp, and when the two boats are full, David pushes them off single-handedly, sweat shining on his forearms. There is a box of clothing and provisions in each boat. All in all, four of the women have the heavily rounded bellies of impending motherhood. Watching them being rowed out to the island, David leans in to me and says, 'At least they will have extra buoyancy if they sink!'

I stand and watch the boats round the point, the sailors in each pushing hard against the wind. Until I can see no more trace of them, not even the wake, I stand and watch and hope and pray.

The sky begins to turn red. Here, the skies are not like Dordrecht; they are full of fire, of orange and red flames burning the horizon. All afternoon I have stayed sitting on the rocks, watching the strip of water where the boats disappeared from sight. My skin begins to prickle from the cold, bumps appearing on my arms and wrists. Further down the shore, someone lights a fire and it burns a dull red. Three or four people are sitting by it and I move down to join them. I had expected the boats to come back this evening, bringing news of how the women and their men fared at finding shelter on the island. Yet soon it will darken and no boat appears, nor can I see how the trip would be made in the dark. Someone is roasting fish and my hunger surprises me. We have some biscuit from our ration left, and also some pickled cucumber. I am beginning to think of fish cooked in the flames, its flesh peeling away.

Myntgie creeps down to the fire, slipping her hand into mine as she sits beside me. We huddle together, barely breathing, as we pick at the fish and, later, as we scramble back through the camp to our tent. Our whispers are so low that they barely rustle the air. All night we whisper, scarcely moving our lips for fear of being heard. We say: what can we do? Then: it is for our safety, surely not a lie. And: but yes, it is a lie, of course it is a lie. And finally, this: you must protect us, Judith. You are the only one who can.

Chapter Thirty-Three

There is no bell or fanfare when the boats return the next day, lighter without the load of swollen women and their men who will seek food and water. David Zevanck and Jacob Pieterz appear to be racing, rounding the point of the bay, calling to each other and laughing loudly. Conraat has taken me down to the south beach and kissed my hand, given his word that the decree is the sole idea of Jeronimus and is purely for the safety of the women on the island. Kissing my wrist, he says, 'But I shall be the only protector of you, Judith Bastiaansz.' His beard scratches at my hand, but I do not pull it away.

Keeping my voice soft, I say, 'It cannot be right, Conraat. To have women taken into men's tents like this.'

'You will be safe with me.'

'But you cannot think this is welcome? For the women.'

'I think nothing. Only that I will obey true authority and so keep myself safe. If I seem double-minded, Judith, it is for our own good.'

I look into his dark eyes, but see only my own reflection.

We hear the splash of oars and look out to see the two boats, keeping pace with each other. Conraat calls out a greeting and begins to run to the main shore, pulling me with him. Limp and empty, I flap along behind, tangling in the wind. Conraat helps David pull the boats to shore and takes him quickly aside, whispering. There is nothing left in the smallest skiff but a length of frayed rope. Hans Haardens, Anneke's thick-faced husband, hauls the other boat up onto the beach. He pushes my hand away when I bend down to help. 'It is not for a woman to drag boats along beaches.' He spits into the sea.

'Surely it is not for a woman to be abandoned with little help, Hans. Nor to be shipwrecked at all. Perhaps it is true that we are in a different time, needing different actions.'

He spits again. 'All sorts of business is done because the circumstances are different.'

'What of those left on the bigger island? Is it fertile?'

He shakes his head. 'They do not need our concerns now.'

Conraat stops his whispering with David and comes back to my side. His skin rubs against mine and a flame crackles up my legs.

Deep in the night Anna leans over the end of my hammock, shaking my foot. I kick her away and she shakes again. I sit up and whisper, 'What is it? Has something happened?'

The moon above us lights the tent, making our shadows long against the sailcloth. Anna shakes her head. 'I heard a cry. I went outside and –' Her words shudder to a stop and she lets out two hacking sobs. 'I followed the sound of the crying. Followed to the sick tent. Eleven people dead.' She draws in a shaking breath. 'Anneke Haardens was crying. Said they were killed. That there was blood, at their throats.'

I look across the hammocks next to me, counting the bumps on each cot: Gisbert, Myntgie, Mama, Father, Pieter, Jan Wylbrecht, Roelant. Yes, yes, yes.

'I do not know who they are. Anneke would not let me go in, and I wanted to –' She stops speaking again, her shoulders moving up and down and her breath coming out in gasps. 'She told me I should run back here or else could go the same way. I asked her why she was there, Judick, and she said, "You should ask your council about that, and about what defence of women should mean." Then she cried again and said I was too young to know about such things and I should not be about at night.'

'What is it?' Father sits up, his shadow winding across the tent roof.

'Eleven people dead in the sick tent.'

'Who is it?' Father sounds annoyed rather than concerned.

'I do not know. I heard crying, I went outside and Anneke Haardens told me that their throats had been cut. Eleven men. Soldiers, I think.'

'It may be one of the tropical diseases. Perhaps it was necessary to bleed them, to prevent the spread of disease. It is possible for some of those diseases to arrive unannounced and leave the next day, with a body left in their shadow.'

I do not know where he has found this information, for Father has never lived in the tropics; this was to be his first time. And the poor man is no medic. When he has a pain in his stomach he believes it to be the work of the Devil rather than the work of the wine.

My mouth feels waterless, airless. 'No. It cannot be, Anna. Please not. Anneke is sometimes – perhaps she imagined throats cut. For why would they? Why that?'

'Because the sick use water, use food. Please,' Father whispers, pleading, 'Anna, do not go out in the night again. We must stay here, stay together. Keep silent. Be useful, always useful. Please. We can do no good by speaking of it.'

'He is right, girls.' Mama leans out of her hammock and gathers up Roelant's sleeping body. 'What can we do, now that we have let them lead us? We cannot get weapons or boat, not even rations without approval. I cannot bear that we should expose you to danger. If we keep quiet, keep calm, we will be safe.' Her voice is pale in the dark as she adds, 'We must not become ill.'

Jan and Gisbert take two tin cups to the rations tent in the morning, ready to fill with ship's biscuit. Father hisses at Gisbert, 'Say nothing. Notice nothing. Be useful.'

When we hear the shouts, we sit on our hammocks, watching each other. Someone – a woman – is shrieking, and still I do not move. Footsteps run past the tent, and a voice is wailing, 'Just a child, a child.' Mama looks at Jan's empty hammock, her lips crumbling like sand.

Wylbrecht is out of the tent before me, but I push past her, gathering up my skirts. Running as fast as I am able, I follow the crying to Anneke Haardens' tent.

Conraat is outside and he holds out his hands to me as I approach. 'No.' He pushes me back. 'Do not go in, Judith.'

The screaming has slowed, has become a slow rhythmic sobbing. I try to push Conraat's hands away.

'Who is it? Jan?' My own voice is turning to a shriek.

Susie Fredericks squeezes out of the tent, shaking and sobbing. I grab her arm. 'What is it? Tell me.'

She pulls her apron up and wipes her nose on it. 'Li—' She stumbles, swallows her words, begins again. 'Hilletje Haardens.' Her sobs begin once more.

Hilletje. Child of the Germans, Anneke and Hans. Joyous girl, her fair hair bobbing as she runs after gulls and sailors. Who would harm her?

Conraat keeps his hands on my arms as I slump forward, my head knocking against his shoulder. Inside the tent, a woman is crying, 'Hilletje-hilletje-hilletje.' The tent is surrounded now, all of us weeping and bewildered. Her throat was slit, someone says. No, says another, a knife through the heart. Again and again: why, why, why? When Anneke Haardens steps out of the tent with a small sheet-wrapped bundle in her arms, the questions and weeping stop as on a sudden breath. She stands at the entrance to the tent and stares around at us.

'You have each killed my girl.' She stops, as if about to fall, and then begins again. 'Each of you with your cowardly ways, letting them take us for whores. Who will scream out and say enough?' She pulls the girl's body to her own, buries her face in it so that her words are muffled, then looks up at Hans, her husband. 'You brought this upon us, you with your lackeying, your cosy clubs and plans of riches. What use are riches now, you fool?'

Hans's face is pale, but he does not weep for his daughter.

Stumbling through the crowd, Anneke spits, 'I hate you all.' We part as for Moses, watching her trip down to the beach. No one goes after her.

The next morning before dawn, the Englishman Jan Pinten finds her body on the beach alongside the blanket-wrapped bundle which was Hilletje. When told the news, Hans Haardens says, 'Then I will pass this damned test too,' and stomps off alone, his fist to his mouth. We do not ask for evidence of the means of death, and the Englishman offers none. Mama says she would never wish to live if her children were taken and spends the day on her knees. Father says that instead of counting days, he is counting bodies and we must be careful, so careful, to make sure that he is not counting the bodies of his own family. We breathe in, making ourselves quiet, and invisible, and useful.

Chapter Thirty-Four

Fever seeps into my nights so that I turn and scratch on my hammock bed, my body tightening until it is rigid at each scuffle or scrape outside my tent. Anna sleeps as deeply as ever, weak snores escaping from her mouth as she turns over. Gisbert mutters in his sleep, dreams of Dordrecht, and one night, of the Company, for I make out the words 'mark it down' and 'exceptional profit'. Outside, footsteps draw close. They stop outside our tent, or nearby. Voices. Whispering. My limbs stiffen until they are carved planks. The whispering stops and the footsteps continue, but my body stays tight. My breath is shallow, I cannot push it into my chest and I begin to hear a shrill ringing. Silence for a moment; air eases its way back into me. From somewhere across the camp, I hear a tin clanging. Perhaps a plate, I cannot tell. Someone is yelling. Something about 'out of tent now'. Two names are called, repeated several times. The yelling stops, and then there are two screams, one after the other. Nothing after that, no yelling, or clanging, no screaming. We do not sit up or speak. A little later, the footsteps pass our tent again, this time accompanied by laughter.

Morning: I count the nine heads of my family and thank the Lord that we have survived the night. Gisbert and I take the jug and bowl to the kitchen tent for the day's ration. Susie Fredericks stops us on the way, her eyes red-rimmed, her lips pale.

'They took him in the night. Did you hear?'

Gisbert shakes his head. 'We heard a scream.'

'They called the Englishman Jan Pinten from his tent and killed him.'

'Why? He was healthy and had caused no harm.'

She glances down at my feet, then back up to my face. 'He was English. That is all the reason needed. They also took Drayer, the lame carpenter, and the gunner, and the cabin boy in his tent. I could hear their laughter after, they are mad on blood.' Susie sucks on her lower lip. 'I would rather be dead than have this endless waiting and whoring. Already I have been used by Mattys Beer and Pauls Barantsz. Pinten was at least kind to me.' She looks sharply at me. 'You are protected, word has it. Perhaps I should have found myself a nobleman, or thrown my lot in with the killers.'

Gisbert takes my hand before I am able to speak, and squeezes it tightly. Susie hates me; I can see it in the way her mouth twists as she looks at me. She nods at Gisbert and pushes ahead of us to the kitchen tent, shaking her empty cup.

Inside the kitchen tent there is a flat bench made from the mast. David Zevanck stands behind it, guarding the wine barrel. On the bench, a barrel of dry biscuit and one of pickled vegetable. David offers every family one scoop of each and three of water. Gisbert holds out the jug and David fills it, smiling as if all the world is well.

When the afternoon sun is at its highest, Myntgie and I walk to the island edge. Our hands are over our eyes, making awnings as we look out to sea, impotently scanning the waves. Myntgie whispers to me, as her head turns from side to side, 'It will come, Judith. There will be a rescue ship, soon, I know it. We will not have to endure this endless torture.'

'Are you hoping for a glimpse as well, Judith?' It is a cool voice behind me. 'Perhaps it is foolish to hold out any hope at all, but I have walked both beaches this morning, hoping that the Lord would hear my pleas and deliver us.' Lucretia steps in between Myntgie and me, so that the three of us stand staring straight ahead, out to sea. She does not turn her head to look at either of us as she speaks. 'The Lord appears to have other intentions. Truly, if I had courage I would throw myself into the waves and pray for death.'

Still looking out to sea, Myntgie says, 'It is a sin to take your own life.' Her words sound as if they have come from someone else, all dull and muted.

'Yes. So I do not. And also I cannot bear that he should win.'

'Who?' I turn my head, watching the sharp edges of her profile.

'Honourable Jeronimus. How I should wish to see him dead.'

'For his protection of you?'

She laughs. 'He spends day and night trying to woo me with words and wine and gifts stolen from the Honourable

Company; so what sort of care is this? And it is clear that he has ordered the killings; you must know that to be true.'

A flash of fury catches me. 'The council is trying to save food and water, is it not? People in these times must protect themselves, must try at least to stay safe.'

'Must swear allegiance to Jeronimus's order? To his new order of bloodshed and greed? Oh, he is a demon, I tell you that. Each night, he comes to me, says he will provide such riches for me, that he has the loyalty of many who will help him steal from the rescue ship, should she come. He is a fool, though, for the Lord will not see him win.'

'They have sworn loyalty to him?'

She looks at me pityingly. 'An oath is signed, written, unbreakable, so he says. More than twenty of them: Mattys Beer; the smith Roger Frederick.' Her lips twist as she adds, 'That worm Hans Haardens, too. His wife still warm. I cannot believe what we do to save our own flesh. Is this the Lord's way? Yet here am I, in his tent for so-called safety. I wish the Lord would take me, yet I cannot help my longing for life.' One tear tracks its way down her face.

Myntgie turns as Lucretia speaks, and calls a greeting up the beach to Andries de Vries. He hobbles towards us, as though he has a pebble caught in his shoe. Though there are dark shadows under his eyes, he smiles when he draws close. 'I tripped on a rock coming round from the north beach and have made myself bleed. I have not been sleeping these last days – indeed, has anyone? And look at me, clumsy as a seal.' His eyes settle on Lucretia and he begins backing away. 'I am not to be seen with you, Lucretia. He has heard that we have been speaking and – he desires you greatly, could you not give yourself to him? All would be so much easier then.'

Lucretia's voice rises with anger. 'How can you ask such a thing, Andries? Is that what you believe of my worth?'

Andries steps back as she comes closer, but she puts her hands out to him, grasping his wrists. Up the beach, by the fire, I notice Lennert Michels lay down a rope and call Roger Frederick over. They look at us, then edge towards the kitchen tent. I turn back to Lucretia who is still grasping Andries's hands. He tries to shake her off, saying, 'I do not know – I do not know what is true and what is false.' She keeps hold of his hands and, voice dipping, he adds, 'It is best not to touch me, please. The punishment is death and—'

There is a yelp from up the beach and Andries looks up, his whole body now shaking. His face – how can I describe this? For though it is marked, oh forever, in my memory, it is a colour and look I have never seen again and never before – white, but not as if only colour had gone, as if everything had gone. It is as though his eyes, nose, very self has dropped from his face, so that everything is folded in, swallowed up by his open mouth. He pushes away from us, so that Lucretia tumbles to the ground, and begins to run into the sea, screaming, 'Nono-NoNO.'

And then after him, here they come, yelping and yelling and each waving a brutal knife, Lennert and Roger, loyal to the High Commander, on pain of death. Andries splashes into the sea, stumbling on his splintered foot. My hands are at my face and I think that I am crying out, 'Andries! Andries!' yet there is no sound other than Andries screaming and the two knife-brandishers yelping like mad dogs. Andries trips into the water, crying as his face goes under. Lennert pulls at Andries's hair, tipping his head back. Andries's eyes, rolling and wine-red, rise to mine, and I can do nothing but hold my hands to my face, oh, Andries. His mouth opens wide, and white froth spits out. Roger steps in front of him and calls out, 'Let this be a lesson to all! Watch us now!' as he slices the knife across Andries's throat. Blood surges into the ocean, spreading around their legs, and Lennert slices again. The knife catches on bone and Lennert grunts, pushes harder, pulling at Andries's hair. Andries gurgles until they release him. He falls forward, blood covering his hands and face, until his head disappears beneath the surface. The sand begins to turn red.

Lucretia is sobbing quietly next to me. 'Is that protection, then? That a good and kind man –' She stops and puts both hands to her eyes, pressing hard. She stands like that for a moment, then turns and walks up the beach, as if on this tiny, damned island there is somewhere safe for her to go.

Lennert looks at Myntgie and me, standing dumb on the beach, and cries, 'And why do you stare, Bastiaansz girls? He was warned and he trespassed. Besides, this is only the way de Vries sliced the throats of the sick.' He passes us, blood dripping from his knife. 'You see? We are all of the Devil here. All of us.' His laughter follows us all the way up the beach, no matter how hard we run.

Chapter Thirty-Five

Sweat pours from Conraat's face as he piles swords and daggers into the skiff. Brown-skinned, soft-tongued Conraat, his eyes as dark as night-time waters. My evening shadow extends over his shoulder, makes a long line across the boat, and he looks up, turning his head in a move so sudden I expect his neck to click.

'My lovely Judith.' He lays a blanket across the contents of the boat and turns to me, hands out. Beside him, David Zevanck rubs at the broad planks.

'Conraat.' I sit on the gunwale of the boat, watching his fingers wrapping round a dagger. An image rises in me, of his hands, touching me beneath my skirts, and my breath catches. Blinking into the sun, another picture comes: Andries with a rusted dagger at his throat.

Conraat straightens himself up. 'We have things – I am busy, my Judith. Please, speak your mind.' His fingers are dirt-brown, like his face, roughened by the sun and salt. Rust-red marks slither beneath his square, flat nails. Eyes still on me, he says, 'What is it? Speak.'

I think of those hands, and all they are capable of. Then of Roelant, dark lashes against his cheeks: *I will keep you safe*. 'No,' I say, 'nothing. Only I wondered what you knew of – did you know anything of why Andries—'

He lifts a clutch of those harsh weapons, morning stars. Their deadly metal points gleam as he slips them beneath the cloth. 'No. I know nothing. Only that he had warning not to speak with Lucretia van der Mijlen and he disobeyed.'

David wipes at his nose, as flat as a door. Says, 'Disobedience is treachery.'

Conraat does not turn his head from me. 'I am going to Seal Island for the night with David, Jacob, some others. To take supplies.'

'Including daggers and other weapons?'

'There are animals on the island as well as plentiful water.' He looks up at the sky, a whirl of grey moving close. 'The rain helps.'

Beside him, David lets out a snort of laughter.

'And you will be gone until tomorrow?'

He bows down to kiss my hand. 'Until tomorrow noon.'

I stand on the shore, waving, as they row out to the blue sea. Beneath the surface, flat and long, stretch the dark grey shadows of the reef.

Through each night, we hear the high screeching of an infant and Mayken Cardoes, his servant-girl mother, desperately shushing him. All night he shrieks, rolling screams which cut through sleep. After three nights, Jeronimus calls, 'Shut that child up.' Nights are the worst. Each morning we count heads, check that those we love are still in their beds. Each night we toss and turn, trying for the deep sleep and deep silence of belief. We have the will to believe, most of us, the desire to believe that good will come. Good will come. Good will come. We must believe.

When Conraat returns the next day, after another night of the infant's cries, the daggers are still in the skiff and a dark red stain marks the length of the boat. Old Andries Jonas is clinging to the edge of the skiff, his pale eyes pursing like dry lips. Looking up at me, he says, 'Just step away, girl. Women should keep away, it is not safe. Stay well away.'

'It was too much for the old man.' David taps on Conraat's arm.

'What was too much? Conraat?' I sound like a shrewish wife, I can hear it, but still I stand, arms folded, in front of him.

He does not answer me, but covers the boat's red stain with his coat.

The sun is so bright that it blinds me. Squeezing my eyes tight shut, I trip up the beach away from him and my unanswered questions, up the beach to the camp. Near Jeronimus's tent I see a cluster of people, bent like bird's legs. Taking slow steps, I draw closer, frightened of what I might see. Closer, I feel my hands flutter to my throat: Mayken Cardoes is crumpled on the ground, weeping, her thin red hair scraping in the dirt. Her fatherless baby boy, still a suckling, is in Jeronimus's arms, no longer screeching. The baby's head is tilted back and a line of vomit trails from his mouth; he lets out a half-cry, but he does not move his head or his eyes.

Jeronimus hands the baby to Salman Deschamps. 'Strangle him.'

Mayken does not look up, but her hands go over her head. Her weeping is quiet.

Jeronimus is still holding the baby. 'Strangle him, Deschamps. The child is half poisoned and will die slowly if you do not. It is quicker for him if you strangle him. Death by this poison could take days.'

Salman takes the baby and cradles it to his face. He breathes on him, shakes him.

Jeronimus throws his head back and yells at the sky; a harsh animal sound with no words. The crowd draws back. He wipes his face and speaks again to Salman, this time as loud as the animal cry. 'Strangle the child or be strangled yourself, Deschamps.'

Salman, his hands shaking, passes the baby back to Jeronimus, then places one palm on either side of its neck. The baby looks up at him through glazed eyes, his mouth pink and open. Salman closes his own eyes and calls out, 'Devil or God help me,' as he pushes his hands together tighter and tighter on the baby's throat. The child's body jerks and then is still. All is silent except for Mayken, weeping so quietly on the ground. Jeronimus drops the baby on the dirt, turns and walks away; Salman follows. Without looking up, Mayken stretches out her freckled arms, grabs at the baby and gathers him in under her own body. She huddles over him, almost still, almost silent; rocking and rocking and rocking. We form a circle round her, heads bowed.

But one by one we leave her there, none of us speaking.

Mama, Father and Wylbrecht are alone in our tent. My father holds the tin kettle, full of fresh, dark seal meat.

'Salman Deschamps strangled Mayken Cardoes' baby. He had already been poisoned, so Jeronimus said. Was dying slowly.' I look away, at my feet, my hands, anywhere.

Wylbrecht's voice is floury, as thick as soil. 'There is but one apothecary on this island: Jeronimus. If her baby was poisoned, it was poisoned by him.' She lies down on her hammock and stares upwards, her mouth loose. 'They are like hounds now, with a taste for killing which will not stop.'

Father puts the kettle of meat on the ground by the edge of the tent, then takes my hand and leads me outside. 'We must take a walk.'

My tongue is still heavy from what I have seen; indeed, my whole body feels weighted down, as if I am wading through thick cake treacle. When I nod my agreement, it seems that everything inside my head is shaken up, but slowly, slowly. Father keeps hold of my hand and leads me away from the camp, smiling at those we pass as if everything is happy, everything is of God. I wonder, these island days, what my father thinks of God. We pass Susie Fredericks and she lowers her head as I pass, does not look at me. Father walks quickly, so that I am dragged behind him and become quite breathless. He leads me over the low mound, past the grass hollow in which I shamed myself with Conraat. We walk and walk and it is only when we are at the far end of the western shore and as alone as we could be on this shrunken island that Father turns to me and speaks. 'Judick, you must earn Conraat's protection. We must have protection.'

I nod. 'I do not know what he can do, Father. For it is not—'

'We do not need to know who or what, these things are only the business of the Lord. No, we need only know that we shall be kept safe.'

'I know he will do all he can. He has done. What about those who have escaped? The latest is Aris Jans. He made a tiny raft, so Wylbrecht says, and though they tried, David and Jacob did not catch him. Perhaps we could—' Yet even as I speak I know I will not leave Conraat.

'And where would we go?'

'High Island, with the soldiers.'

'Judith, those who have escaped are strong men, young men able to fight. Anna, Roelant, Jan are not—'

'What else can I do?'

'A betrothal.'

'He has not spoken yet, though I have hoped. Yet now I am unsure, nothing seems certain.'

Father turns and stares straight at my eyes. His voice is low and desperate. 'We must buy his protection, whatever it costs. Give him whatever you must, Judith. You must give him whatever he wants.'

When he puts his hand in mine it is as cold as a bag of silver.

Chapter Thirty-Six

Susie Fredericks is a tall woman, and solid. Her skin is oddly coloured, some patches red with the sun, others white as if with snow. Her hair, though, shines even now as though it has been brushed with pure oil. Even Conraat does not have such golden flecks in his hair; I can see them glinting as we walk back towards the camp, as though she is a hearth fire, guiding us home. Except this is not home, this is so very far from home. She is bent over so that her face is hidden. Her cap has slipped back on her head. Father keeps my hand held tight and tries to guide me around her as if she is unclean.

She straightens up as we come close, a torn cloth in her hand. 'Predikant.' She bows neatly to my father. Her eyes dart from left to right as though she is following a train of flies. 'I am trying to catch some insects. Perhaps they could be eaten, I thought. My sister has been killed, you know. My sister. Off on the island there, the island with the seals. And here I am, alone, alone, alone.'

Father coughs and smiles with his mouth shut.

Susie waves the cloth about her face. 'There, I have caught

them. No, they have gone. They will not stay still, do you see that, Predikant? Not stay still for a moment and what shall we eat, my sister and I? For I must feed her, now her husband is dead. All killed, all killed on the island. He told me, the old man, Jonas. Who shall take care of us? Who, if not me?'

I take a step away from her, though surely her sudden madness could not spread to me simply by her words.

'My sister Trietje is dead, you know. Did you know?' She lowers her voice. 'He has forced me to his bedchamber and made me lie with him and what shall I eat if not these insects?' She bends down again, flicking at the ground with the cloth. With a sudden flash of clarity, she looks back at me. 'You have other ways of saving yourself.'

Father pulls my hand, dragging me away and offering no words of comfort to the poor woman.

I pull my hand from his and turn to face him. 'Surely it is your place to offer her some words from the Lord, Father?'

'The woman has gone mad. There are no words that she would understand.'

'So the Lord does not have words of comfort for those who are mad?'

He shakes his head at me, slowly, as at a child who has forgotten her lessons. 'The Lord has already chosen those whom He would call, and His words are for His chosen.'

Fury roars in me, and suddenly I want to smack my father as if he himself is the child. I fist my hands behind my back. 'So all this is chosen for us?'

'Judith. Please. This is a time of trial. We must be faithful.' I have heard him repeat these words to my mother and, late at night, to himself. This is a time of trial, this is a time of trial.

'No. That is what they would have you believe, Father, surely. Look around: how many corpses, Father? Surely even you cannot believe the Lord would will this? This is like wine, where the more they drink the more they desire. Only here, it is not wine but blood. And as for Susie, she has not gone mad because she has been chosen by the Lord for madness, nor lost by the Lord; she has gone mad because she has been made into a concubine.' Something wet slips down across my mouth, and I realise I am crying, a long, cold stream of tears. 'Please, Father, please.' I am unsure what is it I am begging from him: safety? Or perhaps this: a word from the Lord.

He wipes his hand across his face. 'We must find Conraat van Hueson. We must seek his protection.'

Behind me, Susie calls out, 'Are you seeking protection? You will not find it, surely you will not find it here, even you with your nobleman will not find it,' so that I wonder whether she really is mad, or has simply chosen to disappear.

Father lowers his voice to a whisper. 'We must speak more quietly. We should not be heard. Where do you suppose he would be?'

I shake my head. 'He does not tell me his movements. He may be with the Honourable Merchant. Or on the beach. Or in his tent. Or collecting food. Or with the soldiers. Perhaps we should start with his tent.'

'He will not be in his tent, surely not at this time. What would he be doing there?'

'Then the Merchant's tent, but I do not want to go there.'

'Then we shall go to the shore and wait for him.' Father paces ahead of me, his coat floating out behind him. He walks so fast that I have to run to keep up.

We are at the edge of the camp when Andries Jonas stumbles out of the soldiers' tent, waving his arms, his legs bending and unbending. He has a flask of wine in one hand, which he spills as his arms fly about.

He stumbles towards us and stops, swaying, as he draws close. 'A dagger for some killing, ha, my turn.' He looks straight at Father and yells, 'Blood is good, yes indeed, it is tasty, THANKYOU,' then staggers off, occasionally clapping his hands and calling out, 'A dagger for me. Where is the dagger for me?'

We stand watching his bee-like path, wine falling in red droplets along the way. Shivering in the sunlight, I think of Susie's words: *All killed, all killed on the island. He told me, the old man, Jonas*, and of the last time I saw old man Jonas: pale-eyed, climbing from the boat, shushed by David.

Father's arm presses against mine. 'We must stay strong, Judith. Whatever has been done, whatever madness they are going to. Stay strong. Stay useful.'

Though I want to slap at him, want to scream, I will not be useful, not for these devils, I keep silence. Holding in my head the scent of Roelant, the feel of his vanilla skin. *I will keep you safe.* I watch the glint of the old man's dagger as he weaves to the shore.

A few moments later, Jeronimus comes from the same soldiers' tent, laughter on his lips. He bows when he sees us and says, 'Van Hueson will be looking for you, Predikant and daughter-predikant. He has been searching all morning.'

'We are grateful, Honourable Merchant. Where will we find him?' Father bows low to Jeronimus, his hand holding his hat firm.

'He is in the kitchen tent supervising rations.' Jeronimus turns towards the beach, takes a step, and then turns back, a narrow-lipped smile oozing across his face. 'You will join me tomorrow night for supper in my tent. We will have much to discuss.' He nods at my father. 'There are things you may offer, Predikant, should you wish to join our little kingdom.'

'We are indeed grateful, Honourable Merchant.' My father sounds ready to kiss Jeronimus's toes. 'All the Bastiaanszes shall be with you.'

Jeronimus smiles again. 'We will not fit all the Bastiaansz family in. Only the two of you.'

Father does not come out of his bow until we can no longer see the back of the Merchant. The light from the old man's dagger has caught in my eyes, so that I feel blinded, cut to pieces with the very air. Grasping at his back, I whisper to my father, 'I do not trust him. We cannot go.'

'We have no choice, Judith. To disobey—'

Yes.

I clasp my hands together in desperate prayer.

Conraat is inside the kitchen tent, his broad arms folded across his chest. For a moment I imagine him holding me, pulling me to his chest, my body becoming liquid. David Zevanck is ladling out wine rations, for yet another barrel has floated ashore, and one of ale as well. Three bodies, bloated and faceless, have also drifted to the southern shore; the first kept floating back although Walter Loos rowed far to sea and threw it into the ocean.

David grins at me when we push past Janneken Gist and Andries de Bruyn waiting in line for their rations. I fancy that he winks, though this could be merely a trick played by the shadows. Conraat's eyes are staring at a distant place, more distant than anything I can see. David prods him with his ladle. 'Your lady is here, Corporal. Calling for your attention, for surely it would not become the predikant to come calling for extra rations, eh?'

Father does not respond, though he is obviously invited to; for indeed my father has often come calling for extra rations, claiming that as we are the largest family we have need of greater succour and he himself to do the Lord's work requires sustenance. Extra rations were granted on two occasions.

Conraat unfolds his arms and jerks his head slightly. He nods at David. 'Thank you, soldier.'

Father coughs a pretend cough. 'We wondered, Lord van Hueson, if we might have a word?'

Conraat opens his arms wide. 'As many as you wish, dear Predikant. Speak away.'

Father looks about him. 'Privately, we hoped.'

Conraat looks at me, raises his eyebrows. I am mute beside my father, my lips held together as though sewn tight with catgut.

Conraat nods and walks towards the tent entrance without

looking back at David. I give a slight curtsey to him, for it does no harm to be civil. Outside, Conraat leads us away, towards his tent. We huddle behind it, and though there are voices coming from within, Conraat assures us both that this is a safe place, as safe as any. He squats down in the dust and looks up at my father. 'Well?'

Father kneels down beside him, while I stand, feeling foolish, speechless. Father draws a line in the dirt. 'We have wondered about your intentions towards our Judith.'

Conraat laughs, a short, sharp shot of a sound. 'Intentions? In what regard?'

'In regard to her safety as well as her honour.'

'Her honour has not been compromised. As for her safety, I have offered her protection and will offer anything to keep her safe.'

'What of this: that any man could take her to his tent if he saw fit?'

'No man would, for each man on this island knows that she is mine.' There is a hard edge in his voice as he adds, 'No man will disobey me here.'

'Yet she has no betrothal.'

I cannot imagine the reserves of courage, or desperation, it takes for my father to challenge him like this, to insist on his way.

Conraat arches his back and looks up at me. Grins. 'Yes. I should take her to my tent so that she shall be protected. Is this what you suggest?'

'I suggest betrothal. We shall all be protected then.'

'And with that, she will be resident in my tent.'

'Not without—' My father pauses, looks around at the scrubby dirt, the edges of the grass, the tents made from salvaged canvas all flapping in the dry wind. 'Yes. She shall be resident in your tent. With a betrothal.'

'Then she is betrothed to me now.'

Though Father's whole body is shaking, and the tremor in his cheek is dancing, he turns his head straight to Conraat and speaks steady. 'No. We shall have a public ceremony. In one hour.'

We are all gathered, all the Bastiaanszes, and this is not the way I wished it to be, for the dirt blows up in my face, my gown is edged with lace borrowed from Jeronimus's trunk, and the ghosts of all the dead seem to sit on the edges of our circle. Father stands with me, holding my wrists with a length of twine. Jeronimus leads Conraat to me, and my father passes the twine to my betrothed, who even yesterday made me tremble with song and now makes me shake with uncertainty. I curtsey, and Conraat leads me back through the camp, followed by our half-willing party. All the way back, people part for us as if we are made of fire. There is silence though; we are watched quietly, with no singing or clapping of hands. And my head is bowed, all the way to Conraat's tent. Outside the tent, Jeronimus gives me a drink of wine; I gulp it down more hastily than I intend, spilling a little on my chin. Conraat wipes it, and laughs, then drinks from the same cup. My family step away, still wordless, and walk towards our family tent. I watch them go, all in a line, wanting to run after them, to be with them. After some minutes I will go to them, there to wait for Conraat to collect me this evening: I am the instrument of their protection and I let them go in silence.

Only my lips are silent, though, for a hum, the beginnings of a song, echoes through my body. When they are gone, Jeronimus and Conraat walk with me, one on either side, all the way back to the family tent. I walk to the music in my body. I make it grow louder, stronger; I will it to drown out the weeping and the screaming I have heard, make it grow so loud that it drowns out even the voice of my father, saying, 'Whatever you have, use it'; so loud that it drowns out even my own uncertainties. I am able to do this, make this song grow. And the song which accompanies me is this: betrothed, betrothed, betrothed.

Chapter Thirty-Seven

Myntgie has pulled my hair back, knotted it and tied it with red cloth, which pokes out below my cap. She sits on the ground, rubbing at my stockinged feet. Her face is calm, all expression carefully wiped away. Instead of the joyous tying of ribbons and receiving of visitors, which the time of a betrothal should surely be full of, my family is gathered around me, unspeaking, wrapped in their own private mournings. Yet this is for their protection, Father tells them, as well as for mine. This is the best way, surely it is. Only Roelant is joyous, unthreading Myntgie's apron ties, babbling obliviously. He takes so little to be happy. Gisbert sits with Pieter, both of them staring at me as they might stare at a stranger. Gisbert has already argued with Father, yelled at him that it is not proper, far from proper, for me to go to Conraat's tent, unwed. My father wept and said that this was the only way to be safe, and what would Gisbert rather see me as, a concubine of any who chose to use me, or the betrothed of the nobleman Lord van Hueson. Gisbert spat out that he did not consider Conraat to be so very noble and then I wept. Myntgie asked for all to be quiet, as we should be better using the time to pray and care for each other instead of bickering as if we were a common family of servants, with no disrespect towards Wylbrecht intended. Wylbrecht quietly said, 'None taken,' and since then we have been quiet. I am listening only to the breathing of my family and my family is listening to mine.

There is a bell to collect the rations. Gisbert, Pieter and Father gather up the goblets and tin bowls, of which we have two. When they return, Father reads a word from the Lord's Book, and we pass the goblets around. We have still some seal meat left, and there are plenty of white peas in the ration, so our meal is plentiful if morose. Every so often, Myntgie strokes my back, and as I am finishing my wine ration, Jan says, 'Why are you going to sleep in another tent, Judick?'

'Because I am betrothed, Jan boy.'

He nods at this, then after a few moments adds, 'Anneke Volkerson in Dordrecht was betrothed and she stayed home with her family, did she not?'

Before I can answer, Anna says, 'Have you not noticed that things are done differently on this island to the way we do things in Dordrecht, Jan? This is the way betrothal happens here. Judith is to go with Conraat tonight, because that is the way things happen here.'

'So what is good in Dordrecht is not good here? And what is bad is not bad?'

Anna lowers her head. 'I do not know. Nothing is good here, nothing that I can see.' She looks at my father. 'Is it so, Father, that what is bad is not bad here?'

Myntgie stops stroking my back and says quietly, 'Here, it is good that we protect ourselves, Jan. We must do all we can to be safe, for you know we are—'

Father shakes his head. 'The Lord knows all the doings of His people. We must trust that He has predestined us for this trial, and that He will guard us through it. We are being obedient. Judith is being obedient. Please, Jan, no more questions.' The tremble is in his voice again and he hands Jan the goblet. 'Drink your wine, Jan. Before Judith leaves, we will have a family reading.'

Jan stops asking questions, but he watches me carefully during the reading, and when the darkness draws in he says, 'And now you are leaving to go to his tent, Judith Bastiaansz?' He sounds like an old man, instead of the young boy he was when we left Dordrecht.

I watch the gold-red shadows cut across the front of the tent; the colours are so deep and bright that they shine right into the tent, making shapes on all our faces. 'I will go when he calls me, Jan Bastiaansz.' I hold out my arms for him, and he climbs up onto my hammock, lets me squeeze him tight. His hair is rough and matted but even so I push my face right into it, wanting to catch the feel and scent of my evasive brother. The sun stripes disappear and Gisbert lights a candle. Outside, a lantern light draws closer, until it is an engulfing whiteness on the canvas of the tent.

Conraat calls from outside, 'I am ready for you, if you are ready to come, my betrothed.'

Mama buries her face in her hands and turns away from the light. I hug her from behind. She lifts her hand up and pats at my head, but does not look up or speak. As I turn, I hear a small sob from behind her hands. Whispering, 'Thank you, lovely sister,' I bow down and kiss Myntgie. Then each one in turn: Gisbert, Anna, Pieter, Jan. Roelant I gather into myself and try to squeeze him tight, but he will not have it. He wriggles out and runs to the other side of the tent, waiting for me to chase him. But I cannot. As he waits for me, giggling expectantly, I take Father's arm and pause as Conraat opens the tent flap. The lantern swings beneath his face and, for a moment, I hold tighter to my father's hand, afraid to leave. Father pushes me towards Conraat, and says, 'Godspeed to you both,' as if we are going on a long journey instead of walking the length of the camp to Conraat's tent.

I bow my head and say, 'Thank you, Father.' Taking Conraat's hand, I leave the Bastiaansz family tent.

Conraat and I do not speak as we walk, though I keep hold of his hand; it is sweaty and hot. As he opens the triangle to his tent he steps aside and says, 'My lady, your home awaits.' I give the laugh he expects and duck my head to go in. Thick rugs and fabrics line the canvas walls, and two boxes are placed to the side, with candles and a whole jug of wine. Blankets and rugs are folded on the ground to make a thick bed. My throat tightens when I see it. Across the tent, dividing it in two, is a long red curtain; I recognise it as one of the curtains which hung in the Great Cabin on the *Batavia*. Conraat steps behind me and puts his arms about my waist. I tip my head back onto his chest. 'Where did all this come from?'

'A gift from the Honourable Merchant. For our betrothal.' He laughs, though I see no joke, then pulls aside the curtain. 'Our dining area.'

A table has been built, tidy and low, and two chairs tucked under it. 'The soldiers make good carpenters.' His hands begin kneading my waist. I twist away from him.

'Conraat. My family. Will they be safe now?'

'As safe as any can be.'

'As safe as me?'

'You are very safe. You are as good as my wife and no one will touch you.'

'And my family?'

'Yes.'

And that is all I require from him, for already he is pulling me to him, sliding his hands along my arms. I hear my mother's sob, Roelant's expectant laugh, and I close my eyes, willing myself to know only Conraat's lips, trailing down my neck, to know nothing except the delicate flames tickling my throat. Conraat puts his hands on my shoulders, tilts my head back and kisses the base of my throat. 'You are my wife,' he whispers, and I tilt my head back further. He begins untying my top-dress; he has to turn me round to untie my apron, and I let myself be turned, as weak as a child. Pressing himself against my back, he slides his hands round to the front of me. Shadows from the candle flicker, and Conraat steps away from me, blows the lantern out and each candle, one by one. As he steps to the last flame, my mouth opens and before I know myself I am saying. 'Stop. Please, Conraat. Please.'

Raising his head, he whispers, 'What is it?' His lips hang slack.

My cheeks feel packed full with needles, each of them ready to poke through my flesh. 'I cannot.'

With one candle flickering behind him, Conraat's shadow is huge, whale-like, swimming on the sailcloth walls. He looms over me, the shadows making him faceless.

The needles have moved to my throat, so that when I swallow, I slice my own tongue. When I speak, it flaps in my mouth, useless. 'Please. I – you – please. I cannot.'

He steps close to me, so that his shadow disappears. Lowering his head, he breathes on my cheek, runs his fingers across my chest.

My hands cover his, stop them moving. 'Please. Not now.'

His lips, his breath, his hands: all stop. Quietly he says, 'Then I will wait. Yes. You sleep, there, on the rugs. And I will sit here, waiting.'

'Conraat –' I shake my head, expecting the sharp rattle of needles.

He pulls a chair from the table, turns it to face my blanket bed, and lowers himself into it. I hide my head beneath a blanket, biting at my fingers until sleep comes. The rugs are soft beneath me and sleep does come, though with it come dreams of my family: my mother, weeping; Roelant, laughing; Gisbert, sailing away on a boat made of cloth.

When I wake, dry-mouthed and sore-skinned, Conraat is still there, eyes bright, still watching me. As if he will never stop.

Chapter Thirty-Eight

I do remember someone giving their water ration to Roelant. It shames me that I do not remember who. Not even the face, or the voice. Only the action. A hand stretching out to my mother, a voice saying. 'This is for the child.' Why can I not remember? I do not remember whether the owner of the hand was killed or not. So few of us survived, though, that I feel I would remember if he, or she, had left the island alive. This irks me greatly, and I have spent these last three days writing down lists of names, scoring them out, trying to recall something, some quality of each of them. Each of the people attached to the names. Lists and lists of names, a long, long list of the dead. Trietje Fredericks gave her wine ration to Anna Jenz who carried a child. I remember this. I remember Trietje looking at her goblet, then handing it over, saying, 'I seem to have lost the taste for wine.' Her voice was low and deep. Her hands marked at the wrist. Why then do I not remember the voice of the person who gave water to my baby brother?

My daughter came into the room as I wrote, the door

clicking behind her. She looked over my shoulder at the lists, and at my hand flexing to ease the strain of writing so many names, the list of the dead:

Mayken Cardoes: solemn-faced, red-haired.
Susie Fredericks: long hair shining.
Trietje Fredericks: long-limbed.
Claudine Patoys: square-jawed, soft-voiced.
Anneke Haardens: brown hands plaiting Anna's hair.
Andries de Bruyn: thunderous deep laugh.
Janneken Gist: delicate arms.
Anneken Jansz: seeker of shellfish.
Hilletje Haardens: button nose, high giggle, three notes.
Gertie Willemsz: hand always on one hip.
Jan Pinten: odd accent and downturned mouth.
Abraham Hendricks: fat and red.
Young Jeronimus Dircxyz: helping Anna across the rocks.
Provost Jansz: his belly collapsing with a wind of laughter.
Sara Jansz: her fine skin gleaming.
Andries de Vries: turning to face me on a precarious skiff.

On and on the list goes. I must remember something of each of them, I must remember a word or gesture or laugh or action. Mostly I try to remember something good of them, even of those who were our captors.

My daughter finds me weeping, for I cannot remember a thing, not a single thing about Isbrant Ysbratsz. Only the name floats in front of me, telling me nothing. Perhaps it was he who gave Roelant his ration? But I remember nothing, nothing of either of them, the nameless person who gave the ration, nor the named Isbrant with no face, no voice and no story. Ink runs beneath my hand and I sob so loudly that my grandchild jumps against my daughter's skin.

My daughter puts her hand on my back and says, 'Why must you do this, Mama?'

'If I do not remember them, who will? Who?' I feel as insubstantial as salt.

Her hand travels down my spine. 'No. Not remembering, blaming. Blaming yourself. Why must you believe in your own guilt, when you were a victim? Why do you carry their shame, as if it is your own?' And then her face creases, sharp as paper, her hand grasping at her belly. Before her mouth opens to cry out, I see the pain cutting across her back and her belly, cutting her as it cut me.

'No,' she says, 'I am not ready, not prepared, I have not –' and then she groans, her hands resting on her knees, droplets of sweat marking her collar.

I stand with my hands on her shoulders; her green eyes are flecked with black, and with fear.

'Breathe,' I say. 'Breathe deeply.'

Her hands stretch out, and I take them in mine. Together we wait, and breathe.

Chapter Thirty-Nine

Conraat pulls his breeches on, dips his hands in the white water bowl and rubs them over his face. He smoothes his hat and bows to me as though we have just met. 'Madam Bastiaansz? Delighted to make your acquaintance. Delighted.' Then he scoops down and gathers me up, rubbing his beard on my neck. Straightening himself, he says, 'Was that improper for a new acquaintance?' He stands for a moment at the entrance to the tent and is, briefly, a tall shape blocking the light. Then a wave and he is gone. I roll over, and wrap my arms tightly across my waist.

All day I stay in Conraat's tent, afraid that if I leave I will be called van Hueson's little whore. Certainly I have heard Lucretia called Jeronimus's whore, though truthfully she is not betrothed to Jeronimus, nor, she says, ever would be. She will survive for her husband's sake, this is what she says she has promised herself, and so she has relented. Lucretia tells it like this and I have no reason to believe that she would lie to me. She has spoken to me of these things, yet yesterday, when I walked through the camp with Conraat, Lucretia was like the other women, turning their faces from me.

Late noon, my father comes to the tent. Pokes his head in before his body, peering around him like a bird, taking in the rugs and tapestries and the small wooden table and my bed of folded carpets. 'Are you being held in here?' He moves the whole of his body inside the tent and stands awkwardly. I have sat here for the entire morning, thinking thoughts.

'Do you see anyone guarding me, Father?'

'Why have you not come out, then? We have waited for you, and your absence at the family prayer begins to look shameful.'

Father still carries on with his morning family prayer, although word has it that Jeronimus declares the Lord is no helper of us, and many have been heard to deny God and the Devil. No person has been reprimanded for these outcries.

Stepping in front of my eyes and snapping his fingers, my father says, 'Judith.'

'I did not wish to be called a whore or concubine. In here I will be called nothing.'

'You are betrothed, girl. How could you be called a concubine? You are not like the van der Mijlen woman, giving in with no—'

'Father, I have no wish to hear you speak ill of Lucretia. If you speak so of her, why do you believe that I should not be spoken ill of?'

He flaps his hands, more and more like a bird, a white hen perhaps, or a chicken. 'Lucretia van der Mijlen is far in character from—'

I stop him again. It is as though I truly am a married woman, able to contradict my own father. 'Her character is blameless. You can hardly chastise me for trying to avoid such talk. For if such a good man as you would speak like this of her, how do you think someone who is less holy may speak of me?'

'Yet surely you are adding to such talk by hiding away in here.' He looks about the tent, lifts the curtain which divides it into two rooms. 'Though it surely is an elegant hiding place.'

'Please sit down, Father.'

He ignores me. 'Your mother is concerned.'

'Why is she not here with you?'

'She is exhausted. Resting. Shall I call for you before dinner? Come to the tent and walk with you?'

'And Conraat.' Though my betrothal was engineered by my father, he seems to have forgotten that I am no longer a child of his house.

'Yes, walk with the two of you.' He kneels so suddenly that a pat of dust flies up. 'Judith. Are you – did he – I am sorry, girl, that we are here, in this place.'

'Please.'

Father has his hands clasped, as though settling in for a long prayer, so I add, 'I need to rest, Father. I, too, am exhausted.' I am the lady of the house! It does not matter that my house is a tent, I am the lady of it. If there were servants, I would command them, and if my father comes to visit, beginning to speak of things I do not wish to speak of, I can ask him to leave.

Such things become so significant in such a time. Pettiness, smallness, meanness, envy. In an ordered, peaceful time, we carry these poor crumbling qualities; but in a time of desperation they swell, fed by hunger and anger and fear. Fear leaves no room for goodness. And so it matters to me that I can tell my father to leave, that I can watch his puffy face fall into itself with disappointment, that I can lie back with my hand over my eyes: an elegant lady in a house on the Nieuwendijk with an afternoon headache; a lady with no uncertainty at all.

It does not please me that I felt these things, became these things. It does not please me that I did not go to see my mother that afternoon. That after Myntgie had tied my hair so carefully, even then I did not step outside my tent to see her, nor Anna, nor my brothers. Forever and forever I am haunted by this, by my own careless nature.

In the evening, Father stands outside the tent coughing and aheming until Conraat calls, 'Is that Predikant Bastiaansz?' and pulls back the tent flap. Father stands outside, his hat carefully tilted on his head and his face full of – what? It seems to me, now, remembering all this, that his face carries hope and desperation and need and deep, deep sadness. Yet it may be that really all his face says is: I am looking forward to my first good meal in many days. For it is no secret that Jeronimus has fare almost as rich as that which was served on the ship, and that he has kept a whole barrel of wine aside for his own use.

We walk to Jeronimus's tent together, Father and Conraat on either side of me, arms entwined with mine. No one calls 'whore' or 'concubine'.

Jeronimus has lined his tent with more curtains and velvets

than I knew had been salvaged. A thick tapestry stretches across the length of the tent. Though it is creased and scored with water marks, the picture is still recognisable. A pale-skinned woman, ripe and plump, her breasts pouring out, and a clothed man with a knife, leering down: 'The Rape of Lucretia'. I cannot tell if it is a deliberate placement, a joke of some kind, or an accident. Or perhaps I imagine it, perhaps it is not Lucretia but another poor wretch.

Jeronimus does not get up to greet us, but waves from the table. Lucretia sits by his side, her head bare, her face down. Jan Pelgrom brings tray after tray of food: good cask meat, white and grey peas, pickled salad, even butter, though I had no idea that butter had been saved. Wine is served not in tin cups, but glass goblets. Jeronimus claps his hands together and says, 'And now we feast to celebrate the betrothal of my trusted assistant and commander, and the lovely girl Bastiaansz. Yes?'

We raise our glasses and tilt our heads. The wine slides into my throat, warm and soft. Jeronimus touches Lucretia's throat. 'Perhaps we should be betrothed, yes?'

She does not look up, only quietly says, 'I have a husband.'

Jeronimus laughs. 'He is not here. Predikant, would you marry me to this woman?'

Father gulps more wine. 'I would not feel – I would, certainly if – that is –'

Jeronimus laughs and claps his hands again. 'We have no need of marriage in this new kingdom. We are free creatures and all is good. You see, Predikant,' he leans forward, wine dribbling from one corner of his mouth, 'all is of God and if all is of God, all is good. You see?'

Father nods and says he does see and, though I stare at Conraat, he does not disagree, so I too am silent.

And so it goes on, all night. More wine and more wine, until my head is spinning and turning, and Jeronimus talking and talking and talking, and I begin to think that perhaps he is right, there is nothing in the world which is not of God, so there is nothing in the world which is not good. My thoughts are all scrambled in my head when Jeronimus finally says, 'Dear Predikant, there are matters I wish to discuss with you, though the betrothed will surely wish to go.'

I nod my head, feeling the wine tumble, and Conraat pulls me to my feet. Outside, the moon is as low as the sea.

We trip into his tent, and all my limbs are as warm as the wine. Conraat lights a candle, then pulls me to himself, laughing. Pressing his face into mine, so hard it scratches, he mumbles, 'Here.' He lowers me onto the rugs. 'Lie here like this.'

I am flat, my arms spread out, my cap still on. He pulls at it until it snags on my throat and I cough, then untie it myself, for I think he will choke me if he keeps tugging. My red cord from Myntgie is still in my hair, and Conraat sits me up, begins untying it. 'I want to see it out. Loose.' It snags in his hand and he throws the cloth across the tent. 'Now. Lie there.'

I allow myself to notice only these things: the softening of my flesh; Conraat's eyes making deep circles in the half-light; the feel of his hands on my skin, the warmth it brings. He lowers himself down my body, rubbing himself against every part of me until he is at my feet. And then, oh, and then (are there words for this?) he kisses my feet and then my knees. I cannot see him, for he has dived beneath my dress. I hear his voice, muffled, saying, 'I learnt this in India,' but I am barely listening to anything except the lap of his tongue on my skin. Briefly, through the haze, I wonder whether this is Godly, whether even married people love like this, and then he has slid my stockings away and I feel his face in my secret parts, can see the mound of his head beneath my dress and wonder for a moment how he will breathe and then I feel a ripe wetness lapping, lapping, up and down and I am rising falling rising falling. Wave after wave of oh, something warm, and then everything rushes down my body so that I am melting and burning both at the same time. Then I am flat again, my breath coming in rushes and before I have a chance to breathe softly again, Conraat is emerging from beneath my dress, and blowing out the final candle.

I lie, still shaking, and listen to him unbuckle; I have heard my father and my brothers undressing in the night and know the sound. There is a sudden weight on top of me, pushing my breath out in a burst, and Conraat's beard, full of a sharp scent, rubbing against my throat. 'Now we will be one,' he says, and his words are pushing, pushing, and each bone of mine is melting, opening, inviting. There is a sharp thrust of pain, and then I am full, each of my edges disappearing, until I no longer know where I end and Conraat begins.

Afterwards, we lie damply together, with the moon casting its shadow over us. Conraat is stroking my cheek, my breath beginning to still, when we hear it: the cry that cuts through the moon. I climb up, pulling my skirts down, the wine sliding about in my head. Conraat pulls me back, says, 'Wait. Let me go.' I shake him off as though he is an insect and run to my father's cry.

The lantern is on in the tent. My father is on the ground, crumpled below my mother's hammock, crying out, 'Judith, Judith,' in a thin voice. I hold my hands out for him and Father folds like a child. I cannot look, I cannot look anywhere but at my father, this is as far as I can ever get to. Even in memory, this is as far as I get, to my father. And there, in that night while the moon drops lower and lower, I keep my eyes on his face, watch my father so that I will see nothing else. Until Father says, 'They came while we ate. While we drank wine,' and unfolds himself from my grasp, hobbling over to my mother's hammock. Hobbles to the shape which should be my mother sleeping, arms out, mouth open. But this is not the shape, not the arms out, the gentle snoring. Mouth open, yes. And thick red across her face, her chest. Thick red blood, and something solid beside her, dark red and wet. Must I? Must I remember this, this image which I have spent my life trying to erase? Here it is then: a pile of shapes in the corner of the tent, arms out, hands splayed, covered in slipping red blood. My family, throats slit, arms hacked, thrown on top of each other like luggage, like rats. Gisbert; Pieter; Anna; harmless, fine-boned Jan. Wylbrecht Claas, hands over her face. And Myntgie, her hair caked with shit, mouth open in an endless, lifeless scream; so that I will see, always, the men bursting in, knives in hand, slicing one at a time, each of my sisters having to watch the other raped, faces rubbed in shit. Oh God, Oh God, why have you forsaken me? Where are you? You are nowhere in this picture. For here is Roelant, fine and dark, his tiny head, his perfect head, smashed in so that his eyes can no longer be seen, only his mouth, small and perfect cupid, still round below the crumpled skull. His hands, his barely beginning hands, dangling from one thread, the one thread which has not been sliced. Here is my father, crumpling on the floor, face in the blood of his wife.

And here am I, shaking again, wanting the sword, desperate now to cut out my flesh, to join my sister; to destroy forever my own treacherous body, the body I can never forgive.

Chapter Forty

All night, I hold the tiny corpse of my brother, stroking his hands, his feet. Father stammers and jibbers, wiping Mama's face. 'Maria-maria, oh, Maria.' When light begins to spread across us, he takes the blanket from his hammock, holds it out to me, saying, 'Please, Judick. Please wipe them. I cannot.' My hands shake as I wipe Roelant's body, dabbing carefully at the brown blood, unwilling to hurt him. He is stiff now, and cold, and as I wipe him, I wet his face with my tears. I want to wrap him into myself, swallow him, protect him; and it is too late. When I touch Myntgie's hand, stone-hard and blood-caked, I feel a stampede in my chest. My face presses against her hand. *Forgive me, forgive me*, but there are no words coming from me, only shuddering sobs which tear at my bones, at my skin. I lie alongside her, covering her, too late, with my arms. Her body rocks with my rocking, shakes with my sobs. How can I do this? Wipe the bodies of my family, wipe the blood and terror from them? But I will not have them buried covered in the marks of these murderers. I dip the blanket in water, drench it and let the drops wet my feet, then dab at Anna, at Pieter, at Jan. Thinking, like Peter washing the feet of the Lord: *I am not worthy*. Gisbert's countenance is somehow peaceful; there is no blood on his face, only on his chest, and his lips rest together as though in sleep. When I lift my hand to wipe him, I hear his voice: *The Lord told me in a dream that I was going to die*. I rest my head on the wound on his chest, whispering his name. Father takes the cloth from me, and I lie in the dust.

In the morning, we wrap each of them in the blankets from the hammocks. Behind my eyes there is stone, grating against my skin, rubbing me raw. Each tiny shred of my skin is worn down, scarred with their wounds. I have wept and wept until it feels that I am made of water, yet when Jan Pelgrom looks into the tent and calls out that we should give the blankets to the Merchant to be distributed, it is as though he speaks to someone else. Another Judith, one with my face but empty inside, as though someone has cut, cut away with a dagger, gutting me like a pig. Father keeps wrapping Mother's body, rolling her along the blanket. Though I wish to run at Jan, screaming at him that I will not be stopped from wrapping my family, though I want to yell that I will squeeze the breath out of him with my blanket if he dares come closer, I lower my head and say, 'We will see the Merchant later,' for I owe them this at least: that I try to keep living.

I wrap Roelant, folding him as though he is a parcel of jewels, and kiss his cold, crushed head. Father looks up at me and I whisper, 'I have lost everything except you, Father.'

Outside, footsteps crunch in the dirt. Conraat pokes his face into the tent. I cannot bear to think of him, of the pleasure I had from his touch which kept me from my family. Bile rises in my throat and I rush outside the tent, pushing him aside and doubling over to spit the poison taste from my mouth.

Mattys Beer helps Conraat and Father to dig a long flat grave. One by one they carry the bodies to the centre of the island while I wait alone at the table in Conraat's tent. Mattys Beer calls to me from outside the tent, 'The grave is ready and you should join your father.' He is loud and hearty. It seems that all voices, all faces, are hearty today. Faces with smiles or half-smiles, faces with a ridiculous lack of sorrow and fear. Raising my hand to my cheeks, I pull at my skin, slap at it. Still the aching emptiness, enough to swallow the whole sea.

Wind is blowing cold on the island, and it begins to rain as I step alongside Father, putting my hand in his, holding my mouth shut. Conraat stands opposite us, looking out to sea. There is no address, only Father briefly reading from the Lord's Book. His voice is a mere whisper and I cannot hear all the words. When Father scrapes dirt across the top of the hole, I long to lie with Myntgie, have him cover me with dirt. Yet I stand, looking down, keeping myself alive.

No one speaks to us as we return to the campsite, no one comes from their tents to shake our hands in sadness and sympathy. How could they? It is good to feel the brief passing of a sliver of relief, ah, it was not me, and it was not my family. And then to hide, not to show any sympathy with those who must bear the loss, for it may catch you. Tomorrow it may be you. I have felt all this, have huddled in my family tent, thankful that it was not me; have stroked Conraat's face, feeling myself safe and not wishing to think of those who were not. I have held silence, have looked away, and so today it is my tomorrow. Today it is me.

For five nights I lie on the blankets in Conraat's tent, while he sits on the chair, watching me. When I try to speak, I croak, harsh sounds unlike words. Father is alone in the Bastiaansz tent and I cannot bear to think of him in his solitary hammock, reaching his arm out for Mama deep in the night. On the fifth night I find words again and I ask Conraat to let me go to my father. No, he says, and then watches me again. On the sixth night he lies beside me, and on the seventh he tries to cover my body with kisses. I taste poison when he lifts my face; see the piled up corpses of my family, with their too-thin arms protruding, when he tips my head back. He holds me so tight that I cannot breathe.

On the eighth night, he begins to peel my clothes away. When I try to push him back his face turns red, his pupils black, and he pushes me down on the bed. I weep, and tell him that I cannot give myself to him, with my family lurking in my mind so closely. He tears my clothes then and says, 'Your family are gone now. I am your family. Remember that. I am your family. Go on, say it. Say it.' And so he goes on, until I repeat after him: you are my only family, Conraat. But they do not leave my thoughts.

He has told me that I am to see Father only once a day, and for only a few minutes. Father has been forbidden to pray or preach. Each morning, he takes his Holy Book to the far side of the island and spends the whole day there. When I asked Conraat why he should ask such a thing of me, he said in a soft voice, 'I want you kept safe, I do not know whether they will harm your father. I thought your family would be safe, but they were not. And surely if they harm him, and you are with him, they will harm you. Please, my Judith, be careful and quiet.'

If my father is gone, what point is there for me to go on? I could not say this to Conraat, of course, for he would say: what of me? Am I not reason to go on? He says that he likes me to think of him as a reason for living, that I am his sole joy. When I spoke of this to Father he wept but then dried himself and said, 'Whatever becomes of me tomorrow, you must care for yourself, Judith, you must survive. Promise me this.'

And so I promise.

Heat bores through the tent, making my throat dry. Conraat has been gone all day and I have stayed either by the shore or inside the tent, not knowing where I should be safe. I am safe with Conraat, safer than anywhere else, for he is my protector. Outside, the heat is stronger, a blanket covering me. Dry dirt spatters out around my feet and I keep walking, keep walking, only wanting to be safe, only wanting to find Conraat, my protector.

He is on the southern shore, and he is not alone. My feet are quiet on the rocks and though I draw close, no one looks up at me. There is a circle of people around the boy Cornelis Aldersz. White hair frames his pink face; it glints in the sun, whiter than the sand. Jeronimus is laughing with the boy, saying, 'Here, look, we tie it like this over your eyes and then you will see the magic.' He ties a black cloth about Cornelis's eyes, pulling it tight, and steps in front of him. 'Now can you see this?' He holds up a hand.

Giggling, the boy, barely thirteen, shakes his head.

'What about this?' Jeronimus makes to punch Cornelis, stopping close to his face. Everyone laughs, even Cornelis, infected by the laughing crowd. I am about to draw nearer, step close to Conraat and take his hand, when Jeronimus puts his finger to his lips and hands Mattys Beer a shining sword, as long as his arm. The boy is still laughing as Mattys Beer, the man who helped me bury my family, swings his arm back and swipes at Cornelis's neck. There is a scraping, shuddering sound, then a spurting of blood. Mattys swings again and slices through the boy's neck. Cornelis's head tumbles to the sand, his eyes wide, mouth open in a frozen laugh.

Jeronimus looks around at the crowd. 'What magic, yes? What relief from our boredom. And now, who will sew the head back on?'

They all laugh, holding their hands over their mouths, or on their bellies. Conraat has his head thrown back, his teeth shining like the boy's hair, his laugh loud and long. He straightens himself up, looks over and sees me watching. For a tiny moment, we stare at each other. Then the laugh stops, his lips close; and I turn and run as though the Devil himself is after me.

Chapter Forty-One

Feet pounding like hooves at the rocks, I run in towards the tents, then back, weaving, to the east beach. There is nowhere for me to run to, no one who will be safe for me; only, perhaps, my father. And if they see me talking with him, they may kill him. So I run in a crooked line, panting heavily and listening for Conraat's steps behind me. They do not come.

Behind me, there are two rocks, side by side like young brothers. They make a tiny corner which I fold myself into, leaning against the cold hardness of the stone. Night colours begin to flash across the sky, and though I am hungry, I tuck myself closer into the rock, arms wrapped over my body like wings. Thirst scrapes at my throat, and as the dark begins to drop, the rock becomes unbearably cold. The sun dips down, the moon rises, and a swarm of insects start devouring my arms and face. Because there is no one else, I stand, shake the blanket of dust and salt away, and start clambering back to Conraat's tent. If I stay here, they will find me. Someone will find me, and I will be slashed like Mayken or strangled like Anneke, and I will do my family at least this honour, the honour of surviving, of keeping their memory. Father held me tight when he whispered: whatever else, you must survive, you must think of tomorrow. For tomorrow, there will be a rescue ship. Surely there will be one soon?

Darkness has come down quickly, so that I must crawl on my hands and knees to find my way along the shore and towards the camp. When I get to the scrubby rock, I stand upright and almost immediately trip. There is a noise behind me, a scraping of feet, someone running. I dive down into the dirt, press my face against the cold earth. Wait. The noise fades. Someone shouts from the far side of the camp. If I raise my head, I can see the lights of the camp flickering. My stomach is empty and cold; I press my fists into it to stop the hunger. It does not work. I stand up and, holding my hands out in front of me like a child playing Mr Blindman, grope my way towards the camp.

Closer to the tents, the lights form a strong haze. Someone is sobbing. Hands pressed into my belly, I stop, my body filled with the noise of my own heart. I look at the dark shadows ahead of me, the stretches of darkness between the tents filled with unknown killers, and worse: known ones. Conraat waiting for me in his tent, his lips pressed together; Conraat throwing his head back and laughing as a boy's head is sliced from his neck. Conraat waiting with a knife.

Wylbrecht said that Aris Jans, the underbarber, escaped on just one plank of wood, deep in the night. I have heard, too, that there is a neat pile of driftwood by the northern shore. Tucking my skirt up in my stockings, so that my legs are half bare, I run towards the north beach, on the other side of the camp. There are figures in the camp dotting back and forth. I run with my head down, foolishly hoping this will make me invisible. Finally, sand beneath my feet, soft and slippery. I can see two solid shapes, square and safe, by the water's edge. Tripping over myself, I run towards the sea. Behind me, footsteps thudding, harder and closer. I run faster, my eyes squeezing together to see by the moon. Arms seize my waist as I near the raft.

'Where are you going, my Judith?' Conraat is breathless in my ear. He turns me round and peers into my face. I can smell ale on his breath. 'Are you running from me?'

Though I am shivering, I make my voice still. 'No, not from you. How would you think that? But if Jeronimus is dangerous – there is no one else safe on this island.'

'Apart from me.'

'Yes.'

'But you do not trust me to protect you.' His words are like nails.

'I do. Yes I do. But I was alone and—'

He pulls me to himself and whispers so close that his beard rubs against my ear. 'Jeronimus is not safe. I must be seen to go along with him, to keep us both safe. We must say nothing, not until he is caught.

'He killed that boy.'

Conraat holds me out, looks down at me. The moon is a white mandala reflected in his eyes. 'You do not believe that I was happy to see the boy killed? Like you, I wished to run and to weep. But if I do – he is, I think, quite mad. I must nod my head and agree and laugh with him. Or he will kill us both, and your father. This is why I do not wish you to speak to your father. Jeronimus must believe that we are all on his side, all his family. Your father is safe, for Jeronimus has a purpose for him. Do you understand?'

Though I do not understand, not at all, I nod my head obediently.

Conraat speaks softly. 'Judick, I am doing this for us.' He holds his hand out for me, and I follow him back to his tent.

We are woken by Jan Pelgrom ringing his foul little bell and calling all out to the shore. He carries his ridiculous box, places it carefully down on the rock, then climbs onto his little lectern. Even his clothes now are unrecognisable, stitched together from the Company's rich brocades and fabrics for trade. Jan has a sweeping cloak, trailed with gold cloth, and long trousers covered with lace. Conraat, too, has taken to wearing lace trousers and a coat with deep sleeves. I have never seen such designs; they may have come straight from the mind of the Devil. Jan rings his bell again and calls out, 'All welcome the Great Honourable Commander General.' There is a smattering of applause, though we know not what we are applauding, and Jeronimus thrusts himself out from the bracken, for all the world as if he is a magic trick. He has covered himself in red and gold, trailing tails of lace.

He holds his hands up. 'Thank you for electing me Commander General. As it falls to me to lead this new kingdom, it is a correct title. A new declaration shall be drawn up today and I require the presence of all officers and senior Company officials on the island. Welcome to the new kingdom.' His eyes are bloodshot but shining with a fearsome wetness.

Conraat and Jan gather a group of men together, including my father, and shepherd them off towards Jeronimus's tent. By which I mean the Honourable Great Commander General's quarters.

Later, I find my father on the far shore. He is sitting upright, but doubled forward so that his head is on his knees. There is no one nearby, so I tap him on the shoulder. When he looks up, his face is red with tears.

'You should not be speaking with me, Judick.' He drops his voice to a whisper. 'They have spies everywhere. Please.'

'Father.' I sit down beside him. 'I miss you.' We have never used such intimate words before.

He nods, then begins weeping again. 'I have sold my soul to the Devil.'

'What do you mean?'

'I have signed a pact of allegiance to him. To Jeronimus. That Devil himself. What could I do? They would kill me if not, and then you. They plan to seize the first ship which comes for rescue, to escape with all the Company's gold. The gold of the Lord himself. He has boxes of Company jewels, you know, salvaged from the ship; he will kill those on the rescue ship and use it to escape, to live in Sierra Leone, he says, rolling in riches. And I have signed myself to him.'

'We must survive, Father.' But inside myself I am thinking: must we?

He turns to face me. 'Yesterday, five went to High Island with plans to trick the soldiers there and then to kill them, in case the soldiers should spy a rescue ship first. For if rescued now, what is there for Jeronimus? The drowning cell, and hanging, surely. So he is determined to seize her, whoever she will be. Yesterday they failed, so tomorrow they go to High Island for battle. They have asked that I go to offer greetings, bring the men down to the shore. Fifteen men will go: Mattys Beer, David Zevanck, Jacob Pieterz—'

'Jeronimus?'

Father laughs, coldly. 'He does no foul work himself, only orders his lackeys. I am to negotiate, to convince the soldiers of the good intentions of these scoundrels. The soldiers, they say, have food and water, plenty, but no blankets, and no wine. You must come with me. I cannot leave you here.'

'But Conraat—'

'Conraat is coming of course. We will insist to Jeronimus that you stay with us. Yes. That is the plan. Perhaps we can hide you on High Island when I come back. Say that you have been killed. Something like this.'

I am about to say: but are the soldiers safe, with their weapons? And I know before I speak that I have made myself believe the lies. Though I have signed no oath, I am as guilty as my father. I have believed the lies because I needed to. The pirates are here with me, in my tent and in my bed: where I wanted them. Him.

I take my father's hand. 'I will tell Conraat that I need to be with him on the boat. I will make sure.'

Huddling inside Father's dark cloak, I listen to the voices of a boat full of men slap around me as harshly as the waves. Conraat rows with Jacob Pieterz, grunting loudly with each heave. High Island rises up, more solid than our graveyard island, flat and long. Near the shore, there is some sort of low rock fort. David and Jacob ground the skiff in the mud shallows and Conraat lifts me from the boat, swinging me high so that I am near his shoulder. He touches my cheek when he lowers me, whispers, 'My Judith.' Ignoring the coiled snake hissing in my belly, I force myself to smile up at him.

The water is cold on my legs and my feet slide from under me. I slip and trip across the mudflats, holding Father's arm. When we come close to the reef-like island, I look up and see the square face of the soldier Wiebbe Hayes looking down at me. A thick curtain covers the snake inside me, quietening the hissing. Wiebbe's face is a solid cave; grey, but full of safe shelter. Three soldiers stand behind him, carrying long pikes made from sticks and metal. Wiebbe Hayes does not lean down and offer a hand up, though my hands are scrabbling on the rock and my dress clinging wet about my legs. My father calls out, 'We come to negotiate.' He looks hard at Wiebbe, holds out his hand. 'If you would hear me.'

When I am free of the water, Wiebbe helps me to stand and watches as I brush the mud from my legs.

'Sad circumstances to meet in again.'

I nod, keeping my eyes on the ground.

Father steps between us, eyes at Wiebbe's feet, mutters as

quiet as air, 'They are planning to attack.'

Wiebbe nods, and raises his hand. A group of his soldiers leap from the nearest fort, cruel pikes thrusting forward. Conraat, David and their grubby gang are still slipping across the mudflats. Seizing my hand, Father runs towards the centre of the island. Another rock fort squats solidly, windowless and safe. We crouch behind its walls, pressing our backs against the cold rock. My father keeps his hand on my wrist, holding me below the fort walls. It is over quickly: we hear shouts, calls, something banging, and then Conraat, calling my name. 'I will not leave without her,' he is yelling. Someone else – David? – is urging him away, calling, 'We will be killed, fool.'

Conraat calls again, 'Judith, Judith,' then there is the sound of wood on water; his voice, more distant, calling, 'We will return, Hayes.'

Slowly, I raise my head above the stone wall. The skiff is beyond the mudflats, minus only Father and me. Conraat's face is towards me and I watch the boat until my lover is a speck, smaller than the dot of Batavia's Graveyard, and then I turn away.

Chapter Forty-Two

The reef glitters; a distant upside-down moon. Even from here, from this island, I can see its shadow, long and treacherous, snaking beneath the surface. Indeed, from this distance, I see it more clearly. From Batavia's Graveyard, the reef is a mere shadow, a slight darkness in the ocean blue.

The moon is rising. Wiebbe Hayes comes close on padding feet. 'Would you like to eat?'

He has mentioned nothing of Conraat, nothing of my own folly. Nothing, indeed, apart from basic courtesies. It is as though we are in an Amsterdam coffee house, or waiting for a concert to begin.

I look at his plain, kind face. 'Yes. Thank you.'

Outside the fort, a hare-like creature, balanced on hind legs and tail, nibbles at the bracken. Wiebbe grins at me. 'You see why we are so well fed.'

Towards the centre of the island a fire is blazing, and the sweet smell of an unfamiliar meat rises up with the smoke. There are clusters of people gathered around the fire: at least thirty men, chattering quietly. Three men spear the object roasting in the fire: two of the hares and several birds. I have never eaten such good food. Wiebbe sits next to me, tearing at his meat with his hands and teeth, though they have fashioned plates and implements from tin and stone.

With a palm-sized chunk of bird in my hand, I turn to Wiebbe. 'You have been ingenious in the making of things. The fort, the plates.'

He grins. 'More so in the making of weapons. Because we will remain loyal to the Company and loyal to our Lord – you see we have some refugees.' He waves his hand round the circle. Aris Jans, the underbarber, nods at me. 'We have had news, so, of the goings on there. Seems they will like to kill us, too. They will not succeed, I promise you that.' He pauses, then adds, 'Congratulations on your betrothal.'

My face feels hot, my hands wet. Though I wish to say, 'I was forced,' how can I explain? I have been forced to love a dangerous man? Instead, I nod. 'My family were murdered. My father sought my protection.'

Wiebbe grunts, neither agreeing nor disagreeing. He tears off another chunk of meat. 'Still, we will be prepared for them.'

I listen to him chew, then whisper, 'They are planning to seize any ship which comes, kill those sailing her and steal the ship. To become pirates, living from the wealth of the *Batavia* wreckage. So Father has told me.' I wipe my hands on my apron. 'Not Conraat. He told me of the plans. Swore his compliance was a pretence.' I want to add: please, do not harm him. But I cannot, for I know nothing of who is right or who is speaking the truth.

Father and I sleep huddled together in one of the low forts. Deep in the night, I wake with a shiver, a long shadow of dread climbing through my body. I stretch my hand out and trace the rough shape of the stone; the cold, ridged rock is somehow comforting and I fall asleep with my hand upright, stretched in prayer against it. In the darkness, I think I hear Conraat's breath, hoarse and deep, beside me. My father's snores sound like mutterings, like Conraat calling my name. Accusingly. He comes into my dreams, stumbling to me across the reef, his feet sliced into red slivers. I stand on the edge of the reef, watching him fall, watching as a sudden wave rises and sweeps him away. When I wake, with a crisp shaft of sun across my face, I still see Conraat's feet, cut and bleeding. My shoulder aches from having my arm raised, and my head aches from my dreams.

Father wakes and stretches his legs out. I stand, raising my arms above my head, and straighten my skirt. My cap is now so loose that it sits on the back on my hair, serving little purpose other than decoration. Still I persist, out of habit, in tying it on, hoping to keep a semblance of neatness at least on the outside, though my hair flies loose now, trailing down my back.

Later, Wiebbe walks towards us, his long arms dangling by his side. He calls to me before he is halfway near, 'Morning, Judith Bastiaansz. Did your father sleep well?' He does not ask if I slept well, as if this is of no concern, or the answer is already assumed.

Father pokes his head up to the sun, like a snail. 'The Lord welcome you, Wiebbe Hayes.'

I recall, all of a sudden, my father on the *Batavia*, pointing down to Wiebbe Hayes. Warning me against him. His plainness, his class.

'Would you lead us in a service, Predikant?' Wiebbe squats down to meet my father's eyes.

'We have had no service on the graveyard island. Banned. All mention of the Lord. Though they speak of the Devil freely enough.' A drop of spittle nestles on the edge of Father's mouth.

'Will you then? Before we break the fast?'

Father stands. 'Immediately?'

'You should wash first. There is a well, do you see – follow my finger – by that clump of bush. Three wells we have dug, all with the sweetest water. That one we keep for washing.'

The water is indeed sweet and cool. Father strips his shirt off and rubs at his chest, splashing the cold water onto his face, while I wash face, hands, throat.

Father leads a short service by the fire; his lips tremble as he calls us to prayer. Wind and water have damaged his Holy Book, so that some pages stick together. Pulling at the pages until one tears, he lifts his face and begins reading: ' "If my people will humble themselves and turn from sin, I will heal their land as they pray." '

We stand and listen, heads bowed, while the sizzle of fish cooking on the fire accompanies his words. When Father finishes his prayer ('O lead us home to safety, dear Lord'), he wipes his eyes.

Wiebbe stands beside him. Quietly, he asks, 'How many dead, Predikant?'

Father clutches the Holy Book to his chest. 'One hundred or more, we think. They killed those on Seal's Island, and Traitor's Island, too. They have developed a lust for killing; that rascal Jan Pelgrom calls out for victims, says, "I can slice a head so nicely." They –' He lowers his face to the book. 'I did not know that man had such evil in him.'

Wiebbe rests his hand on my father's shoulder, then calls, 'After eating, weapons to be made ready. Lookout – that will be Lamberts – on the point. Remember, we must surprise them, not they us, for they would betray us with a kiss. Could be that they will come today, could be days away. Me, I think they are fools and will come today.'

A red-faced man with long wrists hands me a piece of beaten tin. On it is half a pink fish, and a round, white egg. I peel the egg and eat it whole; it is warm and rich, sweeter than a hen's egg, and riper than a duck's. When we finish eating, the same man collects up the tin sheets and wipes them with a damp piece of shirt. Wiebbe claps his hands together, and the soldiers disappear like ants, all to different corners.

I walk with Father to the island's edge and sit beside him, our legs stretched out in the sun, watching for the dark shape of the boat rowing out from the graveyard island, past the reef. When the sun is high above us, we see them. Two dark dots passing over the blue of the sea. As we stand up, ready to call out, 'Seems that they are fools, for they have chosen today,' Lamberts is banging a rock against one of the tin sheets. Groups of five or six soldiers huddle together, lying flat on the rocks.

Wiebbe stands with us, arms folded, watching the shape of the skiffs grow closer: they have brought both boats and a whole company of followers. The first boat rows to a stretch of sand, a lower reef, a little way out from High Island, and Wiebbe pulls us down behind the fort, so that we are lying on our stomachs. Someone tall – perhaps it is Salman Deschamps, for his hair appears red in the sun – drags the boat up onto the low reef and the men climb out. Even from here, I can see the muskets lying in the boat. The men look towards our High Island and I flatten myself against the grass. David pushes the second boat off again, and rows it closer and closer, until it is below us, in the nearest mudflats. Jeronimus sits in the stern with his red cape, hands pointing towards the island as though he truly believes he is a king. David Zevanck jumps out of the boat, followed by Conraat. They call out a welcome, screeching like gulls' calls against the waves. Conraat has a pile of blankets in his arms, David a wine barrel. They splash across the shallows, calling, 'We come to make amends, to offer trade.'

David looks towards the closest fort. 'We realise that we must work in friendship, that we have made an error. So we bring with us wine and blankets which we are willing to trade for water and fresh meat.'

Wiebbe edges back, whispers, 'I am going out to them,' and disappears. My teeth are pressing hard on my lips, so that the taste of salt trickles into my mouth. Before me, on the reef, there is hand-shaking going on, and the passing of blankets and wine. Wiebbe splashes out to Conraat and shakes his hand. As he does so, Conraat raises his hand in the air. On the sandy islet, the men begin to climb into the boat. Lamberts, on lookout, bangs the tin again and a swarm of soldiers dive for the reef. Someone from the islet fires off a musket. Twenty or thirty of Wiebbe's soldiers – I cannot count, they move so fast – swarm like black flies around Conraat and Jeronimus. Perhaps it is less, for another group have surrounded David Zevanck and Jan Pieterz. In their tattered clothes, and driftwood shoes, Wiebbe's soldiers are a ragamuffin army indeed, yet they are as swift and determined as the Spanish. They carry pikes, and large spiked balls on sticks and ropes.

Conraat kicks at Wiebbe and turns to run to the skiff, lifting his feet high in the water and calling out, 'Attack! Shoot now!' The musketeers prime the weapons desperately, but not quickly enough. Wiebbe pulls Conraat's arms behind his back and the red-faced soldier runs at him with a long pike. One musket shot echoes, the smoke clouding across the mudflats. Though Father tries to pull my hand back, I am standing before I know myself, screaming out, 'No! Conraat! No!'

Conraat looks up at me, his eyes a green sea, and the soldier pushes the pike into his chest. Conraat's mouth opens, his eyes still raised to mine, and then it closes. Father is pulling at me and I am kicking at him, crying, 'Leave me, let me go,' but he does not let me go. Finally, I push him to the ground and stumble across the shallow water, tripping several times and bloodying my hands and knees on the rock.

On the mudflat, Conraat lies unmoving, a red gape in his chest, his eyes still wide. Three other bodies lie near him. I climb over them, eyes only on Conraat. Mud and blood cover my face as I throw myself down, slapping him, calling him back. He does not come back; no. He lies there, crumpled as cloth, while David rows desperately away out to the sandy islet. David Zevanck, streaked with dirt and bone and blood, escaping in the skiff which Conraat should have escaped in.

Father calls from the edge of the island. 'They have caught Jeronimus. He is tied with rope and sat on by four men. Coward though, he is weeping with fear, begging for his life.'

Wiebbe lifts up his hands. 'Let him weep,' he calls, crowing like a fat ugly rooster.

I throw myself at his smug flat face, my hands clawing at him, my nails digging at his eyes. 'And why could you not kill him and spare this one? Why save the tyrant?'

Wiebbe holds me out, so that my hands claw at the air. 'They were about to attack us. We would have been killed.'

'Not by him, you ugly, ugly fool. Kill Jeronimus, yes, he is filthy. But Conraat has killed no one. Harmed no one.'

Wiebbe shakes his head. 'Not so, Judith. He has killed several – and when Claas escaped to us, it was Conraat who chased him with a knife. More, it was he who marooned us here, intending us to die.'

'Shut up! Shut your ugly face up!' I slap at him again, and then my body doubles in on itself, so that I am an uninhabited shell, tumbling down somewhere far, sobbing so loudly I sound like the sea, as I disappear to a far, far place, where there is no one left in the world except my own shaking, weeping self.

Chapter Forty-Three

There is no burial for Conraat, nor for the other men. Their bodies are thrown into a low grave, and covered with the harsh grey dirt of this island. Father does not attend, and nor do I. I do not know who does the throwing, or even where my betrothed, my savage betrothed, is buried. I do not leave the sharp island edge, except to eat. Wiebbe Hayes comes to see me, carrying a mug of wine: the wine carried to him by Conraat. I turn my head away, forcing my lips together. Wiebbe places the mug near my feet, as if I am a dog, and says, 'I am sorry you lost your betrothed, Judith. And am sorry for what he was.'

I keep my lips together, staring at the rough shapes on the ground. There is a strange light, as before a storm, which makes everything seem blue, even my hands.

'We did not kill him maliciously.'

'It is not possible to kill without malice.' Though I do not mean to speak at all, the words seem to slip out before I have thought.

'Aris Jans says Conraat planned all with Jeronimus. Even on board they planned mutiny, Judith. Planned to steal the ship, and all her goods. With the wreck came other opportunities. He fooled you well.'

I do not turn my head.

'No. Anyway, I am sorry that you have lost so much.'

'I have lost everything.' My words are barely a whisper.

Each morning, Father brings me food on one of the beaten tin sheets. More of the rich eggs, hare meat, fish and some sort of long vegetable. On the first day, I do not eat. I am full up with sorrow; fasting on my tears. After this, though sorrow still fills me, I am able to eat. Father does not ask me to speak, and for this I am grateful.

Perhaps eight days after Conraat's killing, Father brings me a goblet of water and a plate of fish. He sits beside me with his hands folded around his knees. He is silent while I eat, then says, 'It seems he was a murderer after all, and a willing one. Was in the plan from the beginning, on the ship. They had thoughts to mutiny then. Later, after the wreck, he agreed with Jeronimus that they could simply revise their plan, that numbers must be reduced, down to forty, they said. Only those willing to thieve the Company goods salvaged from the *Batavia* and from the rescue ship should be kept alive.'

I busy myself pulling some white bones from the fish.

My father lays a hand on my knee. 'Jeronimus has said so.'

I spit out a bone. 'Oh, well if that murderer has spoken, then surely it is true.' My head is full of pictures I do not wish to see:

Conraat telling me I must not see my father; Conraat meeting at night with Jeronimus; Conraat's hand running up, under my skirt; Conraat laughing as the boy's head falls.

'You know the truth, Judith. We have been fools, surely.' My father's voice is softer than I have ever heard it; I sit up and look at him. His skin is papery, his lips pale. Perhaps it is the strange light, but he looks like a dead man. Another dead man. I stretch my hand out and put it on his wrist. His skin is cold.

'I do not know what to believe, Father. Or who.'

He rubs his hands across his face. 'No. We have been deluded by so many.' He lets out a long breath. 'And we have no protection now, not at all. With Conraat gone – we must try and stay here on the island. They will come back, sure enough, to try to rescue their Honourable Leader. And try to take us with them.'

I look at his thin blue skin, at his long hands waving about. 'How long have you thought Conraat was a willing killer?'

Silence.

'How long, Father?'

'I do not know. Perhaps since the declaration.'

'Which you also signed. And are you a killer?'

'I could not bear to have you lost as well. When we have lost so much, lost everyone – Judith, I cannot bear it, cannot bear to think of them.'

'No. Nor I.'

'I signed for our protection.'

'And how do you know he did not sign for the same reason?' Though I know it is not true, though I know now that Conraat's heart was not good, I cannot let him go. Not like this, so easily.

Father puts his hand up to his face again. 'It was Conraat's plan to capture those on this island, to kill them and take the skiff. He proposed capturing the first ship which came and swore me to secrecy on pain of death.'

'Perhaps, like you, he was merely playing a part to keep safe. Why are you so different?'

Again, silence.

I push at my father's arm, filled with a sudden fury. 'You are no different from them, from any of them. You have gone along with their plans and preached God only with your mouth, not with your heart. You have become one of them, keeping silent for your own protection. And you did not protect your children.'

Father does not raise his head or his voice. 'I have not shared a bed with a killer.'

'Leave me alone.'

'I am sorry, Judick. I am shocked; I cannot bear to be without them, without her. I am not myself.'

'No. We are none of us ourselves. Please, Father. Let me be alone.'

He clambers up, his blue skin creasing.

For another three days, I stay silent and alone, growing pale and cold. Drawing pictures in my head of Conraat, of Myntgie, of Roelant. Of my mother. Remembering Conraat's slow steps that night, his eagerness to pour me more wine, and more; and all my creeping doubts. On the third evening, I go to the fire and eat. I do not speak to anyone and I do not look at Wiebbe Hayes.

The next morning, I wash by the well and sit by it for some hours, drawing patterns on the ground. Across the sound of the sea, suddenly, there is some shouting. The shouting comes closer, grows louder. And then a musket shot, blasting into the air.

Wiebbe Hayes is calling something about Jeronimus and there is another musket shot. Covered in dirt and dust, I stand up and look out to see, beyond the reef, the two boats from Batavia's Graveyard drawing up.

Another musket shot. I lie close to the earth and peer across. David Zevanck has a musket in his hand and is waving on a cluster of men to the shore, calling Jeronimus's name. Several of Wiebbe's men are fighting David and his followers, waving their pikes and odd-shaped weapons. Men are lying on the reef, blood-spattered. A line of Wiebbe's men run behind me and down to the reef, leaping on the mutineers from behind. Then there are more men, climbing from the larger boat and it is all happening so quickly I cannot tell who is who or what is what. There are cries and shouts and falling in and falling out. Wiebbe Hayes is near me, calling to another line of his men. It seems to me there are hundreds of them, all wading across to the reef in clusters, though I know there cannot be more than forty. Yet they appear and reappear, clever as ghosts. I cannot see my father, though I huddle closer and closer to the edge. I stand and look over, do not see him, even when I turn and run, looking to the other shore. Yet there is something: not my father, but a huge shape, white and billowing, making a sharp line across the blue-green ocean, closer and closer. I clap my hands over my mouth to stop myself crying out, and run back, run in a circle, half lost, half mad. Wiebbe calls out somewhere behind me and I turn, follow the sound. He is by the well with three men. For one moment, I hesitate, thinking: *Conraat*. And then I hurry to him, seize him by the arm and turn him to face the other shore. Pointing out to the ship, blowing and gliding towards us, I say, 'Get there first or they will seize it.'

He does not answer me but turns to the three men, says, 'Keep them occupied,' and runs, runs, runs to the skiff.

And as he rows out, past the north point of High Island, the good and faithful Commander Pelseart is already rowing to us, rowing to the near point of High Island, his arms full of the strength which comes from prayer, his prayer full of hope. He comes closer to the island and begins calling out greetings in the name of the Company. His own voice echoes back to him, futile, until Wiebbe Hayes, rowing like a fever, rounds the point. No time, Wiebbe says, no time to explain. Only this: get back to the ship now or all on board will be killed. And Pelseart obeys, though he cannot understand – how could he? – and they row back to the ship, Pelseart's prayer deflating, his hope slithering into the sea.

Behind them, David Zevanck, who is not stupid though he is foolish and deluded, has noticed Wiebbe gone, has noticed one of the skiffs missing, stolen from under his fat, flat nose. He gathers three men into the remaining skiff, calling, 'Move! Can you not move faster?' They shove against each other, too clumsy with haste, and row past High Island and out to sea, out to the good ship *Saardam*, already anchored in the bay, waiting to offer rescue. When they round the point, they see two skiffs soaring across the sea, closer and closer to the ship, and they strain and swear at each, drawing closer, closer. Pelseart and Wiebbe push against the wind, against hopelessness, against evil; cutting through the swell, looking back over shoulders. David stays a dot behind them, his three men heave-ho-ing with the strength of desperate greed. Hope must win against greed, it must, though it has already lost so much.

So Pelseart and Wiebbe climb aboard the *Saardam*, are dragged onto the deck, panting and breathless. And for a moment, with David Zevanck's skiff a mere dot in a vast ocean, they are victorious.

That night, when Zevanck has been bound and chained, Pelseart weeps into his fine brandy, stored to celebrate the recovery of the wreck and of the survivors.

'I should have stayed,' he says, 'should have jumped overboard, not let Jacobsz and his thugs carry me off. Yet once they had restrained me onto the yawl, it seemed that I could convince them to sail to Java, which we did, and have the Company give us a boat for rescue. We were met by four Company boats in the Sunda Strait, did you know? Waiting for the winds, yet it seemed to me that they were waiting for me, sent by the Lord. When they escorted us to Batavia, with Jacobsz under chain, it seemed that I had won after all. I could not know, I could not tell; what could I have done?'

The *Saardam*'s skipper nods awkwardly, patting the commander's arm.

Wiebbe Hayes returns to High Island for Jeronimus and brings him on board, bound and weeping. Returns again for my father and for me. 'Thank you,' he says. 'We have won.'

I speak so quietly that he has to stop rowing to hear me.

'No,' I say, 'I have lost everything I love. I have won nothing.'

Chapter Forty-Four

Before dawn the next morning, it was over. Jeronimus's rulers in his angry new kingdom were overpowered and taken by yawl to Seal's Island; each of them awaiting trial, chained there without boat or supplies. Empty now of life, the island, like Traitor's Island and Batavia's Graveyard, has a bloody story to tell. Andries Jonas, climbing into the skiff, looked up at my father and said, 'Ask the Lord's forgiveness on me, Predikant, for doing their work, stabbing the women on Seal's Island.' His face crumpled as he added, 'I have been an evil man.'

For days and days we waited for the trial to begin on Seal's Island; waiting for the goods to be salvaged from Batavia's Graveyard. Each evening Pelseart listed the goods recovered, pages and pages of items listed for the Company and not a list of people lost. Finally, still absorbed in his lists, Pelseart ordered the trials to begin. I stayed on the *Saardam*, with Lucretia, both of us staring across at the reef. I had no wish to hear more of them, more of their lies or truths, or to see them tortured. Father reported back to me each evening: Jan Hendricxzs under

Jeronimus's orders killed twenty people; Jan Pelgrom was ordered by Jeronimus to kill Mayken Cardoes and Anneke Haardens, was ordered and also under his own pleasure took Anneke into his tent, under his own pleasure went with David Zevanck and Walter Loos to Seal's Island, stabbing three cabin boys; Salman Deschamps was ordered by Jeronimus to kill Hedrick Jen as he walked; Jacob Pieterz was forced by Jeronimus to kill Hilletje Haardens. Jeronimus himself was questioned with the water collar for four days, until his body and face were bloated like a seal's, before confessing at last. Each of them, except for Jeronimus, the same: obeying orders, saving their skins, doing what they must. Walter Loos forced to kill Andries de Bruyn and Frans Yant, ordered to kill fifteen on Traitor's Island and, finally: ordered, with six others, to kill the predikant's family.

Father sat weeping beside me, his tears making a long line down his face. I said nothing, nothing. And here is where it began: with the first silence on board the *Batavia*, when we watched a bird being broken and tossed to the ground, and did not know what to say; and then later watched the body of Kaaren Hendrickson tip into the sea and said nothing, offered no sympathy, no grief. And there we were, leaching away our goodness with our unwillingness to share sorrow. Turning my face away when Lucretia stood, covered in shit, head low. Yet when Jeronimus was hanged, we cheered, all of us, even my father, even me. When Pelseart sentenced Walter Loos and Jan Pelgrom to be marooned on the shelf of the Great Southern Land, we were silent.

As we sailed off, off to the green island, off to the new life in Batavia, the life my father had promised my mother, I turned back from the deck and watched a plume of smoke rising up from the continent. I expect they are there still, settlers in a desperate land.

My father died in Java; dysentery took him quickly, and his new wife followed. I do not know if he found happiness with her: after we landed in Batavia we never spoke of such things as happiness. Death, I think, may have been the Lord's gift to him, and a welcome one.

And I, I am here, back in my homeland. Grown older, and still with the empty hole where my family should be. And the hole made by a foolish love. It was not silence which made me a betrayer, it was not obedience. It was desire.

I know now who it was, the one who offered the water to Roelant. Jan Pelgrom: murderer, rapist, marooned on the mainland with a barrel of biscuit, three blankets, and a package of trinkets to trade. A small hand, stretched out with a tin cup. A boy's voice: 'This is for the child.'

My daughter's child has been born: a she, confounding expectation. My daughter brings her to me, swaddled in white muslin. My granddaughter has a monkey face: grey-blue eyes, a flat red nose. Behind one ear, there is a brown mark, like a kiss. I hold my finger out and she wraps her hand round it; her lips make a circle as tight as her little fist. Taking her from my daughter, I rub my nose into her cheek; she is rich with the smell of bread, and of honey.

'I am calling her Judith.' My daughter hands me a cup of sugared coffee.

I say, 'You cannot. It would be a curse.'

'Everything good I have has come from you, Mama; curses can be overturned.' She pulls the muslin back from my granddaughter's face. 'Her name is Judith, and if she has as much capacity for love as you do, I will be blessed.' She puts her hand on my cheek. 'Look at her, look into her face.'

My eyes devour this pink-skinned baby, gobbling her startled eyes, her white brows, the single tuft of fair hair.

'What do you see?' My daughter has pulled the muslin cloth right off, so that the child is bare.

'She is lovely.' I inhale her warm scent again.

'She is innocent, is she not? As innocent as you, Mama, and no more worthy of my blame.'

I lift my granddaughter, baby Judith, right up to my face and breathe her in. Her pale eyes are wide on me, and her lips bubble into a smile as I lay her on my lap. With my daughter's hand still resting on my cheek, I smile back and sip at my coffee. It is warm and sweet and good.

Do you remember the drowning cell? It was used in Amsterdam: like the water collar, a tool of torture, or of confession. And therefore, perhaps of redemption. A prisoner would be locked in a cell, a tiny square room, with one pump. And into the room would flow water, faster and faster and faster. To keep the water out the prisoner had to pump the water, keep pumping however his arms might ache, however his heart might burn. Pumping until the water reached his legs, his chest, his neck. Sometimes, he would give in, stop pumping and let the water take him. It must have been a kind of relief. And this is how it is for me. Each day, hate and guilt and desperate, desperate grief flow into my cell. I pump and I pump, desperate to keep the waters out. My feet are wet but my waist is dry and I will not let the waters in; for if I do, I will disappear. I will not let the waters win.

So this is my confession.

Acknowledgements

The Accomplice is a work of fiction inspired by the wreck of the *Batavia* in 1629. Like all those fascinated by these events, I am indebted to Henrietta Drake-Brockman, whose passion for the subject led to the discovery of the wreck in 1963. I have relied heavily on her work, *Voyage to Disaster*, although the most recent research is to be found in Mike Dash's excellent book, *Batavia's Graveyard*.

I have also made use of, or been inspired by, the following material:
C.R. Boxer's *Dutch Seaborne Empire* and, more especially, his article *The Dutch East Indiamen: Their Sailors, Their Navigators, and Life on Board*, published in *The Mariner's Mirror 49*;
J.P. Sigmond and L.H. Zuiderbaan's *Dutch Discoveries of Australia: Shipwrecks, Treasures and Early Voyages off the West Coast*;
Rupert Gerritson's *Their Ghosts May Be Heard*;
Hugh Edwards' *Island of Angry Ghosts*;
and Simon Schama's *Embarrassment of Riches*.

Where these sources disagree, I have allowed the demands of

the fictional narrative to take precedence.

The writing of *The Accomplice* was facilitated by an astonishing amount of practical and personal support. I am especially grateful to the Arts Council of England; the Southern Arts Literature Board; the H.H. Wingate Foundation; and the Royal Literary Fund, in particular to Steve Cook.

I am thankful, also, to the librarians of Westminster College, Oxford, who were unfailingly helpful and endlessly thorough; Richard & Jane Griffiths, for their Devonshire retreat, and the Sisters of St Mary's, Wantage, for the same in Oxfordshire, where much of the early draft was written. Several people enabled – in a number of ways – the work to happen, or offered wise words. I am particularly grateful to: Becky Weatherall; Katrina Fitzsimmons; Hilary Mead; Sarah Leach; Tanja Turtscher; David Langford; Jill Dawson; Jimmy Booth and Judith Murray.

Special thanks to Charlotte Mendelson for wonderfully determined editing; and, as always, to the miraculous Richard Griffiths.